A CHRONETIC MEMORY

A Novel by
Kim K. O'Hara

© 2014 Kim K. O'Hara

All rights reserved. This book or any portion thereof may not be reproduced or used in any manner whatsoever without the express written permission of the author except for the use of brief quotations in a book review.

Sign up for new book notifications at
www.pagesandnumbers.com

Contact the author at
kimkohara.author@gmail.com

Cover design by Sam O'Hara
www.samofsorts.com

Printed by CreateSpace in the United States of America

First Printing, 2014

ISBN: 1-5009-4647-8
ISBN-13: 978-1-5009-4647-0

To Mom, who always encouraged me to follow my dreams.
I wish I had finished this while you were still alive to see it.

CONTENTS

	Acknowledgments	i
1	Collision	1
2	Isolation	3
3	Manipulation	12
4	Agitation	14
5	Intention	23
6	Appreciation	27
7	Acquisition	40
8	Confrontation	42
9	Desperation	55
10	Direction	62
11	Anticipation	72
12	Collaboration	74
13	Disruption	82
14	Alteration	86
15	Detection	95
16	Deductions	100
17	Suspicion	112

18	Realization	114
19	Recollection	125
20	Introduction	129
21	Interception	137
22	Explanation	141
23	Preparation	157
24	Decision	162
25	Neutralization	176
26	Information	178
27	Revelation	196
28	Distraction	202
29	Escalation	226
30	Diversion	230
31	Apprehension	234
32	Explosion	237
33	Confirmation	245
34	Interruption	249
35	Restoration	252

ACKNOWLEDGMENTS

My thanks to **Kellianne Rumsey**, who has encouraged me with just the right blend of belief and ultimatums, and without whom this novel would never have been imagined, continued, completed, or published; to my husband, **Michael O'Hara**, for doing without me for long hours as I worked to complete this book and carrying many family obligations on his own during that time, and also for being a sounding board for my ideas and questions; to my daughter, **Sam O'Hara**, who read my final draft, gave me feedback, and showed me how much she believed in me by pouring her considerable creative talent into my cover design; to my other daughter, **Jennifer O'Hara**, who inspires me with her own writing; to my twin sister, **Kathy Kreps**, who offered me practical feedback during numerous stages including reading the entire final draft; to friends **Kermit Kiser**, **Daniel Myers**, **Annie Bouffiou**, **Peggy Holstine**, and **Zerna Beebe**, who served as my beta readers and proofreaders and gave me both corrections and suggestions (which undoubtedly improved the book you hold in your hands); to **Grace Friberg**, who graciously donated her time for the cover photo shoot; and to the **NaNoWriMo** community as a whole for inspiring this venture in the first place.

COLLISION

HARBOR AVENUE, Seattle, WA. 0120, Monday, January 20, 2205.

A helicar horn blared at the bottom of Fairmount hill and kept blaring. For seven long minutes, it cut through the icy early morning air. A blast of wind hit an icicle-encrusted evergreen branch; the brittle limb gave way and plummeted earthward. With an ear-shattering *whump* it hit the hood of the crumpled red helicar. The horn stopped.

The faint sound of emergency sirens crescendoed. Helicars with flashing lights landed carefully on the frozen roads. Their occupants emerged and swarmed away from the red helicar, focusing instead on a larger blue vehicle that lay crushed on the beach below.

After a few moments, one of the rescuers backed away from the blue vehicle and peered around. He spotted the other car and pointed toward it, yelling. Another paramedic joined him, and the two began picking their way up the icy slope, heads down.

They didn't see it when a gloved hand with metal rescue knuckles smashed through the back passenger window of the helicar. Brushing the glass aside, it grasped the front door handle and yanked. The door opened. A lone woman lay slumped over in the driver's seat.

The stopsafe force field that had saved her life had deactivated after the impact, settling her against the cushioned wheel.

The man who had opened the door shook her shoulder. "Marielle."

She opened her eyes and blinked. "Wha—?"

He had taken out his hand scanner to check for nerve or spinal damage. It whirred for a few seconds, then turned green. He stuffed it back in his coat pocket. "Marielle, can you move your legs?"

"Yes, I thi—wha—happ'nd?" Her mouth wasn't working right. "Am I drunk? I feel drunk."

"You were in an accident. You overshot the landing and hit another helicar."

"No! Were they—was an'body hurt?" She struggled to get the words out.

"I'm afraid so."

"Iss so dark. Izzit late?"

"So late it's early. What were you doing out at one in the morning?"

"I—don' know. Can't 'member."

"You don't remember hitting the helicar?"

"No. Nothing. Who—who was in it?" The grogginess was dissipating. If she concentrated, she could make her tongue cooperate.

"It was…" He hesitated, looking at her carefully, assessing her ability to hear the answer.

"Who was in it?" she demanded.

"Marielle, it was Elena and Nicah."

"Are they— are they okay?"

He shook his head. "I'm sorry. Nicah didn't make it. Elena is hanging on, just barely. They're taking her to the hospital. Can you walk?"

"Yes."

"Let me help you to my car. I'm taking you home."

ISOLATION

RIACH CAMPUS, Alki Beach, Seattle, WA. 0740, Monday, June 5, 2215.

Danarin Adams threaded her way through the holographic picket signs on her way to work. As she bumped and jostled between the sign holders, she muttered quiet apologies to most, with friendly nods for those she recognized. Some of them had been there almost every day of the six months she had worked at the institute. There were even a few of the protesters she'd call friends.

Oddly enough, she couldn't say the same of any of her colleagues. The research scientists reminded her daily, in a thousand little ways, that she was only an intern. She might have found friends among the interns, but they were all isolated from each other by individual task lists.

"Hey, Dani!" Katella Wallace waved amid the sea of signs. "Are we still on for lunch today at that new sandwich place?"

Dani laughed to see that Kat had changed her own sign into a giant waving hand to get her attention. "I'll be there," she replied, "and I want to hear all about Jored's game last night."

Kat made a face as Dani caught up to her and started to check through the security gate. "I'm not sure you do. It was even worse than the last one."

"Tell me anyway. He'll expect me to know." She paused to let the irisscan identify her while her bag went through the scanner. The gate opened. She waved to her friend. "See you later."

The noise of the protesters died away as she walked the thirty-five meters from the gate to the main entrance. On her left, block letters identified the massive building as the headquarters of the Research Institute of Anthropology & Chronographic History, home of the famous TimeSearch project. Chronographic history was a window to the past, one that had fascinated her ever since the first reports of the breakthrough had played on her family's viewwall.

In those days, all the newscasts had been optimistic. "Inventors Seebak and Howe," they said, "have patented a device that will allow us access to the past in ways we are only beginning to imagine." The details were even more intriguing. Any inanimate object could generate sensory streams of events that had occurred near it when researchers tuned in to selected times from its past. Talk shows interviewed scientists on national broadcasts, and soon such phrases as "chronetic energies" and "temporal quantum entanglements" were common household words, though few knew the science behind them.

It hadn't taken long before the business community jumped on board. As a child, Dani wasn't even aware of businesses vying for sponsorship opportunities. It wasn't until later that she found out about the plans of a performing arts center to recapture the sights, sounds, and smells of Shakespeare's openings or the plans of packed vacation resorts to offer the sensory inputs of a long-gone pristine beach, forest, or mountain. Universities wanted the new technology for research. Law enforcement and courts wanted it to find and convict murderers and kidnappers. But Dani didn't know all that back then.

Eleven-year-old Dani knew only that her teacher laid aside his lesson plans in science to explore the new possibilities. In history, they discussed what historical events should be recovered first.

She heard about a national essay contest for high school students:

What object would you choose? What moment would you recapture? The winning essay writer would be flown to Seattle with his or her parents to watch the chronograph in action.

Dani smiled, remembering how much she begged to enter that contest. At that age, she wasn't eligible, but that didn't stop her from trying. She sent in her essay anyway.

The heavy iron doors of the institute swung open at her approach, and her smile faded. With a last, wistful look outside, she entered the cavernous maw to begin her workday.

RIACH LABS, Alki Beach, Seattle, WA. 0750, Monday, June 5, 2215.

The door whooshed to a close behind her as the lights adjusted from "dim" to "softly lit," a preference she had indicated at her initial orientation, when her bosses were still acting as if she would be a valued employee. She reached into her bag for her lab coat, powder blue to mark her status as an intern. It was a smooth routine by now, putting on the lab coat, pressing her left temple to switch her connexion device from the city's nexus to the institute's private one. Signals from outside didn't reach well through the thick cement walls without a boost.

On the opposite side of the entry, a small segment of the viewwall shimmered into focus to reveal her daily task list. She knew the task list would be repeated when she got to the chronolab, but she looked at it anyway, out of habit, while she donned her lab coat.

For all the secrecy that shrouded the institute, most of its electronic documentation would have been unintelligible to anyone who gained unauthorized access. But Dani glanced over her first two tasks and deciphered them easily.

MORNING SCHEDULE—Lab D, station 3
1. Ob:103192 19940606:131500-131520/FC EI+47.5 Rec:V Samp/Routine
2. Ob:103192 19940606:133000-133020/FC +47.5 Rec:V Samp/Routine

She sighed. More tedium. Routine sampling of object 103192 at her usual scanning station, beginning where she left off yesterday, at

1:15 P.M. on June 6, 1994, for twenty-second durations every fifteen minutes. Full circle visual recordings at a 47.5-degree angle of elevation. Because all the visual recordings used a 95-degree angle of view, 47.5 degrees ensured that everything would be captured from the horizon up, with a ten-degree overlap directly overhead. Those settings provided a full upper hemisphere of visual data. She skimmed ahead. The rest of the morning was filled with more of the same, jobs for an intern, no creativity required.

Ah—here was something more interesting. Actually, it was a little astonishing to see it on her task list.

AFTERNOON SCHEDULE—Lab D, station 3
1. Ob:097113 22060917:114417-114441/N36W±10 El-15. Rec:VAO Inv/Hist-Comm

A historical investigation! And commissioned, no less. Normally, investigations were "Inv/Event-Potential," where someone (with a title way above hers, she thought wryly) spotted a conversation or encounter from an earlier sample that should be recorded with audio for later analysis. But a commissioned investigation meant that an outside agency had brought in a specific object and wanted a recording to study a genuine piece of history, one that was meaningful to the client. These would require that all the recording devices—visual, audio, and olfactory—be engaged.

The barest touch of her childhood sense of wonder brushed her consciousness. Perhaps today wouldn't be so bad after all.

She turned left down the corridor toward the chronolab. The marble walls reflected the muted glow from the recessed lighting. Four framed images displayed scenes from history alongside the objects that had revealed them. These were the famous promotional images that had first heralded the invention, twelve years earlier.

First on the right was a signed baseball in a clear protective case, in front of an image of the fast-approaching outfielder's glove from the 2089 World Series, just before the game-ending catch. The cheering crowd in the background captured the triumphant moment, and bold lettering above the image proclaimed, "FRESH

PERSPECTIVES."

A few steps farther, on the left, was the photo of an old fiddler in the Appalachian mountains in 1934, taken from below, and the tile fragment that used to be part of his floor. Dani read the title, "HERITAGE RECLAIMED," and remembered how the whole song had been played on the viewwalls at school. It had inspired a resurgence of fiddlers and fiddle music.

Dani moved more quickly past the next display on the right. Even though she understood its importance, it was a little too gruesome for her tastes. She already knew what was there. Under the title, "CRIMES SOLVED," there was the famous axehead. The photograph from the morning of August 4, 1892, was of a blood-spattered Lizzie Borden calmly washing her hands, thus forever putting to rest the mystery of who killed her father and stepmother. Although she knew there was value in solving such things, Dani didn't see the point of displaying it so prominently. She shuddered and moved on.

She loved the last photograph on the left, of Chef Solveig Rendahl, from July 2146. She lingered to absorb a bit of the chef's contagious joy at creating a perfect pound cake, smothered in simmered summer blueberries. Her image was displayed next to the whisk that sourced the shot. Chef Solveig's sugary confections were still considered the crème de la crème of desserts for special occasions, and the exhibit was the delight of schoolchildren, not just because they got to see and hear the famous chef, but because when they sniffed the air, they could actually smell her creation. The photograph displayed under the title, "AUTHENTIC ATMOSPHERES," didn't include scents, of course. Scents were "played back" using chemicals blended according to the specs on digital recordings.

Back before the controversies started, these photos were part of a traveling exhibit and the main spark for Dani's fascination with the new technology. Again she wondered: How could that excitement have faded so quickly?

As she passed through the doors at the end of the hallway, she got the barest nod from the three scientists clustered near the diagramwall. Before she had ever met them, their names were familiar to her. She had seen them on the spines of her college textbooks, scanned for them in scholarly journals. They were the authorities in her chosen field. Calegari. Brant. Tasman.

When he spotted her, Dr. Nikoli Calegari frowned a little and moved his ample body sideways to hide his scribbles from her view. Not that she could read them anyway—his handwriting was notoriously illegible.

Dr. Marielle Brant's soft eyes flitted in her direction without focusing. Dani liked the dark-haired doctor, with her gentle nature and easy laugh. She had, in fact, long admired her as one of the early pioneers of the new science. Dr. Brant had been an assistant to Dr. Mitchum Seebak and Dr. Elena Howe when they had first invented the process. The only names more well-known than Calegari, Brant, and Tasman were those of Seebak and Howe.

Dr. Howe had been a bright star, the warm voice that convinced the multitudes that new worlds awaited discovery. She had taken the photos that Dani passed every day in the entry hall. Hers were the video, audio, and olfactory tracks recorded and played for potential investors and schoolchildren. But a helicar accident one frozen morning in late January 2205 had put her in a coma and claimed her life twenty-eight months later. She had never awakened.

Just a few months after the accident, while Dr. Howe was unconscious, her longtime partner had been discredited and dismissed, for reasons that had never been explained, even to insiders. Dr. Seebak's abrupt departure left a void that Dr. Brant stepped into reluctantly. In Dani's studies, she had learned that the other researchers in those early years had enormous respect for Dr. Brant's scientific expertise. A few protested that at twenty-five years old she didn't have the maturity, but there was no doubt that she knew the technology. She continued in the paths of her predecessors, with work that was both innovative and revelatory. It soon became obvious, however, that she was no Elena Howe. She disliked crowds and avoided public appearances.

The resulting lack of good publicity had left room for others with less favorable opinions to step into the spotlight. Pundits and commentators had started putting into words what everyone was thinking: What would be the fruits of unbridled access to the past? Politicians took up the cause. Who among them didn't have some dirty laundry? Those who lived on the shady side of honor feared the freedom given the scientists and campaigned to limit viewing windows to a hundred years or more in the past. Even those with nothing to hide objected to the invasion of privacy.

Dani shook her head. Now that she was involved with the project, she realized that the likelihood of happening upon an indiscretion while scanning an object was so tiny as to be almost nonexistent. But the honeymoon had ended with Dr. Howe's accident, and the project was now in the dark phase of its existence where researchers were relegated to the bottom of the "most respected professions" lists, just above used helicar salesmen and just below lawyers.

Scientists at the institute still held Dr. Brant in high regard, of course. But Dr. Brant was no more social than she had been in those early years. When Dani had first arrived, she had made two attempts at casual conversation with the doctor, but she got only brief nods in return. Dani had never seen her acknowledging any of the other interns either. Her mind was probably so occupied with planning and analyzing, she reasoned, she had little time available for human interaction. On rare occasions, scientists and interns mingled at social gatherings, and Dani had not seen any evidence that the doctor even knew which interns were hers.

Dani realized she was still standing near the researchers. Now who was being unfocused and oblivious to her surroundings?

Dr. Dural Tasman, in contrast to Dr. Brant, had piercing blue eyes that missed nothing. He always made her nervous, and now she'd been caught hovering. Any moment now, he'd be asking her where she should be.

"Where should you be, Ms. Adams?" he asked her, with the voice of one scolding a wayward child.

"I'm scheduled for the chronolab," she replied, blushing, grateful that she had taken the time to read over her schedule in the lobby.

He waved his hand in that general direction, dismissing her brusquely, and turned back to his fellow researchers. As she picked up her pace and headed for the lab, she sighed. These people were supposed to be her mentors, and she couldn't get more than a few words from any of them. How was she supposed to learn?

At the lab, she started the chronoimager. It would take its usual four or five minutes to run through the daily checks and set up backup files. She checked to make sure the storage rod still had room for the morning images, and glanced at the small copy of her schedule on her eyescreen to remind herself of the object number before going to the library to retrieve it.

"Object 103192...103192...103192," she muttered to herself as she walked down the long aisle, past row upon row of movable cases. Case 103 contained the newest acquisitions, but in a month's time they would be identified, scanned, and cataloged. She would move on to case 104, then 105. There seemed to be no end to the objects.

Ah, there it was. Dani reached up to retrieve a long iron rod with a handle on one end and two curvy points on the other end. "Object 103192: Fireplace poker, manufactured c. 1991," read the sign. She carried it back to the imaging chamber where she placed it carefully to match the orientation from the day before, closed the airtight doors, and checked the sensors. All was in order.

She stepped into the observation box and waited while it integrated seamlessly and silently with her synapses. Her next motions would have been a blur to an observer. In five seconds from start to finish, her right forefinger pulled up the settings screen, her other fingers scrolled through the available dates and times with precise movements until they bracketed the requested time frame:

June 6, 1994, at 1:15:00 P.M. Duration, twenty seconds. Angle of elevation, 47.5 degrees.

As she set the full circle scan, Dani shook her head at the waste. She had discovered yesterday that the fireplace tools had been kept against a brick fireplace in June of 1994, and for 160 degrees of the full circle rotation that brick was the only thing in the viewing field. For a good part of the rest, other iron tools partially blocked the view. Once such blockages were identified, wouldn't it make sense to narrow the scan to just those parts of the rotation that would yield good results? It would be so simple to make adjustments as she watched with the integrated sensory input.

For that matter, wouldn't it make more sense to just pick objects that were in the center of the action and get views all around, like the baseball in the famous photo she passed every day? But such decisions were reserved for fellows and research scientists, and above the pay grade of a mere intern, no matter how intelligent or capable that intern might be.

Dani worked efficiently, using interval settings to record visual scans. After the first few minutes, she had settled into a rhythm: Set, scan, adjust. Set, scan, adjust. She kept half an eye on the images flashing past at an accelerated rate. In the four hours she had before lunch, she was able to gather seven days of readings at the requested intervals. She was the quickest chronop in the building, which would have felt pretty good if she had had even the slightest hope that she was doing something remotely useful.

She shrugged. She had wanted a career; this was just a job. Then she chided herself. At least it *was* a job. And this afternoon held something more interesting, possibly even significant, if her schedule didn't change while she was at lunch with Kat. By the time she had saved the backups, and returned Object 103192 to its shelf in Case 103, she had begun to feel better. She left the lab humming a cheerful fiddle tune that had hit the top of the charts just the month before.

MANIPULATION

HUNTER'S OFFICE. 1200, Monday, June 5, 2215.

The connexion icon on the viewwall buzzed. The tall, impeccably-dressed man turned abruptly and waved his hand at the icon, which expanded to become a hologram of the caller.

"Right on time, Ms. Lowe," he commended her.

"Hunter." She acknowledged him with a look of resignation. Her posture was proper and professional. He could read her expression easily: Make this a business transaction. Let it be over quickly.

After months of these meetings, her initial fiery defiance had succumbed to fear, and the fear had turned to surrender. She had seen the futility of resistance, and her acquiescence made it easier to control her, but he missed the terror he had inspired in their early meetings.

Sometimes, he toyed with the idea of exposing her husband's real background to the world despite the payments she had made so regularly. It would destroy her family, he knew. Lowe would be imprisoned, the company he had built from the ground up would fail, and their finances would crumble. He thought of the children, still in elementary school. They idolized their father. He scowled. He hated their smug trust. He wanted to see them suffer as he had suffered, living in a shabby studio apartment in the worst part of town. He wanted to see them cry. He wanted the man to watch his family be reduced to abject poverty, knowing he was powerless to help. The more he thought about it, the more difficult it was to restrain himself. It would be so easy to leak the news.

He decided she would have to pay more.

"The funds have been transferred, Hunter. I trust the group's discretion will continue."

The group. He would have to get the increase approved. He chafed at the delay, but knew he had no real choice.

"As always, Ms. Lowe." He waved his hand again and the image vanished. A few more gestures opened a banking icon and confirmed the transfer: 400 million global credits. The corner of his mouth turned up slightly, just short of a smirk. The money was coming in, from hundreds of highly-placed sources, and a good portion of it was his.

Soon he would be one of the richest people in the world.

4
AGITATION

BATELLI'S DELI, West Seattle, WA. 1205, Monday, June 5, 2215.

Kat had already ordered for both of them when Dani got to the sandwich shop. "You have your choice between beef with provolone or turkey and Swiss," she offered. "They'll be here in a few minutes."

The restaurant had an old-fashioned feel to it. The owners had decorated the deli to match a two-hundred-year-old photograph. Walking through its doors was like walking back in time. Dani watched as waiters took orders by hand and brought meals to the table. "I'll take the turkey," she decided, "although the beef sounds good too. How much do I owe you?"

"Don't worry about it. You can buy next time."

They settled into the antique chairs that made no adjustments to their body temperature or shape. The unyielding plastic felt strange on her back, but surprisingly comfortable.

"So the game was bad?" Dani prompted her friend, wanting to talk about something that didn't involve settings and scans. Most of the interns ate in the cafeteria at lunchtime to gossip and gripe, but she depended on these forays into the outside world for her sanity.

"Oh, you wouldn't believe it. None of these kids has ever telecompeted before this year. Including Jored, of course. It's worth watching, though, if only because it's so funny."

"Well, he's only seven. It's mostly about sportsmanship and having fun at that age, isn't it?"

"Exactly. And he does that part really well."

At that moment, their waiter arrived with the sandwiches and a complimentary apple turnover. It looked delicious. Excellent way to inspire loyalty in new customers, Dani had to admit. As if the whole two-hundred-year-old atmosphere thing wasn't enough. "Where are his teammates from?"

Kat shrugged. "They don't really like to tell you that. Underage players and privacy, you know."

"You'd know all about privacy," Dani teased. Kat's whole reason for protesting was to keep private lives private.

"Well, yeah." Kat grinned. "But the kids talk, and Jored has a vague idea anyway. There are a few from China, two or three from the Balkans—their families have known each other a long time, it turns out—and only a handful from the western hemisphere."

"Impressive! Truly international, and at that age! I don't think any of my telegames, when I was a kid, involved anyone from out of the country. Well, I mean, they would have, if we ever got to championship levels, but we were never that good." Dani shook her head. "Kids these days don't realize how much the world has changed." Then she added, almost as an afterthought, "How do they communicate?"

"Sometimes in English, sometimes in Croatian, but mostly in Chinese." Kat laughed at her friend's expression. "Kids pick up languages so fast."

"But he likes it, right?"

"Oh, he loves it. Almost as much as he loves playing chess with you."

Day brightener, right there. "I love spending time with him. It surprises me how much I look forward to it. When we play chess, it's not really about chess. It's mostly about talking. He's so smart. And he likes to hear about the parts of my job that I still enjoy. Reminds me of what attracted me to this field when I was his age."

"He asked me this morning when you were coming over again. Want to have dinner with us tomorrow night?"

Dani didn't hesitate. "What else have I got going? Six-ish?"

"That'll work."

They ate companionably for a few minutes, saying nothing. Kat was comfortable like that. But Dani felt like talking after her silent morning in an observation box. "How was your day?" she asked her friend.

"Great! The fair-weather visitors have starting showing up, so we get to educate them about how dangerous your work is." She winked.

When the two had first met, they had kept their conversations to neutral topics. They both instinctively realized that a new friendship had to find common ground before venturing into potential discord or conflict. But now they were sure of their bond, and there were no rules to their topics.

So it was with no trace of defensiveness that Dani replied, "Do you know how many yottabytes of information you'd have to sift through to find one damaging piece of information? And it's all so boring." She yawned, then laughed. "I didn't plan that yawn, really."

Kat smiled. "Jored never hears about that part of it, does he? He thinks your work is the most interesting thing in the world. It's my job that he gets bored with. To him, it's just standing outside and waving a sign."

"You're doing what you believe in. That's what counts." Dani reassured her friend. "Honestly, I'd squirm just like anyone else if someone decided to look at my life with a chronograph."

"There, see? That's what I mean. People never think it's about them. It's about all of us, as much as it's about any of us."

Dani looked at her fondly. "You have such a big heart, Katella. You're always looking out for people, always making people's lives a little easier or a little better. Does Marak know how lucky he is?"

"Well, yeah. That's how we met, you know. He was doing

something the hard way, and I made it easy."

"What did you do?"

"He was standing outside a fence, clearly wanting to be inside, testing the bars for potential footholds, trying to figure out if he could climb it to get one of his famous insider reports. I watched for a while and then I couldn't help it; I laughed."

"Did you know who he was?"

"Not until he introduced himself, but then I knew. He had already made a name for himself, and his stuff was really good. He'd gotten it into his head that he wanted to interview my uncle for some story he was working on. Hadn't been able to reach him through the usual channels, so he decided to go see him in person. But when he found the locked gate, he hadn't a clue what to do. I guess he'd just figured the gate would be open and he could walk right in." She snickered.

Dani could just see that. Honest, earnest Marak, who didn't have a deceptive bone in his body, faced with a locked gate. "Did he ever get inside?"

"That was the ironic part." The glint in Kat's eye was unmistakable. She so loved a good joke. "My uncle wasn't even there that day. He was down the road, waiting at the marina for me to meet him so we could spend the afternoon on his boat."

"What did you do?"

"I brought Marak along, of course. And I introduced him as the man I was going to marry someday, which was not what he expected at all. But he warmed to the idea pretty quickly." She activated her eyescreen to view the time. "Hey. Don't you have to be back at work in a few minutes?"

"Yes!" Dani gathered her bag, tucking the uneaten dessert into it for later. "I'd better run. See you tomorrow morning?"

Kat nodded. "Don't forget about dinner!"

RIACH LABS, Alki Beach, Seattle. 1310, Monday, June 5, 2215.

Back in the lab, Dani was in a considerably lighter mood. She glanced at her eyescreen to check her schedule again, just in case there were any changes.

AFTERNOON SCHEDULE—Lab D, station 3
1. Ob:097113 22060917:114417-114941/N36W-15. Rec:VAO Inv/Hist-Comm

No changes. Good. A real investigative recording awaited her. She caught herself humming again as she went to the shelves to retrieve Object 097113, which turned out to be a small iron padlock. She looked it over, trying to imagine its history. "What have you seen?" she asked it conversationally. "What have you heard and smelled, that might make them want to get sounds and scents from you?"

It hadn't escaped her notice that the time frame she was about to bracket was within her own lifetime. Even if this hadn't been a commissioned investigation, that aspect alone would be interesting. She smiled to think of Kat's reaction if she knew. Anything more recent than a hundred years ago would make Kat start preaching privacy invasions. She placed the padlock within the imaging chamber, activating the seldom-used audio and olfactory recorders, and sealed the door.

The requested time frame was for a little more than five minutes. She waited for the sensory integration, set the viewing elevation, beginning time, and duration, then flipped the switch to begin.

Immediately, she realized her mistake. The view surrounded her on all sides as well as overhead. This was supposed to be a narrow angle, not a full-circle image! She reached to turn off the switch and start again when she caught something around S30E that startled her. A hand reached for the lock and jiggled it, evidently testing it to see if it was locked. Viewing and hearing it as she was, from the lock's point of view, everything around her jiggled side to side, and the fingers obliterated pretty much everything else. Normally, she'd only be able to see the fingers, with the view angle that had been requested. But because of her mistake, she could see the whole hand. Apparently, the lock had held. As the hand retreated, she got ready to change the settings, when she saw the face behind the hand, and realized it was a face she recognized. That hand belonged to someone she knew very well: Marak Wallace.

She snatched her hand back from the screen. This wasn't supposed to happen. Time searches were tedious, boring, and completely devoid of anything personal. How many times had she told Kat that?

Guiltily, she changed the settings to reflect her assignment. As she finished the five-minute recording, barely aware of the events she was seeing, she tried to console herself. It was an honest mistake. No harm done, right? It just felt really strange. She realized that, up to this moment, she hadn't actually believed these images were of people who had lived and breathed, not really. They had felt more like characters in works of fiction.

But now? Her whole perception had changed.

All afternoon, while she completed and dismissed items on her checklist, she wrestled with the possible implications. All Kat's cautions and worst-case scenarios from the last few months suddenly held new meaning. Nearly every relevant conversation they had had came back to beg for reconsideration. Every time another one popped up, she shoved it under a mental rug and deliberately made herself concentrate on the task at hand.

But somehow, she knew those thoughts wouldn't put up with being ignored for long.

DANI'S APARTMENT, First Hill, Seattle, WA. 1750, Monday, June 5, 2215.

The rest of the day had gone by in a blur. Dani vaguely remembered checking out of the institute and awaiting her usual tube car to take her under the water and up to her apartment on Seattle's First Hill. She felt relief that she wouldn't have to face Kat tonight, and then decided that avoiding her friend was ridiculous. Kat was the essence of open acceptance when they were on opposite sides of her most passionate issues; why would she have any trouble with these new misgivings? She fixed herself dinner and had the apple turnover for dessert.

Enough of this. A good night's sleep would settle her down. Tomorrow she would be fine.

It felt like she had barely closed her eyes when she had the first dream. She was in the school cafeteria, grade seven. She knew the year because the tables were set to blue for most of that year. Her best friend Kirtana had finished lunch and was checking out something on her worktablet. Dani leaned over the table to look and suddenly she was wearing a dress that was too short. A boy from the next table came over and tapped her on the shoulder to tell her he could see her underwear. Embarrassed, she straightened up. That's when she saw them: forks with blinking eyeballs, spoons with ears. Watching and listening.

She woke herself up somehow and sat up in bed. Her heart was racing. It took a few minutes for the fog to clear so she could convince herself that it was a bad dream. She got up and splashed some water in her face. Maybe if she read for a while. Something soothing. She activated her eyescreen reader and blinked to page through until she found Sarama.

> we remember
> the past for
> its gifts of
> what we can
> no longer touch
> taste hear smell
> or see
> but when we
> burrow deep
> in remembering
> we find
> we can still
> feel

She sighed. Sarama could pack all the reasons she chose her career into just a few words. He helped her focus. She read another.

> soft shells
> crunch beneath
> my feet and
> grains wash
> away with water
> that comes
> and goes
> in and out
> but the grains
> are rice
> and the shells are
> only pasta and
> the beach is
> a beach
> no more

Her heart rate had slowed to something close to normal. Her eyelids drooped. She nodded in the chair, and the chair's sensors detected that her breathing had slowed. It tipped her gently back into slumber.

She was back at the university sitting numbly in the dorm lobby while Jhon Rhys told her he never wanted to see her again. He was dark, beautiful, and everything she wanted until he opened his mouth to berate her. His kindness extended only to finding her alone, in the early hours of the morning when he knew she would be finishing out the night shift. He held back nothing; he was comfortable with brutal honesty. He was a rising star in international finance, she was a lowly academic, studying a field of science that should be banned. He was destined to stride through the world as golden pathways were laid beneath his feet, she should resign herself to stumbling along a gravel road that would soon be a dead end. She was an embarrassment to him. She was too tired to believe he was wrong. In her dream, he left, and that was when she noticed that all the student mailboxes were open, revealing hundreds of audio-video cams, busily filming her humiliation from all angles.

She turned in her sleep, and the chair adjusted to her new position. Now she was in New York on spring break, and the gigantic screens in Times Square were playing all her most shameful moments. She awoke, shivering from the lack of covers, chiding herself for not bringing one over to the chair. Her eyescreen revealed that the workday would start again in a little over an hour. She got up to shower and dress.

As the water warmed her and the foamy shampoo oozed out from the curved wands that massaged her scalp, she managed to let her fears wash away too. This was ridiculous. She was a young professional with a promising career. Even if everything about her past were revealed to some snoopy scientist somewhere, he would find nothing worth exposing. Her life was not a big deal to anyone, and she was silly for getting so emotional over something she'd known all along to be possible.

Besides, even though she had only been to Times Square once, she was almost certain that advertisers would rather pay to feature their products on its huge viewwalls, not to feature embarrassing scenes from her life. And it was totally unlike her to have bad dreams, and even less like her that she would let them bother her. By the time she was ready for work, she had put her misgivings behind her.

Or at least, she had figured out how to pretend they weren't there.

INTENTION

SEEBAK LABORATORY, Vashon Island, WA. 1430, Monday, June 5, 2215.

"Lexil! The sensors found another one."

Lexil Myles looked over quickly from a viewwall full of figures and formulas. The disturbances had been coming more and more frequently in the last few years. "Big one?"

"Not so far, but it will bear watching." Dr. Mitchum Seebak pushed a strand of graying hair back from his forehead. "How are you coming with those calculations?"

"Every time I run them, I find the same thing." The younger man shook his head. He had been trying everything he could think of to resolve it. He pointed to some equations on the viewwall. "These countering forces only occur when a disturbance takes place."

"How about the size? Is it predictable?" His mentor asked him.

"It's roughly proportional, but ..." His voice trailed off. It was frustrating not to be able to give a specific answer.

"Nothing you can come up with a formula for?"

"No, Doc. Not an exact formula. An estimate is easy, but when I go to pin it down, the numbers don't quite mesh. It's as if there's some kind of intentionality behind the application of the countering forces." He would need the older man to see what he saw. Maybe if he created a visual display. "Here, let me show you."

The two men sat down together at a table. Lexil pulled out some paper. Somewhere in his childhood, he had found he preferred pen and paper to electronic devices, even the mathematical ones with the built-in equation editors. By age ten, he was distinguishing himself among his peers enough that his parents indulged him in his eccentricity. He never outgrew the practice.

But this time, pen and paper wouldn't be enough. He wanted Doc to be able to see the effects clearly. So he worked out his equations, then used the results to generate graphs for the viewwall with a few quick motions.

"Here. A disturbance, see?" The graph looked like a glowing pebble in a phosphorescent pond. The ripples began radiating outward uniformly. They watched as the waves spread, their amplitude dwindling to nothing within seconds.

"I see. And immediately, it was opposed by the damping force," said the doctor.

"Correct. That progression is easy to predict. But look, here's another one." This time, the pebble fell in the pond, and the ripples radiated irregularly. Two bright blips on the outermost ripple, and new disturbances started radiating outward from them even as the original ones faded. When the surface settled into smoothness again, the places where the blips had occurred still glowed. "These spots, I've found, are much more likely to be the site of a new disturbance later."

"How much more likely?" Doc asked him.

"Approximately a hundred times more likely."

Doc sat up straight. "What? That could cause the timestream a lot of trouble."

"I know."

"Is that the intentionality you were referring to?"

"No. These blips I attribute to human actions, many of them related to the chronography institute. Their influence can be quantified, and the ripples behave in predictable ways."

"I'm puzzled, then. Is there a third type of force involved?"

"Yes. Watch this one."

Lexil moved the graph up onto the wall. The pebble dropped. The ripples spread outward, produced a single blip, then faded. As they watched, the single glowing spot started to pulse, and then new ripples appeared, moving inward toward the blip, gradually reducing it in size until it disappeared.

He heard Doc's sharp intake of breath. "Is this an actual event, or a simulation?"

"An actual event. The initial disturbance occurred about two months ago. It took three days for those ripples to subside, including the ones from the blip. Twelve days ago, this inward ripple started. It took it about six days to repair the blip. As far as I can determine, there was no human agency involved."

The older man leapt up and returned to his own work area. He yanked out boxes of memory rods, reading labels and casting them aside. Lexil heard him muttering to himself. He couldn't quite make out what he was saying, though.

"Doc?" he asked, walking toward him.

By now, the older man was surrounded by displaced boxes. His head popped up for a second. "Looking for something!" and then he was back at it. A few more minutes passed. Finally, he emerged, triumphantly holding up a tattered box in one hand and a memory rod in the other. "Found it!"

"That box looks old."

"It is. This is from back when we had just set up our third time disturbance sensor. That gave us, as you know, the ability to triangulate to any point in history, although we couldn't be very precise at great distances. I thought I had seen a pattern like this before. Let's put these numbers in your nice little visualization here and see what we get."

They sat down together in Lexil's work area and plugged in the memory rod. "Haven't used this format for data in a long time," said

Doc.

"I have a conversion program that can handle it." Lexil swiped a few screens to run the data through it, and soon, they had enough to create the visualization.

It started with four or five of the bright blips on the screen. As they watched, the inward ripples started, first with the blip on the far left, then moving to the next closest one, and progressing sequentially until all the blips were gone.

They sat in silence for a few moments after the visualization ended. Doc cleared his throat. "What do the spatial dimensions represent on your graphs?"

"Physical dimensions on these two axes, and time on the third axis," Lexil answered. "I can locate these blips on the earth's surface within a few feet."

"Because that looked for all the world like something was deliberately moving from one blip to the another, doing the repairs, then moving on to the next."

"Yeah. Like I said, intentionality."

They looked at each other, not knowing what to say.

6
APPRECIATION

RIACH CAMPUS, Alki Beach, Seattle, WA. 0740, Tuesday, June 6, 2215.

Dani emerged from the tube car that had taken her from First Hill under the surface of Elliott Bay to Alki Point North. She loved living in Seattle, with its view of the mountains and the ancient Space Needle, clearly visible from the institute campus, even on a cloudy day like today. The cloud bank made it harder to see the Olympic Mountains, but she knew they were there, just waiting for a patch of blue sky.

There was Kat. Dani knew her friend's schedule almost as well as her own: Take Jored to school. Stop by the office to pick up extra signs for people who might join them during the day. Drive to RIACH. Rain or shine, Kat would be there, educating people.

This morning, she was busy talking with someone Dani recognized as another protester, but not one she had ever gotten to know. It looked like an intense discussion. Probably better not to interrupt. Besides, right now, Kat was simultaneously the one person Dani most and least wanted to see. She knew she would need to have a serious talk with her soon. But not here. Not now.

Just as she was about to walk past her to the security gate, the heated discussion ended with the other protester stomping off toward the tube station. When Kat turned, Dani could see her friend was frustrated. She decided to wait for her. Kat had cheered her up so many times, and it seemed as if she could use some encouragement.

"Oh, hi, Dani. Looks like I almost missed you."

"Yes, almost. You doing okay? That didn't look pleasant."

"Oh, yeah. It's all right. That was Neferyn. He's just a little...misguided." She wrinkled her nose. "Some of them are getting tired of educational demonstrating and want to make a bigger noise. No big deal, but I feel responsible, because I recruited him."

"You got it settled, though?"

"Yes. He's just not entirely happy with the whole thing. So are you coming for dinner? Jored is eager to see you."

"I'll be there. What can I bring?"

"Chocolate," Kat answered without hesitating.

"Of course. But besides that?"

"There's something besides chocolate?" Kat shook her head, but she was wearing a big grin. "I guess you could bring yourself. And something for Jored."

Dani paused, tilting her head thoughtfully. "I think I can find a way to bring myself. I'll see if I'm free." She laughed, then sobered. "I have something I want to talk to you about, too. Something ... different ... happened yesterday afternoon."

Her friend sensed her seriousness immediately, and walked beside her to the security gate. "I'm here to listen, whenever you need me."

"I know."

Dani submitted herself to the irisscan and bag check, then gave her friend a quick hug. Kat headed back toward the tube car station to intercept travelers as they emerged. Even on a cloudy day, there would be visitors, and she would have passionate words and a compassionate heart to share with them.

Inside the heavy iron doors, she went through the steps of her familiar routine. Bag. Lab coat. Schedule. Oh, what was this?

MORNING/AFTERNOON SCHEDULE—Off Campus
1. Equipment needed: School Presentation Kits, projector
2. Sign out helicar
3. Local Schools Tour: Alki Elem (0900), West Seattle High (1300)

It had been several months since she had done school presentations, although her internship had originally highlighted them as a big part of her job. She loved the contact with kids and the excited ways they responded when she painted her visual pictures of the many ways chronography could enhance understanding of the past.

She packed up school presentation kits for the two different age groups, grabbed a hovercart, and set off to get a helicar.

ALKI ELEMENTARY, Alki Beach, Seattle, WA. 0830, Tuesday, June 6, 2215.

A slight haze diluted the brilliant blue sky as Dani lowered her car into the orange-painted outlines of a parking spot. Parking lot descents were easy now, but she remembered how difficult they had been to learn. Her driving instructor had made her practice every time he rode with her. "People forget to check what's below them," he had said. "Anything could move into your spot: an animal, a rolling ball, a child. You can't see it, unless you use your underview screen." She remembered learning to center her car over the parking spot. That was easy. The trickiest part was turning while she hovered so the corners lined up. Parking spots abutted each other on four sides, with only enough room to open doors and walk between. Her early attempts had resulted in smashing more than a few holographic cars.

As she entered the brightly-colored door to the elementary school, an efficient secretary greeted her at the desk with a pleasant, if preoccupied, smile. Dani read her name on the counter nameplate: Ms. Lawrence.

"How can I help you?" asked Ms. Lawrence.

"Danarin Adams. I'm here for the Chronography presentation."

Immediately, the secretary's smile warmed. "Oh, the children love you! Do you have the fiddle player with you?"

Dani fought off the urge to say, "Yes, right here, in the side pocket of my bag," and decided to behave more professionally. She'd save the silly humor for the kids.

"Yes, and several other recordings," she answered instead. "Could you tell me how many children to expect?"

"We have about two hundred children scheduled for your presentation, with a mix of ages. Even the ones who usually telestudy have made the trip in for this." Ms. Lawrence gestured to a room behind her. "Would you like some coffee before you set up? Or something to eat? One of the parents brought in a fruit tray this morning."

"That actually sounds nice. Thank you. And then, if you could show me where to set up?"

In a few minutes, Ms. Lawrence had escorted her to the auditorium, setting down a cup of coffee and some strawberries on a nearby table, and Dani was preparing her presentation. The kids would sit around her in a semi-circle on the floor, little ones in front and older kids in back. She would need a certain distance for the holographic projections to have the best effect. The little kids would want to touch and feel the things she had brought, so they needed to be close.

The older kids would be more standoffish, but she knew exactly how to reach them if their attention wandered at all: She would ask for volunteers to operate the controls of a portable image reader that the institute had adapted to read real-time images from any location in the room and project them somewhere else. Kids liked to pretend they were flies on the wall, or bugs on the floor, and observe the presentation from other vantage points. They especially liked it when they could watch themselves in holographic form.

She arranged her samples for the touch-and-feel part of the presentation. A metal disk. A small round stone. A scrap of leather. A plastic leaf. She set up the holographic projector and tested its projection height. She liked to raise it a foot or so off the floor so that the ones in the back could see it all. She pulled out a stack of touch-and-color handouts for the youngest audience members, and a box of holographic matching card games for the older kids. The holographic cards were popular for kids in middle school too.

The kids filed in and seated themselves. A murmur of excitement rippled through the room as they spotted the image recorder and holographic projectors. When they were all seated, she stood, and the kids quieted instantly.

"I'd like to welcome you all to my chronography show," she began. "How many of you have heard of chronography?"

Hands shot up all over the room.

"Who can tell me what it is?" She pointed to an eager little boy in the second row from the front.

"It's where you can see and hear and smell things from a loooong time ago." He beamed with the confidence of a child who knows he's got the right answer.

"That's right. But we've been able to make recordings of those things, which we call 'visual,' 'audio,' and 'olfactory' recordings, for many years. Does anyone know what is different about chronographic recordings?"

A little girl from the other side of the semi-circle waved her hand. "Because way back then they couldn't make reco-decordings like that?" She stumbled a little on the word "recordings," but Dani mentally gave her big points for trying.

"Yes, that's a big part of it. Now we can see and hear things from hundreds of years ago, before they even had movies. What would you want to watch from way back then?"

Two of the boys shouted out without raising their hands first. "Big trucks!" "Airplanes! The old kind!" The latter suggestion was accompanied with arms spread out like plane wings, and she half expected him to stand up and make motor noises. She was always glad when nobody mentioned wars and bombs during these presentations. She knew, from studying history, that earlier generations had had a preoccupation with warfare and violence, and she was encouraged that the intervening years had refocused some of those energies.

A hesitant hand went up from an older girl near the back. "Forests and beaches? I'd like to see what those looked like, before all the buildings went up and the pollution made everything all yucky." Many of the other kids nodded their agreement. Even their parents hadn't seen forests and beaches, although here in the Pacific Northwest, some private homes still had clusters of trees.

"Those are all really good ideas," Dani said, "and we often record those kinds of things. Would you like to see and hear and smell a forest?"

A chorus of agreement greeted her offer.

"Okay. You'll have to be very quiet to hear the birds and crickets. Ready?" The room fell silent.

She turned on the projector, and trees sprang up in the middle of the room. The scent of Douglas fir trees and decomposing needles and mosses filled the room. Along with the crickets and birds, they could hear a stream in the distance. The kids were awestruck. Suddenly, a little squirrel popped its head around a tree and chirped at something just outside the range of the recorder. Then the projection ended with a voice over: "It's not just seen. It's heard. It's smelled. It's PastPerfect."

The kids applauded.

Dani continued. "Sometimes we look at things that weren't so long ago. Does anyone know why we might want to see things from your grandparents' lifetimes, or your parents', or even your own?"

An older boy raised his hand. "To find out things that people might not have wanted to record?"

"That's very good! Can you give us an example?"

"Like if you wanted to find out who took your bike, or who left the milk out on the counter. Or find out who *really* started an argument." Some of the older kids laughed at that one, and Dani did too.

"Yes, we use chronographs to solve crimes, too. Even bigger crimes than those, like kidnappings." She paused to gauge her audience's attention, then asked, "Do you know that ninety-eight percent of kidnappings are solved now—that's almost all of them—because we can see and hear the bad people right when they are committing the crime? We hardly ever have to find and arrest kidnappers any more, because they know they will be caught, and that makes all of you a little safer."

She turned to get the source samples. "I'm going to pass around these four objects, and I want you to get into small groups of about ten kids each and come up with guesses about which ones make the best recordings."

Three kids in the back rows were already raising their hands. "And if you already know," she added, "don't spoil it for the rest. Let them think about it."

She held up the first object. "This is a plastic leaf. We find lots of plastic things: bottles, toys, bags, mixing bowls, and serving utensils, for example. Before we made laws that plastic had to be biodegradable, they made the kind of plastic that took centuries—or even longer—to break down and go away, unless it was melted or burned. So when we go hunting around for old things, we see plastic everywhere. Do you think plastic makes good recordings? Pass it around and figure out your guess. But don't say anything until you've seen them all."

She handed the leaf to a little girl with long braids in the front row. As the leaf was going around her audience, Dani turned to pick up the next object. "Here's a leather scrap. Leather is made from animal skin, and it has the same properties as other things that were once part of something living. Who can think of some other examples?"

The little boy in the second row waved his hand. "Tree bark?"

"That's a good example, but we don't find it very often. Trees are constantly building new bark, and the pieces that fall to the ground decay pretty quickly." She glanced around for more eager hands, then pointed to a girl in the back row with wavy red hair.

"Books?" the girl asked.

"Excellent! Yes, we take very good care of books, and both the paper in their pages and the cardboard and cloth in their bindings are good examples of material that was once part of something living. Now don't forget, you're guessing which material makes the best source for our recordings." She gave the leather scrap to the little girl with braids, who looked at it solemnly before passing it on.

She held up the small round stone. "This stone represents things made of non-metallic minerals. Other examples are things made of clay, like pottery, china plates, and ceramic tiles. Glass, which is made mostly of sand, is the same kind of source as clay, unless it has a metal, like lead, in it, and then it depends on how much."

She handed the stone to the little girl in the front, who by now was taking her job very seriously. Then she took the last object from the table and held it up. "Here's a metal disk, but it represents all the metal things that we might find, like doorknobs, lamps, car parts, or other things like that. Can anyone tell me something that's shaped like this metal disk that used to be very common?"

From somewhere in the middle rows, a young boy in a blue tee shirt put his hand in the air tentatively. "Coins?" he asked, when she called on him.

"Yes, exactly! Have you ever seen a coin?"

He looked down shyly. "My dad collects coins. Sometimes he lets me hold some of the ones that aren't all shiny."

"How about the rest of you? Have you ever seen coins?" A smattering of hands—she estimated about 20 or 30 kids—said yes. "Several hundred years ago, school children paid for their lunches with coins and paper money, and grocery stores would take your paper money and give you change."

Dani handed the metal disk to the pigtailed little girl, who took it and asked her in a whisper, "Is this a real coin?"

She whispered back, "No, not a real one. But it's shaped the same."

Facing the assembly again, Dani reminded them of their assignment. "In your small groups, as you look at each of these and feel them, guess how well they would work for my job. Decide what order they should go in, from best to worst. And then we'll have a little game."

She gave them a few minutes to talk about it, then moved among them to listen to what they were saying, collect the four objects after they made their way to the back of the room, and hand out the game boards the institute had developed for presentations.

"When you're ready to play, touch the red dot along the edge to turn it on. We'll all start at the same time. When I say to start, you'll see the four objects you just looked at as small images above your game boards. Your job will be to arrange them in order, starting with the one you think is the worst source on your left, to the best source on your right. When you have a guess, press the blue triangle. If your guess is right, I'll see your answer up here. Let's see how fast you can solve the puzzle. Ready? Start!"

The first one got it in thirty seconds. It was the group of older kids in the back who had raised their hands when she first started passing around the objects. But it wasn't long before they all had it.

"You guys are really fast. Good job. So, yes. Plastic makes the worst source. We can't get any images at all from plastic." She held up the plastic leaf while she was talking about it, then went on.

"The once-living things like leather and paper are a little bit better. They let us get snapshots of visual images, but not much else." She held up the leather scrap for a minute, then put it away in her pocket with the leaf and touched the "next" button on the holographic display. A three-dimensional image of the baseball glove at the 2089 World Series shimmered and stabilized. "This was sourced from a leather baseball that a collector let us use. He was so impressed with our photographs, he let us keep the ball for a museum display. It's a very famous ball."

She held up the rock next, and continued. "Better than leather and paper are the non-metallic minerals, like this rock. We found a loose piece of floor tile in a very old building and recorded this sight-and-sound moving hologram." She pushed "next" again, and as the old-time fiddler began to play, she stuffed the rock away with the other objects. The kids were mesmerized. Everybody loved fiddle music from a master.

That clay tile had been an amazing find, one that still inspired her. How many sample recordings they must have had to take before they found that one moment of history where the fiddle-player was playing. It was even possible that he played there every day for several years, but not at all hours of the day. She was sure it had required months and months of taking samples, and she knew all about that kind of tedium. Some things made it worth the boring stuff, she had to admit.

When the music was over, she asked her audience, "Do you remember what the last item was made of?"

They all said it at the same time: "Metal!" That was an easy question. They all still had their game boards in front of them, with the objects correctly arranged.

"That's right, and metal is the best source of all." She held up the metal disk. "What do you think we can record with metal that we can't get from stone or leather?"

A few voices called out, "Smells!"

She pushed the "next" button again, and there was the famous chef. "You can watch and listen to her as she talks about her blueberry dessert, but don't forget to sniff." She dropped the disk into her pocket as the chef did her thing. The kids all breathed as one when she poured the simmering blueberry sauce over the pound cake, sniffing the fruity, heavenly scent till their mouths watered at the thought. She turned off the projector, but the scent lingered until the projection chemicals dissipated.

This group of kids was so good, she didn't even need to use the hologram projector to keep their interest. But it was a great ending to the presentation, and she still had about five minutes left. "Now, who would like to operate our portable image reader and make the rest of us into holograms?"

The girl with the wavy red hair stood up immediately. Dani smiled. That would have been her, twelve years ago, if they had had the simulated image recorder then. A boy on the other side of the room with an appealing grin also stood up. She invited the kids to come up front with a wave of her hand. "What are your names?"

"I'm Minna," the girl answered.

"Sommy," said the boy.

She turned back to describe the device to the others. "This isn't a true chronograph, because it just displays what is going on right now. It doesn't reach back into the past. The machine to do that is much larger—about as big as the stage up here. We're going to let Minna and Sommy pick a spot in the room that they'd like to look at us from, then we'll broadcast it in miniature from the projector here."

The two kids whispered for a few seconds "From the very tip top, please," Minna said, pointing to the center top of the domed ceiling above them.

Dani showed them how to use a laser pointer to set the direction and distance of the originating point. Then she helped them adjust the viewing direction and angle on the machine itself. Together, they turned on the projector, and there they all were, little tiny people gathered around a little tiny stage, no more than a foot across. They all clapped, and the tiny figures clapped with them. That made them laugh, and the tiny figures laughed too.

While the kids were watching the hologram of themselves, Dani passed out the touch-and-color pages for the younger kids, and offered the decks of matching cards for those who wanted to come up front to get them after the presentation.

Finally, she turned off the projector, and her audience whooped and hollered. She had won two hundred new fans for the institute and its work. It had been a good morning.

Ms. Lawrence, who had been peeking into the auditorium every ten or fifteen minutes, stepped all the way inside to join in on the applause at the end. She dismissed the students to their classrooms to get ready for lunch.

"Would you like to stay and eat with the children? I know they'd enjoy that," she invited Dani after the students had left.

"Oh, no, but thank you," Dani replied. "I really need to get over to the high school to set up for my afternoon presentation."

But she accepted help with gathering her things and packing them back on the hovercart. She nudged the whole batch out to her helicar, loaded it up, and soon she was on her way. She spotted a food dispenser hovering along the main flyway, maneuvered next to it, selected an ergonomic wrap sandwich, and paid for it with her irisscan. She always laughed a little at the "ergonomic" part; granted, it was easier to hold the sandwich while she was driving, but what a lot of fuss for something that would be in her stomach in ten minutes!

As she finished the last bite, Dani spotted the West Seattle High School parking lot, just outside the newly remodeled high school. She landed her helicar gently. For the high schoolers, she took a large stack of interactive question-and-answer sheets and some puzzle pages that would challenge them to determine the correct historic period from the audio and visual clues. Almost as an afterthought, she gathered some more of the holographic matching games, just in case the high schoolers wanted to try them. They were pretty easy to solve, but they still looked intriguing. She was ready.

7
ACQUISITION

HUNTER'S OFFICE. 1200, Tuesday, June 6, 2215.

Today Hunter was wearing a new suit, a dark blue Rafe Zerdo with charcoal pinstripes and a red pocket square. Before leaving his office for lunch, he paused to check the drape of his pants and straighten his tie pin, making good use of the full-length mirror he had had installed for just this purpose. Satisfied, he stepped out, locked the door carefully, and noted that his executive secretary had already left. Good. He had manufactured a pretense to send him away: He required financial records, immediately. Not at some time in the distant future.

The chronography repository would be empty at this time of day. One of the rules he had insisted on, right after the institute was opened, was that all employees must take a full hour for lunch, away from their assigned workplace. This policy gave him the reputation as a caring employer who looked out for the good of his employees, and he found that reputation useful, but his real reason was to clear certain parts of the building for specific purposes.

It was one of those purposes that led him to the repository now. The investigation he had requested yesterday would be completed, and the information it provided would be instrumental in acquiring more essential funding. Despite being near the top echelon of a research institute, he himself was no researcher. If truth be known, he despised the researchers, except for what they could provide him. They had no idea of the goldmine they sat upon. Morons. He was satisfied to let them do the work for him. Except, of course, for this part. He needed to do this himself, to ensure there were no witnesses. And he had to do it with no one nearby, because the process itself made a very distinctive noise, and it would interfere with his goals if someone heard it.

He removed the investigation results from the rack. It would need to be converted to a playable format for his purposes. He had learned that the investigation records were pointers to the real data. Pointers were helpful, because they were so small as to be almost undetectable, and they allowed the real information to be kept intact. The Video-Audio-Olfactory converter allowed him to access the raw data and edit it judiciously to remove any evidence of its source. The same device would then convert the edited information to a format that could be accessed, through another pointer, by a holographic VAO projector. He had never bothered to learn exactly how it worked, but he was pretty sure the noise came from reading the chemical signatures of the scents.

The multiple steps required to produce the incriminating evidence, any of which were quite innocent on their own, enabled him to obscure his tracks effectively, and the resulting holograms, carefully trimmed and edited, could be very persuasive.

8
CONFRONTATION

WEST SEATTLE HIGH SCHOOL, Seattle, WA. 1235, Tuesday, June 6, 2215.

A few clouds drifted lazily overhead as Dani found a spot in the high school parking lot. Visitors got preference here, with a cluster of spots open near the front entrance marked to deter students and faculty from their use. Transporting all her materials in would be easy.

Her first clue that something might be a little more challenging was the abundance of political posters along the entry hall under the heading "PRO or CON?" She saw posters arguing both sides of environmental issues (harvesting energy from the sea, protecting endangered crustaceans, global cooling), civic issues (lowering the voting age to 16, protesting the city curfew), economic issues (working hours for minors, raising the minimum wage), and international issues (balance of trade, involvement in the Asian wars).

Surprised, Dani had to admit that she was impressed. She didn't remember anywhere near this level of involvement in the issues of the day when she was in high school, and that was less than ten years earlier. She looked forward to some interesting questions on her presentation, and wondered whether the giveaway items she had brought—really little more than toys and busywork—would find any takers after all.

The school office was on her right, and she was spotted immediately.

"May I help you?" asked a student office aide with no name tag.

Dani introduced herself. The student asked her to wait in the reception area. It took several minutes, but finally a woman in a sharply tailored suit came out to greet her. Her tone was businesslike, with no trace of warmth, when she spoke.

"Good afternoon, Ms. Adams. I'm Ms. Harris, the principal at West Seattle. I'm sorry to make you wait." She brushed aside Dani's reassurances that it didn't matter and continued in that crisp tone of voice. "I asked them to have you stop and talk to me so we could be sure we had the same ... goals ... in mind. Please step into my office."

Dani's eyes opened a little wider. This was new. She followed the principal to her office, then offered, "I'm sure we do. Do you have some concerns?"

"Ms. Adams, I'm well aware that your institute uses these visits for public relations opportunities. I have no objection to that, but we need to understand each other."

Dani just waited. She was pretty good at thinking on her feet, but still, she hoped this wouldn't mean too many changes to her presentation.

"Many of our young people pass your campus on the way to school in the morning. The picket signs are evident, the political implications easily discerned. I have no wish to be inhospitable"—her tone said otherwise—"but I have to insist on a balanced presentation."

"What do you mean by balanced?"

"We'll need you to restrict your general presentation to demonstrating the technology and explaining its limitations." Still, that tough tone of voice.

"I can do that." Dani wasn't sure what had stirred up the bad feelings here. It baffled her.

"After the presentation, for those students interested, you'll have an opportunity to talk about how you use the technology in a question and answer format. I have to warn you, though, some of these students have studied the privacy issues and they won't pull any punches. They will have prepared some difficult questions."

Dani swallowed. She really wasn't the confrontational sort. She responded the only way she could. "They may have prepared questions, but I haven't prepared any answers. I can only be honest about what I know and what I don't know."

Ms. Harris's no-nonsense expression softened. "How old are you?"

"I'm twenty-three."

"Not much older than my seniors."

"No. In some ways, those days seem like just yesterday," she confided.

"Well, do your best. If they get too antagonistic, I'll see if we can get them to debate each other to deflect some of it."

Dani flashed a grateful smile. "I'd appreciate it. I didn't expect this. I really like kids, and I respect their concerns."

The principal studied her. "You're different. They usually send one of those polished corporate mouthpieces to the high school. Do they know that you're so straightforward?"

Surprised, Dani felt herself being drawn to the older woman. Perhaps she didn't need to be on her guard after all. "Actually, I don't think they know me very well at all."

The two women eyed each other thoughtfully for the space of several seconds. It wasn't long, but it was enough. Dani realized she had found a friend—in a most unlikely place.

Ms. Harris turned to open the door. "Let me show you where to set up."

Dani had barely enough time to arrange her props and equipment before the high school students started filing in. She managed to smile at most of them as they entered, but only a very few of the kids smiled back. She could feel the tension in the air. She would just have to be as charming as she could to win them over.

Once they were settled in their seats, she began. "Welcome to my chronography presentation. Your principal, Ms. Harris, has told me that many of you are studying the science and the social implications of chronography. Good for you! We'll be spending the first part of our time together examining the technology and the science behind it, and we'll have a time to talk about the social implications later for those who are interested."

She saw some nods, but not everyone seemed receptive. "Who would like to tell me what you already know about the science of chronography?" she asked, emphasizing the word "science" just enough to direct their answers.

A young woman off to her left raised her hand. She was neatly dressed in a crisp white shirt with short, cropped bell sleeves. Dani nodded in her direction.

"Chronography," she said, "gives us the ability to analyze history through direct observation, reducing the subjectivity that we find even in original documents like letters."

"That's true. Does anyone know how it works?"

A dark-haired girl, lounging against her seat back, dressed in a rumpled tee shirt, spoke up without raising her hand. "You use old things as a source for sights and sounds and smells. When you put them in the box, they act like they've been little recorders all along, but you don't get their stuff until years and years later."

"Yes, exactly. So we can use them to find out what happened when no recorders were present. And then we can save the recordings for other people to analyze and interpret. If historians disagree about how something happened, they can go back to the same source that the first researchers used and draw their own conclusions. Does anyone know what we call that kind of research?"

A boy in the middle with bright blue hair leaned forward in his seat. She invited him to speak with an open hand held out in his direction. "That's original research, right? Not based on anyone else's research? And that's supposed to be more reliable."

Dani nodded. "It's very important to our view of the past to be able to establish things as true or false, or as simply someone's opinion of what's true. What are some things that you can't learn from a recording?"

More of the students were getting drawn into the discussion. Maybe they were realizing that this wasn't going to be the propaganda talk they had expected. Answers started coming more quickly.

"People's motives." "People's thoughts." "Anything that happened out of the room, or out of the line of sight," which gave rise to, "anything hidden in any way."

Dani smiled. There were some sharp minds in this group. "You've thought this through already, haven't you? Let me tell you what we find when we analyze a typical object."

She showed them the plastic and leather samples and told them the former wasn't helpful and the latter yielded only still photographs, which could be useful for establishing dates and times.

The girl in the white shirt asked, "How can you learn when something happened? If I look at a photograph, I can't tell when it was taken."

"One of the most important developments in the science of chronography was when we first learned how to calibrate for dates and times. Today, when we examine an object, we can zero in on a specific minute—even second—in time."

"How do you know what time to zero in on?" blurted a girl in a dark hooded sweatshirt who, until this moment, hadn't spoken.

Dani was impressed. It was a question she rarely heard, but it was so much a part of her job. She was starting to like this talk-only-about-the-science stuff. It got her into topics that she didn't usually get to address. "We don't. Not at first, anyway."

She reached over and picked up a ceramic vase from a nearby bookshelf. "Let's say someone donated this vase, or that we found it in an old house or museum. We have a vague idea that it might be useful because of where it was found, but we don't really know if it was always in that house, or museum, or anywhere, really. Let's say it spent most of its existence in a school like this one, but we don't know that."

She had their attention. "Ceramic is a good material to use as a source. We can get complete visual and audio recordings from it, with moving images, for as long as we want. If we pick a random time, and we happen to end up in the summer, what will we see and hear?"

There they were, on the cusp of summer. They didn't have to think long at all. "Nothing." "We're all gone in the summer."

"That's right, and we could have assumed that if we knew this vase was from a school. But we didn't. So we see nothing except this room, with nobody in it. Once we see that, we might be able to guess that it's in a school, and our second try at a recording will be more useful. What day and time would you pick?"

Hands went up. "You—when would you pick?"

"Well, I know that class meetings are here on some Wednesdays at 2:00 P.M., and those are usually pretty active, so that would be a good time." This, from a boy with short dark curly hair.

"Okay, but what if you didn't have that inside knowledge? What would you do?"

"I'd look at the room at regular intervals until I found something interesting."

"That's exactly what we do. Our initial scans are for a few seconds every fifteen minutes or so over an interval of a month or more at a time. I can set the scanner to automatically jump ahead and take these samples, but we restrict those to just visual recordings. Do you think that would be enough to tell when something interesting was going on?"

They were nodding, except the girl in the hooded sweatshirt. Now she spoke. "Not always, I think. What if someone stole something or got shot or something else that takes less than a minute from start to end? You wouldn't see anything."

"You're right. You wouldn't see anything at all. We'd look right over the top of that little incident, unless we knew right where—and when—to look. If we are trying to solve a crime, we can fine tune our calibrations a little better, to catch things like that, but the likelihood of our stumbling onto it randomly is really small. Anyone want to do the math?"

"I already have." The boy with bright blue hair looked up from scribbling on his worktablet. "If you assume five-second scans every fifteen minutes, and an event that takes about one minute from start to finish, you will see five seconds of it only about six and two-thirds percent of the time. If you only looked at one month a year, that percentage goes down to a little over a half percent chance of seeing anything at all. I assume you'd need all five seconds to get anything useful."

"That was quick, and you're exactly right. Would you like a job?" The students laughed, but the boy sat up a little straighter. Dani was impressed again. She hadn't expected anyone to actually take up her challenge. Not only had he done the math, he had taken it beyond the original question. She realized that she was beginning to really like these kids and starting to look forward to the political part of the discussion coming later.

"If we do happen to find something interesting, then we narrow down our time window and go back and take a second look. With this second look, we usually include the audio portion and the olfactory portion, if the material permits, but we narrow down the viewing angle for the visual to just the part we're interested in. With this vase, for instance, we don't really care about what the wall behind it looks like, and we'd probably have a general idea in which direction the action was taking place."

"What do you mean when you say, 'if the material permits'?" asked the boy who had done the figuring.

"We can't get scents from anything but metal. We could turn on the scent scanner, but it wouldn't give us anything. We didn't find that out until we'd been doing recordings for several years. We're a little more efficient now."

A girl in a bright yellow shirt was waving her hand. Dani nodded at her. "How do you set the viewing angle? I mean, I know there's a number you type in or scroll to or something, but what if someone turned the vase? Would you have to adjust for that?"

"You know, no one has ever asked me that before. We don't have to adjust, and the reason is simple: The angles are absolute angles, related to the earth's magnetic field. So 'north five degrees east' is always the same direction, regardless of whether someone has turned the vase or even upended it."

She looked at the clock on the viewwall to her left. It was already 1:45, and she hadn't even gotten out her equipment. "Would you like to try out the holographic projector before we get to the political questions?" Several students did, and she invited several of them to come up and learn how. Once she had showed a few how to point at the source location, set the direction, and turn on the projector, she left them experimenting and moved over to talk to Ms. Harris, who had sat quietly but approvingly through the whole talk.

"I think you'll be just fine during the political discussion," she said.

Eight students and Ms. Harris followed Dani into the conference room for the political discussion. She sat near the middle of one side of the long table, leaving the head of the table for whoever might want it.

She looked around to see what—and who—she might be facing. "Will you all introduce yourselves before we begin? Maybe one short sentence about why you're here today while you're at it. I'll start. I'm Ms. Adams, but I'm not much older than you and it's okay to call me Dani, if you want, with Ms. Harris's permission?"

Ms. Harris nodded her permission, and Dani went on. "I'm here today because I believe in the institute that I work for. I believe it has done some wonderful things, but I also know there are concerns about what it could do, so let's talk about those too."

She looked to her immediate left at the girl in the bright yellow shirt. "I'm Alanya. I'm here because chronography seems really exciting, but really dangerous. I want to know more."

The girl in the dark hoody, to her left, said, "Meredin. I love learning about the past. I just don't want everybody to know everything about my past. Or really, about anyone's past, without a very good reason."

The math whiz with the bright blue hair had claimed the spot at the head of the table just beyond them. "Joph. I like numbers. I want to be sure we're all getting the truth." He looked at her very directly as he spoke. She could tell he meant business, and she liked what she saw.

The dark-haired girl with the casual tee shirt was next to him, opposite Meredin. She had pulled one long leg up under the other and was attempting to sit cross-legged on the chair, which was falling short of adjusting to her posture. She gave up and decided to be satisfied with one leg up. "I'm Tejaswi, but people call me Jazz. I see things other people miss. This chronography stuff weirds me out. It's bad news. You're from RIACH, right there in the middle of the weirdness."

"Why are you here?"

"Honestly, I'm here to throw it in your face to see how you respond. No offense."

Dani laughed, amused in spite of the girl's challenge. Here was the opposition she'd been warned about, and she was keenly aware of the nods of agreement scattered around the long table. "Fair enough. I'll remind you that I'm an intern. I'm not in the middle of anything, really. I'm out on the edge. But I'll do my best to listen and answer what I can."

She turned to the curly-haired boy, who was sitting on the left of

Jazz. "Your turn," she invited.

"I'm Shard. I'm interested in everything, but I'm here mostly to get out of sixth period." His admission made everyone laugh, and lightened the tension.

An athletic-looking boy who hadn't spoken up during the technology discussion, and who had slipped in late to this one, sat directly across from Dani. At her nod, he spoke. "I'm Beck." He hesitated, trying to find words. "I don't really want to say why I'm here, if that's all right. It's personal."

"That's fine, Beck." Two more kids to go. She hoped she'd be able to remember these names. Ms. Harris was sitting next to Beck. Her gaze skipped past her to the next position, the other end of the long table.

"I'm Lora," said the girl in the white shirt who had defined chronography. "I think chronography should be regulated. I want to know if anyone is watching the watchers. And if nobody is, I want to make a lot of noise until people wake up and do something!"

Dani nodded. She'd almost gone full circle now. "And you?" she asked the slender young man sitting on her own right. His brown eyes held a friendly look.

"I'm Ronny." He had an engaging grin that took a little of the sting out of his next words. "Lora said exactly what I think, but there's more. You may be a really nice person, and chronography may be this exciting new science, but I don't think the people you work for are either nice people or pioneers. My grandfather is a detective, and he always says, 'Follow the money if you want to know what's going on.' I want to know how the Institute gets its money. It's privately held, and nobody seems to know who is financing it."

Dani cleared her throat. Where should she start?

Ms. Harris must have noticed her hesitation, because she spoke up. "I think most of our concerns center around the privacy issue. Would you like to address that first?" A murmur of agreement gave Dani the floor.

"You've all seen the four posters, I suspect?" she asked. They nodded. "Fresh perspectives. Reclaimed heritage. Solved crimes. Authentic atmospheres. Those slogans, along with the idea of our recordings being PastPerfect because we can see, hear, and smell them, form the public face of RIACH. But there's a lot that goes on behind the scenes, and if you were there for most of it, you'd find it to be really, really boring.

"Earlier today, you heard a little bit about how we sample a time period to try to find something of value. Let's imagine we were looking back on today from several hundred years in the future. Perhaps this discussion we're having now will end up being the long awaited catalyst that produces new laws. People from the future want to know what we said here. Is anybody recording this?"

They all shook their heads at her. "Neither am I. And for most historic events, that's the case. So a team of researchers from the future will have to use chronography if they want to know anything about what happens here. They may or may not know that we had our discussion at West Seattle High. They may or may not know that it was in June. They probably have no idea what room it occurred in. Also, most of the objects in this room will have been replaced or moved by the time they get interested. Look around. Do any of you see an object that would still be here in two hundred years?"

"The chairs?" suggested Meredin.

"They're mostly made of biodegradable plastic," said Beck.

"The metal parts, then?" asked Lora.

"Possibly, if the chairs are still intact, this research team might know that they came from this high school. But think of all the chairs in all the rooms. Should they sample all of them to try to find one that was in here?" Dani could tell they were beginning to understand the immensity of the TimeSearch project. "Also, if they've been damaged, they will have gone to a recycling station, and there will be no way of tracing them back here."

Other suggestions came in. The flag. The clock. A piece of

carpeting. In each case, Dani explained the difficulties. She summarized, "This is why we don't worry very much about privacy issues. The things we find, we just happen on, and it's not usually because we're looking for them."

Jazz hadn't said anything for a while, but now she spoke up. "If you're not worried, you're wrong not to be." They all turned in her direction. "The fact is, we're not worried about whether people two hundred years from now can find out what we did or said. We're worried about whether people today can find out. And any one of us could borrow a chair or even take our own clothing—natural fabrics work, right?—and take it in for analysis. Can you tell us truthfully that this is never done?"

Dani flashed back to the object she had investigated the day before. She didn't know why they had scheduled a recent object, and after seeing Marak, she hadn't really paid attention to the particulars of the images from the five minutes she recorded. She shook her head slowly. "I really don't know. I know that I seldom see anything newer than a hundred years, but it does happen, and I'm not the only one scanning objects. Besides the interns, sometimes the fellows and the researchers use the labs. I ... I can't really answer your question. I'd just be guessing."

Joph was scribbling. More math, Dani thought. He looked up. "Hey," he said. "You know, the reverse is true too. If you're not looking for a particular person's secrets and you'd be satisfied with anybody's, the odds favor finding something worth some money from all those objects. The newer the object, the better the chances."

"That's what my grandfather says." Ronny was nodding his head. He looked immensely gratified. "Follow the money. That would be a hard opportunity to resist, if you had a crack at it."

The room fell silent. Dani felt sick. The kids were right, and she realized she had buried thoughts like these far too long. They had hit on a piece of the truth from outside, but only an insider would have a chance to find out the rest. It suddenly hit her that she might be the only one in the institute willing to dig deeper.

"I think I need to do some research, and not the chronographic kind," she said. "When would you all like to meet again?"

"Actually," said Ms. Harris, "this group meets regularly on Saturdays, with me as their adviser. Ronny is the president. I think, under the circumstances, you would be welcome to join us. What do the rest of you think?"

As Dani looked around for their response, she saw eight heads nodding. Ronny, in particular, was enthusiastically in favor. He stood and stuck out his hand to her. "Welcome to the West Seattle High Political Action Club. See you at ten o'clock Saturday morning?"

Dani shook his hand. "I'll be there."

DESPERATION

SEEBAK LABORATORY, Vashon Island, WA. 1700, Tuesday, June 6, 2215.

"Doc? Doc! Your machine is buzzing," Lexil called, as he emerged from an observation room to the main work area. Dr. Seebak, though, was nowhere in sight. The younger scientist turned off the buzzer and checked the machine to be sure it wasn't signaling anything urgent.

Well. It was five o'clock. Maybe the doctor had decided to observe a normal quitting time for once. Lexil decided to check inside the house. He walked across the wooded pathway to the home they had both shared since Lex had lost his parents as a teenager and Doc had been named guardian.

Oh—what was this? An unfamiliar helicar on the parking pad. The number of people who knew where to find them were so few he could put them all in a four-seater helicar and still have room for the driver.

He entered the house cautiously and found Doc with a visitor in the main living room. His caution became delight. "Marielle!"

She turned at his voice, and the look of distress he glimpsed on her face turned quickly into a smile. She stood to give him a hug. He covered the distance between them in three long steps.

"Lex! You've grown even more since I saw you last. What are you,

190 centimeters by now?"

"No, not even close. Only 186." She was almost unchanged from the last time he saw her. Almost. "Your hair's longer."

She tucked a wayward curl of dark hair behind her ear. "Yes. I don't really get out much, so I've let it grow."

"It looks really nice. *You* look really nice." He had missed her. Back when his mom and dad had dinner parties, she was one of his favorites. He had actually had a little bit of a crush on her, even though she she was older. In her mid-thirties now, she was every bit as striking.

"So, Lex. Let me look at you. How long has it been?" She stood back to get the full effect and nodded approvingly.

"Four years? I think I was twenty-one. We were celebrating something."

She laughed. "You make it sound like it was nothing. That was your first degree, wasn't it?"

"Yes, but in a sense, it really wasn't anything big. I was working in the lab here before the degree and just went on doing more of the same after I got it."

Dr. Seebak agreed. "The degree was just a formality. He'd been doing groundbreaking research for years before that."

Lexil pulled a chair over to join them, but before he sat down, he hesitated. "Am I interrupting anything? You two looked pretty serious when I came in. If you need to talk privately, just say so."

He waited while they exchanged looks. It would be Marielle's decision, ultimately. Finally, she nodded. "It might be useful to have your perspective. We are both used to thinking in terms of what we're allowed to do and what we're not allowed to do."

And that simply wasn't right. He stuffed down the angry feelings out of habit. These two were brilliant, and they should have free reign in deciding what to study and what to publish. But there were patents, and there were copyright laws, and he knew there had been some arrangement, years earlier, before he was old enough to contribute an opinion, that curtailed some of their research.

He sat down. "I'll be happy to help, if I can."

Doc started. "Marielle was telling me that she has become aware of some intrusive practices by the board members at the institute."

"Aware of them!" Marielle exclaimed. "Try: subjected to them!"

Lexil could feel himself getting angry again. He didn't like seeing people he loved being victimized, no matter how they felt about it. "What are they doing to you?" he asked, prepared to leap to her defense, however ineffective that action might be.

"I've been told not to interact with any of the fellows or interns. My work must be restricted to fine-tuning existing technology, with no original research permitted. I'm watched all the time at the institute. I wouldn't be surprised if I were watched when I'm not there as well."

"How can you let them do that to you?"

She locked eyes for a second with Doc. "Well, I'm being blackmailed, essentially."

"What do they have on you that would make you so afraid of them?" Lex was incensed. Then he realized how personal that question might be. "I'm sorry. You don't have to answer that."

"It's okay. Some of it I'm not really comfortable sharing, but I'll tell you, in general, what they have. You remember that I used to be have a problem with substance abuse? You were a young teen back then."

"I heard about it, but I can't remember ever seeing you that way."

"One evening, I was involved in something. Making it public would have destroyed my career and ruined relationships. I could have dealt with the personal aspects of it, but the field of chronography would have suffered lasting harm." She spoke frankly, but he could see that it still hurt her to remember.

"Is that what you've been worrying about all these years?" Doc exclaimed. "The field of chronography has become no better than a mill, churning out data. Other than what we are doing here, all the great intellects have been buried in tedium. Not just you, either,

Marielle. I haven't seen anything from Calegari or Tasman for years."

"Unless they are making breakthroughs that aren't being published?" Lex offered. "Have you seen anything there?"

"No, and I would know. The three of us work really closely together. Nikoli—that's Dr. Calegari—has come up with some equations recently, but they are far from final form, and he has no equipment to adequately test them."

"So why worry about it? Come clean. Get out from under their influence."

"Ah, Lex." She looked at him fondly. "What I wouldn't give to have some of your youthful sense of invulnerability. I'm glad you grew up here. You've had so much freedom in your research."

"We all would benefit from that," Doc interjected.

"You made the right decision, Mitch. I should have bowed out and worked with you. You are still learning, still forging new ground, while I struggle to endure tedium."

"It is no picnic, though. I can't publish anything. The journals will have nothing to do with me."

"Will Lexil be able to publish?"

"He might. We haven't tried. His name has never been overtly associated with mine, but it can't be associated with anyone else's either, so he might not get the attention he deserves."

"My name's not my own, or I'd gladly lend it."

"I know." Doc patted her hand. "You have enough to worry about."

"I feel better, knowing that you know what is going on," Marielle said. "I worry about all of us going down in flames and nobody having any clue. But enough about me. What have you two been working on?"

"We've continued developing the sensors. We're still getting readings from the old machines that we started back at the turn of the century, when you were still a grad student." Doc was going to start reminiscing. Lexil could tell by his expression.

"Before chronography," she said.

"Yes, but chronography wouldn't have happened without them! And now they, and their brothers and cousins, are forming the basis for entirely new discoveries. Tell her, Lexil."

"We've been able to put equations to all the time disturbances. We can distinguish now between the random ones and the deliberate ones. Most of the deliberate ones are accompanied by peripheral events that generate their own effects."

"The timestream ripples." Marielle nodded. "I remember those. But these deliberate time disturbances—have you been able to trace their source?"

"Almost one hundred percent of them come from the institute," Doc contributed. "We really need someone on the inside, so we can compare our findings with what's happening over there."

"I can't," she apologized. "All my incoming and outgoing communications are tightly monitored. And I dare not try to contact someone else in there, someone less noticeable, because the person I choose would have a high likelihood of reporting our conversation."

"We understand," said Doc. "We're not asking you to. It would just help us a lot to have that contact."

"Ideally, we'd want someone in the lab, anyway," said Lexil. "Right down there in the middle of the action."

"There really isn't much action there now. You'd be disappointed, Mitch, at what it has become. The interns are doing busy work, more than anything. Not like your work here."

Lexil nodded. "Just this morning, I was showing Doc the results of my new equations. We've discovered—"

"You've discovered." Doc corrected him. "Credit where credit is due, boy."

"Well, then, stop calling me 'boy,'" Lexil countered with a feigned look of injury. "I've discovered distinct indicators of a third force, beyond the initial disturbance with its peripheral blips, and beyond the natural damping force, that appears to come in and clean up after the event. It repairs the damage caused by the blips."

She sat up and leaned toward him. "It can repair blips?" She sounded like she couldn't quite believe that.

"Not only can, but does repair them. And Doc found evidence that it has been happening for thousands of years."

She whistled. "Maybe I should just give them my notice and come work for you."

Lexil wanted to say, "Yes! Do it!" but Doc spoke first.

"You'd be welcome, of course, and your contribution would be invaluable. But I'm afraid attention would follow you over. We've been able to operate relatively free from interference here. Also, I think you may be the only one left there that has any kind of conscience."

"For the little good it does."

"Someday it might," Doc encouraged her. "How was it that you were able to come see us today?"

"My mother has been ill. I spent the day with her, down in Central Oregon, then flew back here a little faster than I should have to make time to stop and see you. My helicar needed a tune up anyway, so I used the excuse to rent one. I suspect they have a tracker on mine, but I picked up the rental just before I left."

"Are they going to those lengths now?" Doc frowned.

"I don't know. Maybe not. But I didn't want to risk focusing any of their attention on you."

"That was good of you."

"I try." A quick upward glance activated the clock on her eyescreen. "It's late. I need to get back to town before they figure out that I've strayed off my itinerary."

The other two stood and took turns giving her hugs. "You're welcome any time," said Doc, when they got to the door.

"I've never doubted that," she said with a grateful smile, and stepped out onto the porch.

"We need to keep in touch more," Lexil stopped her, with a hand on her arm. "Especially if you're being blackmailed and controlled like this. You have to have an exit route if things get rough."

"I can't call. I know they monitor that."

"Is there anyone at the institute that you trust that has more freedom to move about after work?" Doc asked.

"No. The only people they let me contact on a regular basis are Calegari and Tasman, and I think they are more likely to report on me than carry a message for me."

Lexil made a frustrated sound. Marielle didn't deserve this, no matter what she had done. "If it gets really bad, don't worry about us. You just come. Promise?"

"I promise," she said, giving his hand an affectionate squeeze, then headed out to the rental helicar. She waved through the window as her car lifted upward.

"So," said Doc, turning to Lexil. "What sounds good for dinner?"

10
DIRECTION

WALLACE HOME, Lower Queen Anne, Seattle, WA. 1800, Tuesday, June 6, 2215.

Dani paused at the edge of the slidewalk to let the irisscan identify her. She juggled her folders of activities for Jored, none of which she had used at the high school. She'd almost forgotten to bring the chocolate; good thing there was a vendor's stall in the transfer tube station. She was sure Kat would like the truffles she had picked out.

This was the home of her three closest friends, but she felt like a stranger meeting them for the first time. They hadn't changed a bit, she realized. She was the one who had changed. All her careless words that had dismissed Kat's concerns echoed accusingly in her head, but it felt like they had been spoken by someone else entirely. How could she have been so blind? How could she have been so duped?

The door had already announced her arrival. Jored would be opening it to welcome her. He would be excited. She needed to put all her misgivings out of her mind for his sake. Later, when he was tucked into bed, she'd pour out her heart to his parents.

"Dani!" Jored didn't wait for her to reach the door; he ran against the motion of the slidewalk to meet her and gave her a big hug. She couldn't believe how tall he was getting; his head almost reached her shoulder now. She was pretty sure he had been thirty centimeters shorter just a few months ago. Slight exaggeration there, but still: Were seven year olds supposed to be this tall? Well, his dad was a bit over 180 centimeters, so maybe.

"Hey, bud! I have some things to show you, but first, let's give your mom her chocolate, okay?"

"Sure, no problem." He knew, and she knew, that soon they'd be putting their heads together over a puzzle or a game, and he was content to share his Dani with others, for now.

"Hi Dani," said Marak, when he caught sight of her. "How's our favorite corporate minion?"

She made a face, but answered cheerfully, "Healthy and surrounded by my best friends. How can I complain?"

"Here's a knife. Want an apron?" Kat offered. "Barbecue's hot and we're making shish kebabs."

Dani put down her bag and folders. As she tied the apron and smoothed it down in front, she realized she still had the four objects in her pocket. She pulled them out and showed them to Jored.

"What are those for?" he asked.

"Why don't you try to guess? I'll set them up here on this shelf where you can see them, and you can tell me later."

"The knife's over here, when you're ready," said Kat. "We saved the onions for you."

"Of course you did."

"Hey, Dani! Do minions like onions?" asked Jored.

"Minions love onions. And they love Joreds, too! Yummy!" Leaving the knife on the counter, she ran after him with her tickle hands ready.

He ducked around a corner or two, but let her catch him. This was their game. "The onions!" he managed to get out between bouts of giggling. "They need you!"

Dani stopped suddenly and managed to assume a very serious

expression. "Oh. You're probably right." Her abrupt change brought new giggles from him, but she maintained her solemn demeanor as he followed her back out to the kitchen.

"Onions," she announced. "The onions need me."

Kat smiled and handed her the knife. They chopped and sliced companionably for a while, Marak on the beef, Kat on the peppers, and Dani on the onions. Then Dani thought of something.

"Skewers," she said. "The skewers need Jored."

"Oh, they absolutely do," Kat agreed. "Jored, they're over there on the counter. Here's a plate of what goes on them. Just separate the beef chunks with layers of peppers and onions, and be careful not to poke your finger."

"I won't," he scoffed. "I'm not a baby."

"Even older people can get poked, son," said Marak. "I don't know if you're ready for this."

He struck a stage pose and assumed a W.C. Fields voice. "Why, I remember when I was a lad of, oh, eighteen or so..." He whispered parenthetically to Jored, "before I ever met your mother," then continued, "I poked myself a time or two while I was making this very recipe!"

"There he goes again with one of his silly soliloquies." Kat rolled her eyes.

"It's the way they communicate," Dani observed in a whisper.

"There I was, standing all innocently in the kitchen of my own domicile..."

"What's a domicile?" Jored was intrigued.

"A house," explained Marak. "Do you want to hear this or not?"

"Not."

"Oh, well, okay. On with the skewering, then."

In another ten or fifteen minutes, they were finished. Marak told Jored, "These kebabs are ready to be shished! Or maybe it's these shishes that are ready to be kebabed. Anyone have a dictionary with etymologies in it?" He was still talking as he moved out of earshot to put the shish kebabs on the grill.

"Set the table, Jored, and then Dani can show you what she brought for you."

Jored was already opening drawers and cupboards. Marak came back in to help him reach the plates, and Kat helped him get the places set.

Dani went to get her bags and folders, and remembered to retrieve the four objects that had been part of her morning presentation. That seemed like a world away, now. She was eager to talk to Kat and Marak, but first she would milk every moment of joy out of the time she got to spend with Jored. She adored him, and she didn't care who knew it. She set them on the far end of the table.

"Here are some more of those touch-and-color pages. You can do those whenever you want," she said, as she brought out the pages, then reached for the game cards. "But I think you'll really like this new game. It's a holographic matching game. In each brown box, you touch the little blue circle in the center, and you might see a 3D image, hear a sound, or smell something. You can set it for sights, sounds, smells, or all three. Your goal is to turn over two that match at the same time, then you get to keep them turned. Otherwise, they flip back to the brown boxes."

"Will you play with me?"

"Sure! We can take turns. Marak? Kat?"

Soon the whole family was playing. Jored quickly realized that it was actually easier when he put the settings on "all three," and harder when they had four game boards going at a time, one for each type of sensory input and one mixed. Pretty soon they were sitting around the coffee table, turning over pairs, then passing the board to the next person. By the time the "sight" board got back to any of them, they had forgotten what was on it. They exulted over small victories and pretended someone had reset the squares when they couldn't remember. The game cards kept them happily occupied until the meal was ready.

"Hot off the grill," said Marak in his best waiter voice, and soon they were enjoying the results of their kitchen teamwork.

"Best barbecue ever!" said Jored, rubbing his tummy. "Now can you tell me what those four things are for?"

Dani brought the plastic, leather, stone, and metal objects over where he could touch them. "Do you want to guess?"

"Are they samples of stuff that can have chronographic recordings in them?" he asked, with that cute little look that his face took on when he was thinking. Was this boy smart or what?

"You're exactly right. Except three of these objects are made of materials that can retain a chronographic recording, and one can't. Can you guess which one can't?"

"Um...the plastic one? Because it's synthetic? Or the leather one, because it's from an animal?"

"The plastic one is right, and you guessed the right reason. You can think of all the rest of these objects as little miniature recorders. They aren't actually doing the recording, of course. They have to be placed in my chamber at work, and the chamber uses their chronetic energies to focus a recording device on some specific time in history. That's how we see things."

Jored touched each sample, except the plastic one, with a look of awe on his face. Dani laughed. "They're not anything special. They're a rock, and a metal disk, and a piece of leather."

"But that's what makes them special," he said, earnestly. "Stuff we see every day can do all that."

Dani told herself again how lucky she was to know this kid, with his untainted sense of wonder. She mussed his hair and gave him a hug. "Hey, how about a game of chess before bed?"

She had barely mentioned the idea and he was already pulling her down the hall to his room to get the chess set. She guessed that was a yes.

It was a cute room, decorated with scruffy-looking dog images hovering in a slightly raised 3D effect on several of the bright yellow walls. When he turned on the light, they chased each other and fought over a couple of tennis balls. She'd been in his room many times, and each time the pups did something different. If she ever had kids of her own, she thought, she'd have Kat come help her decorate.

"Do you want to play here?" Jored asked.

"Let's take it back out to the living room, okay?"

Kat came back from tucking Jored into bed. She shook her head. "I still have to remind him to brush his teeth. He never remembers."

"Probably has a lot of other things on his mind," said Marak. "He's always thinking about something."

Kat glanced over at Dani. "Speaking of having other things on your mind, what happened yesterday afternoon? Do you want to talk about it?"

Dani sighed. She almost wanted to say, "No, we can do that another time." It had been so nice to just behave normally for a few hours, but now all her doubts came rushing back and she knew she needed to talk. Now. Tonight.

She started slowly, watching their reactions. "I saw something yesterday that shook me up. A lot. I don't know who else to talk to about it."

"What happened?" asked Kat.

"I was doing an investigation—that's usually a second, more specific look at something we did a sample scan of earlier—of an object. The date specified was not quite nine years ago, which is unusual because, as you know," she looked at Kat, "I'm usually sampling things from hundreds of years ago."

Kat nodded.

"This object was a padlock on an old iron gate." Still no sign of recognition. "Marak, I saw you there."

He looked puzzled. "With a padlock? Where was this?"

But Kat was getting it. "Nine years ago? Did it happen to be

September 17?"

Dani nodded, miserable. She felt ashamed, like she had intruded on a private moment without being invited. "Marak, all you did was shake the padlock and put it down. But I felt like I was spying on you."

A look of realization spread across his face, and he looked over at Kat. "September 17. That was ... that was when we met, right? And the padlock must have been ... the one on the gate to your uncle's estate."

Kat patted his hand, "Very good!" She turned to Dani. "He always has a hard time remembering dates."

"Yeah, I remember that date. But, Dani, why would you feel like you were spying? There wasn't anything personal about that moment. I was just shaking a padlock."

"I know. It wasn't that. It's just that these scans I do are always so far away, so long ago, that they've only been interesting historically. This was within my lifetime. And of all the objects and places and moments within those years, what are the chances that I'd see someone I know? It shook me." She brushed her eyes, willing the tears away. "Maybe I'm being silly, but I had nightmares all last night."

"You're not being silly," Kat said firmly. "You're just realizing what a lot of us have known for years."

Encouraged, Dani continued. "And then, this afternoon, I went to give a presentation to the high school. I used to do those all the time, back when I was first hired. All my starry-eyed enthusiasm won over whole crowds of kids. We see them as potential scientists, you know, and potential investors and publicists and film writers who will shape the attitudes of the world in years to come. I've always felt like a missionary, and I'm pretty good—really good—at it."

"But today was different?" Marak asked, keen on the story. In a family setting, she rarely saw the investigative journalist, but she could see it now. Marak was also really good at his job, mostly because people trusted him. They spilled their guts to him.

"Today, the high schoolers won *me* over. They had questions I couldn't answer. They'd done research and dug into the math of the whole thing, and I realized...." She took a breath. How to say this, exactly? "I realized that there is not only the potential to abuse this whole technology, but there's an overwhelming probability that it is, in fact, being abused. I came away from that meeting determined to try to find out where the institute gets its money, and why it's looking at things that happened so recently. I actually kind of joined their club."

Her two friends glanced at each other warily. "Dani, be careful. Sometimes it's better to just let things lie."

"Or let people lie? And keep lying?" Dani exclaimed, with fervor. "Don't you see? I'm worried about people I care about. I'm worried about you, Marak! Why would someone be asking me to investigate something you touched?"

"Dani, really, don't worry about me. Nothing happened there that day, except I walked away from the padlock, thought about climbing a fence, and greatly amused Kat in the process. There's no vulnerability here. Really. Nothing to worry about."

"You're sure?"

"Positive."

Her tension began to melt away. She felt her shoulders relax. And then, perversely, the tears began to flow. Kat moved over to sit next to her on the couch and gave her a reassuring hug and a tissue. She blotted her eyes, wiping off most of her makeup in the process. The moment passed.

"I'm sorry. I don't know why I did that."

"It's all good. You're loved here and you know it." Marak smiled. "If we can put up with you acting like a maniac, running down our halls after our son, we can take a few tears."

"Will you guys help me figure out what to do?"

"Why do you have to do anything?" asked Kat. "If you find

something incriminating, you could come across people that wouldn't be happy about that."

"Says the person who stands out with a sign, persuading people, every day? How can you ask that?"

"Dani," Kat said gently, "my role is pretty benign. I'm not really a threat to anyone. I can influence public opinion, but nobody can go to jail from the things I do. With your insider's access, you could become a real threat to them."

"These are scientists! They're not going to hurt me. I just need to find out if somebody is using the technology wrongly and let them know. They'll want to do what's right."

Kat and Marak exchanged glances again. "I think we should tell her," said Marak. "She needs to know." Kat hesitated, then finally, reluctantly, nodded.

"How much do you know about the inventors of chronography?" Kat asked.

"Seebak and Howe? A lot." Dani was on familiar ground now. "Dr. Howe was this exciting, brilliant woman who lit up the whole field for me until her accident—I was only twelve then. Dr. Seebak stayed mostly in the background, but he was really gifted. In college, I heard stories about how he'd walk into the room where everyone else was struggling with some complication—maybe an equation that wasn't working out or an unexplained equipment glitch—and within a few minutes, he'd have it all figured out and they'd be up and running again. But he became sort of a mystery himself. He did something that caused him to be banned from the project—and from any other project that I know of, for that matter. We never hear about him any more. No presentations, no articles in the journals, nothing."

"Actually, he's still working in the field," said Kat. "He just keeps out of the public eye—by design."

"What? How do you know?"

"I have contacts," said Marak.

His wife continued, "It's better if you don't know any more, but I do want you to know this: Dr. Howe's accident was no accident, and Dr. Seebak's departure was a compromise he accepted so that he could live without fearing for his own life. Scientists or not, you can't just go blundering into this."

Dani shook her head, refusing to believe it. But she was once again hearing the numbers in her head, and once again seeing Dr. Calegari turn to hide his scribbles when she came into the room, and once again feeling her isolation from those that headed the project. Could it be that they could be involved in something deeper? Were they being threatened? Or worse—she caught her breath—were they threatening others? She was suddenly very certain that Kat and Marak were right. And who was she, an insignificant intern with no power of the press behind her, to challenge something that was powerful enough to end Dr. Seebak's career?

And then, on the heels of inadequacy and intimidation, an indignation rose up, a fierceness that surprised her. Chronography was still an amazing science. How dare they use it for corrupt purposes? She set her jaw. "Then tell me what I can do to help."

11
ANTICIPATION

HUNTER'S OFFICE. 0700, Wednesday, June 7, 2215.

Hunter enjoyed the early morning hours, before the functions of his real business bowed to the necessities of maintaining a professional façade. Soon, office routines would get their grip on the little people who served him, and they'd be scurrying around like bugs, intent on their petty purposes without a clue about what was really going on.

He hated them equally, the people who sat securely in their palaces of wealth and influence, and the insignificant ones who served them, directly or indirectly. He hated the powerful ones because their comfort had its foundation in the agonies of others. As a child, he had dreamed of taking them down. He hated the weak ones because they were so easily victimized and did nothing to step out of their squalor. None of them had had the backbone to stand up to him. Any initial resolve had crumpled beneath his threats.

He waited by his desk for the call he knew would come. Besides collections, part of his work involved acting as the bridge between the group and their depositors. Periodically, he reported to them, letting them see that he was in control of the variables in their mutual enterprise. His practice was to anticipate their concerns and have a solution in place before they contacted him. It helped to have cultivated the loyalty of their own confidential secretaries. Nothing happened in their offices that he didn't know about first.

He hated them, too, of course.

Another part of his job involved collecting the information that served as such an effective inducement, the basis for everything, without which their goals would have been impossible.

Today, he would launch another demonstration, and they would be satisfied again, leaving him in unquestioned power. When it came time for him to apply the same pressures on them that they urged him to apply on others, it would be too late.

The connexion icon buzzed. He steeled himself. They must not suspect his true opinions of them. He waved at the icon. Two separate figures appeared on his viewwall, each displayed from the waist up. They were seated behind desks, of course. He preferred to stand, and he had subtly positioned his camera and the focal point on his viewwall at slightly below eye level, so that from their point of view he continually looked down on them. He remained silent, forcing them to make the first move. He knew his silence would be taken as subservience, but it was anything but.

Bradford spoke first. "We're seeing signs that the screws need to be tightened on the central fixture. And the monitoring equipment will need to be expanded as well."

"We haven't been able to track its whereabouts as efficiently as we should," added Griffin.

Their guarded words told Hunter more than they knew. They didn't trust their own staff members. And they were wise not to.

"I've located the necessary tools already," he assured them. "I'll have them later today and I can use them before the end of the week."

Their relief was evident. Both were nodding. "Very well," said Bradford. "Proceed. Your methods have been quite effective to date."

The connexion closed.

12
COLLABORATION

RIACH LABS, Alki Beach, Seattle, WA. 0800, Wednesday, June 7, 2215.

When Dani entered the institute Wednesday morning, she had two assignment lists. One was built from the suggestions that Marak and Kat had given her the night before. The other was the one displayed on the viewwall.

MORNING SCHEDULE—Lab D, station 3
1. Ob:082036 21800216:091505/N-47.5. Rec:N Check/Decay
2. Ob:082037 21781130:152005/N-47.5. Rec:N Check/Decay
3. Ob:082038 21810314:134505/N-47.5. Rec:N Check/Decay

She groaned at the list, which filled the screen and displayed a blinking "continue" triangle. These were the most tedious of assignments. Unlike the routine samplings and investigations, the "Check for Decay" assignments required her to retrieve scores of objects, one at a time. She would not be making recordings at all, but just letting the observation box integrate with her to see if a recording could still be made.

She knew they were necessary. As the scope of the TimeSearch project had grown, a new—or initially undetected—phenomenon had come to light. Some objects, when reexamined, had been unable to reproduce the recordings made from them the first time. The earliest, and most notable, of these instances had been two of the four objects in the hallway display cases. Important people had come to tour the institute soon after it opened, and a highlight of the tour was to let them step into the observation boxes and experience the famous recordings for themselves.

Dani had to admit that there were few better ways to impress potential investors or lawmakers than to let them relive a moment from the distant past through neurological links. People never expected it to feel as real as it did.

But that first attempt at showmanship failed miserably. After months of flawless sensory output, suddenly it was gone.

As a student, Dani had read several accounts of the event and the studies that had followed it, trying to determine what had happened. Two of those objects that had become so famous, the wire whisk and the tile sample, yielded no sensory information at all. The machines behaved as if they had no object to read. The baseball barely saved the day. It gave a satisfactory view of the crowds flying past at 96 miles per hour before glitching out just before hitting the glove. Nobody tried the axehead. The photo was gruesome enough, without the live action aspect of it.

The phenomenon of the sudden loss of access came to be known as "time decay," and the objects that failed to give a reading were known as "blanks." Dani enrolled in a graduate-level research class with the same name and worked with her fellow students to pin down the cause. Their first clue came when they realized that the first time an object was scanned, it was never a blank. Blanks came from the second, third, or fourth scanning, and sometimes not at all. Also, an object that was a blank for a particular interval might give a full reading if its scan interval was adjusted to a day, an hour, or even a few minutes later or earlier.

They tried different ways to make an object go blank. They tried exposing it to extremes in temperature or pressure and ruled out those factors. No surprise, since all the objects were stored under the same environmental conditions. They ran analyses to see if the compositional material influenced the decay, and came up negative. Finally they tried using the VAO converters on the recordings from the object, first making photographs, then moving images, then adding sounds and olfactory information. The photographs didn't seem to cause decay, but they began having positive results when they tried to convert any recording that lasted more than a fraction of a second and then played the converted recording on an auxiliary device.

That was the breakthrough. Once the scan of an object had been recorded, converted, and replayed, the interval in the finished product was no longer productive for scans, ever again. Dani's class had won an award for the paper they presented on the topic. They didn't offer the class the next quarter; the deans declared the problem solved, even though the paper had proposed further research on exactly what happened to the chronetic energies of the objects to make the scans fail. Someday, they had said. For now, it was enough to know how to prevent it from occurring.

It wasn't until Dani had graduated and had come to work at the institute, that she found out there were discrepancies. Her neat little set of conditions still yielded blanks, but there were other blanks too, and nobody knew why. Some objects with only original recordings, or both original and converted recordings, were experiencing time decay without ever having the recordings replayed. It was a puzzle. It made it up to number twenty-three on the list of topics to be studied further before slipping down as more important topics were proposed. Last she checked, it was at number forty.

Thus, the periodic checks of objects, the rescans to document whether each object was still productive. Tedious and frustrating for Dani, but necessary to gather data in case that topic ever made it to the top of the list. Also, it gave researchers more confidence when requesting objects for their projects.

She had arrived at Lab D. She consulted her list of objects again, and went to the library to retrieve the first ones. She had learned to save steps by bringing the objects back to the box with her in groups of ten or so and swapping them out as needed. She didn't even have to disconnect from the integrated sensors. Labels on the objects themselves made it easy to put them back in place when she was done. She went back to the lab with a whole tray full of objects.

Then she stepped in the box to begin.

As lunchtime neared, Dani remembered her assignment. Her other assignment, the one Kat and Marak had cautiously agreed to let her undertake. She hoped it wouldn't be too obviously out of character for her to get lunch in the cafeteria. She would need to start by making some friends, and, after accessing the general employee files, she knew just the person to start with.

The Financial Services intern looked up, startled, when she set her tray down on his table. "Is this seat taken?" she asked him, with her most winning and disarming smile.

"Uh, no." He hastily moved some of his mess to the other side of his tray. A mess which included, she noted, an actual book. Made of paper. Which he was trying to hide.

"Wow. Where did you get that?" she reached over, boldly, pretending to an interest that wasn't altogether pretense after all. Where *did* he get that?

He tried to slide it just out of her reach, then realized the futility. "Uh, I, uh, can't remember?" he tried. Then, all of a sudden, he relaxed and looked straight at her with his own, surprisingly gorgeous, strikingly blue eyes.

"Truth is," he admitted, "I borrowed it from the library."

Sure enough, there was a tag on the back. "Ah. 085212," she observed. "I should have recognized it, I suppose, being an intern down there and all."

He laughed, but there was still a trace of nervousness. This was a huge lapse, one that could get him fired, or worse, and they both knew it. It was also, she realized, the perfect opportunity to further

her assignment.

"There are a lot of them down there," he said. "Imagine that. There are books in the library, along with all those other objects. I'm guessing it's hard to keep track of them all."

She gave back the book and sat down, making a show of looking over the food on her tray, deciding whether to start on the salad or the sandwich.

"Are you going to turn me in?"

"Depends."

"I never take them out of the building," he blurted. "I just read them here."

"Them? This isn't the first one?" She kept her tone casual and unaccusing. She wasn't really interested in getting anyone in trouble, and besides, this was the most intriguing thing that had happened to her in the six months she had worked here. Maybe she should have stepped out of her little bubble sooner.

"No," he confessed, sheepishly. "I guess I really incriminated myself there, didn't I? In my defense, I take really good care of them."

"Oh, I can see that," she glanced sideways at his pile of napkins and food wrappers, under which he had been hiding his book earlier. "And nobody has ever noticed? How long has this been going on?"

"Nobody notices me at all, actually. I'm an intern."

She knew the feeling. "Nobody notices me either."

"I sure haven't. I'd have remembered, if I did!" His ears turned a little pink at the tips.

Dani flushed. She'd forgotten what happened when she let down her "don't talk to me, I'm busy" defenses. Still, a little infatuation could be useful too, if she didn't let it go too far. Besides, she could do worse.

She smiled, shyly and a bit, just a bit, flirtatiously. "So you'll be remembering now?"

"Oh yeah. Definitely."

"I'm Dani."

"I'm Anders." Anders Peerson, she knew from the personnel records, but she didn't say anything.

"So, Anders, what are you reading? Anything good?"

"Actually, yeah. It's kind of a sci-fi spy novel."

Better and better. He might actually want to help her even without the threat of being reported. "Would you recommend it? Maybe I'll borrow it when you're done," she teased.

"I only recommend books to people I know well."

Was that an invitation or a rebuff? She wasn't sure.

His voice grew a little softer. "I'd love to recommend a book to you, actually, when I know you a little better. You're the best thing that's happened to me in months."

"Me too." Inexplicably, she felt more lighthearted than she had in a long time. Whoa, girl. Remember your assignment, she reminded herself.

They conversed over vegetable barley soup and sandwiches with tall piles of deli beef. He found out she was on her own, without parents or siblings. She found out he had an older brother whom he idolized. He bought her a coffee. She tidied his mess while he was gone. He ignored his book, leaning forward to absorb every detail when she talked about her favorite old movies. She laughed at his stories about growing up in a family that packed up and moved every two or three years.

As the hour drew to a close, Dani wished it could continue. Suddenly, she remembered her assignment. "Hey, you work in Financial Services, right?"

"I'm flattered you noticed."

She laughed. "I had a student ask me the other day, in one of my presentations, something I couldn't answer."

"What do you need to know?"

"Where do we get our money from? Who funds the institute? Is there a public record somewhere, or even something general that we let people see?" There, that sounded like a legitimate reason for asking, without any trace of a hidden motive. And it had the added advantage of being completely true.

"I can probably dig something up for you. Does it have to be public? I can access some files that the general public can't. I have a talent for ferreting out useless pieces of information in places most people wouldn't think to look. I was kind of known for that in college." He laughed sheepishly. "Thus the fascination with spy novels."

"Oh yeah, I suppose." She squelched the eagerness that she felt bubbling up inside her and tried her best to appear only casually interested. "I can get a general picture from it and summarize for the kid."

"Sounds good. After work, then? Do you get off right at five?"

As they talked, they were standing up, gathering belongings and trays. Preparing to go their separate ways.

"Yes, right at five. I'll meet you outside the security gates, on those benches under the clock tower."

"It's a date, then," he said. "I mean ... let's do it."

But as Dani dumped her wrappers in recycling, deposited her tray on the rack, and headed back to work, she entertained the lingering conviction that he meant something more.

She felt astonishingly upbeat, even when she looked over her afternoon list and discovered more—many more—time decay checks. One thing about boring task lists: They gave her time to think.

Back at the library shelves, she was happy to discover that the next twenty-two items were small enough to fit on one tray. She could fit one more into her lab coat pocket—whoa, what was this? She realized she still had the four sample materials in her pocket from yesterday. She'd have to remember to take those back to the supply room. Oh well, they had probably twenty more sets there, so these wouldn't be needed any time soon.

She carried the items back to the scanner station. This batch could keep her occupied for at least an hour and a half, and she could plan out her next step. Kat and Marak would be pleased with her progress.

Dani was a little surprised that she was enjoying this so much. Maybe she missed her calling, she thought wryly. She wondered idly what the market was for academic espionage. She was half-qualified; they'd have to consider her, anyway. Whoever "they" were.

She stepped into the observation box and placed the items on the small table there, arranging them in order by their tags, then stepped into the box and let the sensors integrate with her brain. The rest of this she could almost do with her eyes closed, if she didn't have to set and check the parameters.

She placed the first object in the chamber.

13
DISRUPTION

HUNTER'S OFFICE. 1320, Wednesday, June 7, 2215.

It was time. Hunter stood and moved out from behind his massive desk. Its size was meant to make him less accessible and more intimidating, but he always preferred to stand.

With a quick gesture of his hand, he pulled the connexion icon over to the center of the sparsely populated viewwall. Another twist and a microphone icon pulsed, awaiting his spoken command. "Dr. Brant," he spoke into the air. The microphone vanished. He waited only seconds before the scientist's image appeared on his wall. His own image to her was blank. They expected that. It protected their privacy, he always assured them, should anyone look over their shoulders and see the screen.

He waited while she stood and closed the door to her office. That was good. What he had to say would not be overheard.

"You are alone?" he asked her.

"Yes. They just left. What did you want me to see?"

"Something has come into my possession that might, shall we say, dredge up old memories. It's not the sort of thing you'd want out where someone might access it inadvertently—or intentionally."

"Someone already has, obviously."

"I have gone to the trouble of ensuring that I have the only copy. I just want you to know the enormity of what I'm protecting you from. You have a holographic projector there, as I suggested?

She tapped the desktop device to her left. "I have it. Here's the icon."

A small rotating image of a hologram appeared on his viewwall. "Will you have privacy long enough to watch it?"

"Yes, my office door is closed. I won't be disturbed."

He waved again at a corner of the screen and sent the recording to her projector. As he played the recording on his projector, she would be able to view it simultaneously on hers. Another quick glance through the glass door assured him that his executive secretary was busy with a list he had given him earlier, his back to the soundproof office, oblivious for the moment as to anything that occurred within.

"Watch." He touched the start button.

A garden bloomed before them, late summer flowers and tree branches nodding gently in the breeze. A fountain gurgled in the background, and birds chirped. The scents of late-blooming lilacs, hybrid tea roses, and honeysuckle mingled with faint smells of city exhaust settling down from the air overhead. On a cobblestone patio to the right of the hologram sat a bistro set, two white wrought-iron chairs and a matching table.

A distinguished-looking middle-aged man emerged from the left, his hand on the elbow of a young woman in a fluffy pink sweater. His gesture was one of support, not control. His expression was sympathetic, his actions considerate. He pulled out a chair for the woman, who was clearly shaken.

On the viewwall, he could monitor Dr. Brant's reactions to what she was seeing and hearing. As he watched, her face hardened, which was not what he'd hoped. He did not want to strengthen the hint of resistance she had been showing. He frowned. She would know this scene well, would remember sitting in that chair some nine years earlier. She would remember Dr. Mitchum Seebak and the conversation they had that day. He could only hope that the memories would stir up the guilt she had buried.

There it was now: another emotion crossing her features. He saw shame, followed by regret, and those responses, in the principled woman that he knew her to be, would be enough to secure her firmly in his grasp. Ironic that he could use her very principles against her this way.

In the hologram, the other scientist was speaking. "Please, sit, Marielle. Relax. I'm here to listen, but not until you're ready."

"I'm ready, Mitch. I have to talk to someone."

He nodded. He brushed her hair back away from her face, and gently wiped a tear from her cheek. With another man, this might have been a presumptive or possessive move, but with him it seemed almost fatherly. He handed her a tissue and waited quietly for her to compose herself.

She breathed quietly and deliberately for a few moments, closing her eyes and inhaling the peace of the garden, clearly willing it to calm her before she spoke. Finally, she opened her eyes.

"I killed him, Mitch."

"Killed him? Who?"

"Nicah Myles. I drove the helicar that hit him and Elena that night. I killed him, and I put her into a coma." She looked up suddenly, alarmed. "Please don't tell Lexil!"

"Of course not!" He reassured her. "But surely, it was an accident?"

"That's the thing. It wasn't. I mean, I didn't do it on purpose, but it was preventable. It should have been prevented! Oh, Mitch ... I was drunk!" She buried her face in her hands, weeping, trying to stop.

When he draped his arm over her shoulders, it made her melt down completely. He pulled it back, wanting to give her space, and patted her back reassuringly, if a little awkwardly.

The hologram ended. Dr. Brant turned her attention from the projected image back to her viewwall, looking at him directly. "What are you going to do with this?" she asked.

"Not a thing, Marielle. I'm looking out for your best interests—our best interests. By showing you this, I've forced the source object to experience time decay, and you know of course that that makes it unusable."

She nodded.

"No one else can view this scene, unless they get it from me. Surely you can see that I'm doing this to protect you."

"As long as I continue to cooperate."

Good. She was getting the message clearly. "Yes, unfortunately, that's what they want. But I told them you have every intention of cooperating, so there is no point in even bringing that up, is there?"

"No, no point at all. Are we done here, then?"

"Yes, done, except for one thing that they've requested. I'm certain you will want to help with it, for our, uh, mutual benefit. To keep all this contained."

"Name it."

"It is time to cut personnel, strategically. We've observed certain, shall I say, extracurricular access to files. Such access could threaten us—all of us—personally. You'll take care of it?" He waved a list of names from the corner of his viewwall to the icon that represented her screen.

She studied it, making note of each name. Since she had gone through the treatment, her incisive mind and photographic memory had returned fully. She wouldn't need to refer to it again. By morning, those employees would be gone. "Yes, I'll take care of it."

"Good. It has been a pleasure, as always. I don't have to remind you to say nothing of our conversation?"

She shrugged. "You're the man who's keeping it all together."

He nodded. As she signed off, he returned to the chair behind the wholly unnecessary desk. People were amply—and very satisfactorily—intimidated without it.

14
ALTERATION

RIACH LABS, Alki Beach, Seattle, WA. 1430, Wednesday, June 7, 2215.

When Dani emerged from the observation box, she had a moment of vertigo. She steadied herself on one of the support pillars nearby. She shook her head to clear it. Things felt strange, although she couldn't put her finger on why, nor be any more specific than that.

"Things." What things? The light seemed different somehow. The air smelled funny. "Strange." How, exactly? She couldn't explain, and she was glad no one was asking. She wondered if she might be getting sick.

Steadied, she turned to take the tray of items from the observation box. Time to replenish her supply. She was an hour and a half closer to getting those financial details from Anders. Two-and-a-half hours to go.

She got three more batches done by the end of the day, and had only found one instance of unexpected time decay. That was a good ratio. Someone would be pleased. Her steps lengthened as she approached the exit, willing herself forward more quickly. She didn't even notice that the pale blue walls were strangely and inexplicably a subtle shade of teal now, or that the air held a slightly more tangy scent. Her mind was preoccupied with the meeting ahead.

They both got through security without acknowledging one

another. She reveled in the cloak-and-dagger feel to their arrangement. Anders was first, and Dani noted that he walked purposefully around the corner toward the clock tower and the tube station. She followed him, rounding the corner. There he was, waiting on the bench.

"You ready for some interesting reading?" He gestured to a screen full of small numbers on his worktablet and chuckled. "Numbers don't scare you, do they?"

"Not at all. Which tube are you taking?"

"Blue line. I live on First Hill."

"Really? So do I? Well, let's ride together, and you can show me."

They waited for a chance to get a tube by themselves. It was rush hour, so most of the six-seater tubes were filled rapidly. They barely noticed the delay. After he transferred a copy of the data to her worktablet, they continued their conversation from lunch. He talked about places he had traveled. She talked about places she'd seen through chronography. Finally the station had mostly cleared out, and they found a tube to themselves.

They settled into the seats and let them adjust to their posture. Anders got out his worktablet and started scrolling through the data. He might have been joking when he first showed it to her, but after a few minutes of study, Dani realized it was interesting reading. With their heads together, he pointed out several generous influxes of funds that were attributed only to "investment" or "contribution."

"A lot of the rest of the funds came in marked like that too," he said. "But when I traced them back, they all had sources listed; some several, some just one. I plugged the details into the data fields. When I followed these, though, they were dead ends."

"So, donors who wish to remain anonymous?"

"No, those are listed as anonymous donors and given a number for tax purposes. These are deliberately obscured."

She tried to estimate the total from the pages of data, then gave up. "Approximately what proportion of the funding comes from these unnamed sources?" she asked him, hoping he might have done the math earlier.

"Approximately? How about exactly? It's forty-three point six percent."

She was stunned. "Almost half of the institute's operating expenses are from unnamed sources? How could anyone not have noticed this?"

"It's possible someone has," Anders replied. "I saw signs of people having gained access to some of these files within the last few weeks."

She frowned at him, worried. "You're leaving a trail when you look at these?"

"Oh, no, not me." He dismissed her concerns with a laugh. "I don't leave trails. I'm like a ninja. I come and go and nobody knows."

He was so nonchalant, she relaxed immediately, and she laughed with him. Then she sobered. "Anders, I can't tell this to high schoolers."

"No, you can't. Seems like somebody should know, though."

"That's a huge amount of money. Somebody might care if others found out."

"And we don't have anything specific. It might be all innocent, although I don't see how it could be."

"I can't think of any innocent explanation either."

They sat in silence for a few moments. "Here's my stop," Anders said.

"Mine's the next one."

"Let me do a little more digging, okay? Maybe I can get something more concrete, some names or something. Then we can figure out who to go to with it." He stood up. "Tomorrow at lunch?"

She nodded. "See you tomorrow."

After Anders got off the subway, Dani called Kat. She wanted to talk to her and Marak, but she had to do some thinking first. Much as she'd like to see Jored, it would probably be better to wait till after his bedtime.

"Hello?"

"Hi Kat!" She tried to make her voice sound natural, in case anyone was tuned in, and shook her head at how she was fitting so comfortably into this spy-novel-turned-to-life. "Hey, I'd like to come see you guys again tonight. Could I come by around 8:45 or 9:00?"

"Sure! We'll have a glass of wine and some dessert."

It was Dani's stop. "I'll see you then." She disconnected and stood up.

It wasn't until she got out of the tube and started home that she remembered back to what Kat had said and realized something was a little unusual. Since when did Kat and Marak have wine at night? Usually, they only brought that out for fancy meals. And as far as she knew, they always waited for her to bring the dessert. Was there some special occasion they were celebrating that she had forgotten? She was usually so good about remembering dates.

Dani was still puzzling about it when she got to her apartment. But she put the thought aside until later. For now, there were things to do.

She fixed a quick stir-fry dinner and ate while she thought things through. She set her worktablet off to the side and set the switch to project windows above it. She moved the panel with the numbers Anders had gathered to the left, and set up a notes panel to scribble her observations. She wanted to have some specific information to give to Kat and Marak, besides that almost unbelievable forty-three point six percent.

The names and numbers would come, she hoped, from Anders's further research tomorrow morning, but there were patterns she could look for in the data he'd already provided. When did the undesignated funding start? Had it been growing? Had it been consistent all along? Was there any possibility that it could be contributed by the board of directors or someone else in charge? She didn't know that much about accounting practices. She was glad

Anders was so eager to help.

It appeared that the contributions and investments had begun within months after the new technology had been announced and the institute had been established. The first unattributed donation was dated September 2204, with another in October. Then they had stopped, until March of the next year, when the third contribution had come in. The next was not until June, and then they started coming in multiples, two at a time, three at a time, in amounts that varied from mere thousands to hundreds of thousands of credits. In the last few years, the contributions had increased both in number and size, so that now some of them amounted to millions and hundreds of millions.

Another question occurred to her, one she would have to ask Anders to check when they met tomorrow. She knew the institute had hundreds of employees, and if she were to judge from her own extremely generous stipend, they were well paid. But with the amounts of money coming in, she wondered where it went. Quick estimations of salaries, equipment, operating expenses, and various government fees and taxes came far short of the total money coming in. Was it being spent? Or was it being stored for some other purpose? How wealthy was the institute, exactly?

Ronny's exhortation to "follow the money" echoed in her mind and prompted her to consider another aspect. Who benefited from all this wealth? She knew, vaguely, that Drs. Calegari, Brant, and Tasman were technically just three more employees of the institute, and a board of directors sat in oversight. Were the directors the beneficiaries? Or did they even know about the immense fortune that was, presumably, being accumulated for some unknown purpose? She realized, suddenly, that she didn't even know who sat on the board of directors!

Another question for Anders. Or, perhaps, for Kat and Marak. They knew more than she had expected. Somehow, they were still in contact with Dr. Seebak. She would ask them tonight.

WALLACE HOME, Lower Queen Anne, Seattle, WA. 2045, Wednesday, June 7, 2215.

"Come on in!" Marak greeted her at the door enthusiastically.

Dani smiled. She always felt like she was coming home when she entered this house. She had no illusions about the actual building; it was the people in it that made her feel so welcome.

"Kat's in the living room. We've got the wine out and a chocolate torte waiting to be sliced."

"Sounds like I'd better get in there, then!"

The living room was neater than she'd ever seen it, and more elegant in some subtle ways that she couldn't quite place. Was that a new vase on the mantel? A new window treatment? Something seemed different.

Kat jumped up and gave her a hug. "We want to hear all about what you found out, but first, let's celebrate."

Dani returned the hug, then pulled away with a laugh. "What are we celebrating?"

"You sound like me!" Marak said. "I can never remember dates."

Dani pondered. June seventh? Was this a date she was supposed to know? They met on September seventeenth. They were married six months later, in March. Jored was born in May the year after that. June? Nothing came to mind.

Kat must have seen the embarrassed confusion in her expression and came to her rescue. "June seventh was the day we met, in 2208."

"Met? Met where?" Had they been apart for a time, after Jored was born?

Marak swept into the room with a grand gesture of placing plates and forks on the coffee table beside the chocolate torte. "Oh, now that's a story that needs to be told! Have a seat and I'll fill you in. I'm a lot better with story details than I am with dates." He glanced at Kat, and her nod confirmed it.

"I'm surprised Kat hasn't told you this story."

"She probably has, and I've just forgotten it," Dani said, coming to her friend's defense.

"I have. But she hasn't heard your version, so go ahead."

"It was one of those beautiful June days, not all that common in Seattle, as we all know," he began. "I had an appointment to have lunch with a story source who had become a good friend—you'll recognize his name, actually—Dr. Mitchum Seebak, and his son, who had just graduated from high school."

"Dr. Seebak has a son?" Dani realized she knew nothing of Seebak's personal life.

"Well, a ward, actually. There's more to that story, too."

"We can tell her that later," Kat interrupted. "Go on."

"Okay, well, Mitch got an invitation to go meet a old friend of his, one of those pillar-of-the-community types, with lots of useful contacts in city government. He thought I'd like the guy, and invited me along."

"You never turn down a good contact, hon."

"Well, no, I don't. Best way to get the facts straight. Good for my reputation. People like being able to trust me, strangely enough." He winked. "Anyway, this pillar of the community had a boat, and it was a beautiful sunny day, remember, so we headed off for the marina."

Dani was beginning to see where this was heading. Marak thought he was going to meet some stranger, and it turned out to be his wife's uncle! Sounded like a great story. She settled back to listen.

"We got to the marina, and found his boat. I was expecting a boat, you know, small cabin and room for a couple people below decks. But we saw a *boat*..." Marak drew out the word and spread his hands out to indicate something enormous. "I was intimidated, I'll tell you. This guy had Money. With a capital M."

"Oh hush." Kat was laughing. "He's just a regular guy, and you know it very well."

"To you, maybe." Marak said, with a conspiratorial glance in Dani's direction. "Some of us aren't that privileged."

Kat slapped his hand affectionately. "This story is so long, I'm getting thirsty. Anyone else want wine?" They nodded, and she poured, with just the perfect roll of the bottle after each glass to catch the drips. *Where did she learn that skill?* Dani wondered. But Marak was talking again.

"So we made our way up this showpiece gangplank—who keeps a gangplank that nice?—and when we got up on deck, there was this gorgeous creature standing there, with flowing auburn hair that sang of seawater and mountain air and bird songs."

"My hair sang?" Kat turned to Dani. "I've never heard this part of the story before, I assure you."

"Oh yeah! And you were standing in that sexy pose that you do"—he tried to demonstrate, with comical results—"and I just stood there, with my mouth gaping open."

"Yeah? I saw this hunk of a man with a smile that sent my world rocking. Or maybe it was the boat rocking." She paused, considering. "Anyway, that's when I knew..."

"That's when *I* knew," he corrected her.

And they finished together: "I was going to marry him/I was going to marry her."

Dani had been relaxing back into the soft sofa cushions, but now she sat up straight. "What do you mean, marry? You guys were already married!"

Kat and Marak looked at her oddly. "No, sweetie," Kat said, "this was 2208. That's when we first met."

First met? Dani's mind raced through the dates she knew. The milestones of their marriage. Of course Kat was wrong. But how could she make a mistake like that? "That's impossible. You can't have first met a month after Jored was born."

Marak looked utterly baffled. "Jored? Who are you talking about?"

"Jored! Your son, Jored!" Dani rushed down the hall to his room, his bright yellow room with playful pups.

Only it wasn't yellow. It was a tasteful brown, with a textured border. The walls were viewwalls, displaying a continuous stream of updating news reports. An efficient-looking desk sat dead center.

"Whose son are you talking about? And why are you looking at my office?" Marak asked.

That's when Dani started screaming.

15
DETECTION

SEEBAK HOME LABORATORY, Vashon Island, WA. 2130, Wednesday, June 7, 2215.

Lexil glanced up at the corner of the viewwall, which was currently displaying a clock. It was going to be a very late night. Bits of the dinner they'd ordered from the Heli Deli three hours earlier still remained on the worktable: a container of Italian olives and artichoke hearts, some hothouse strawberries, and their water globes. The meal had been delivered through the airtube above the house by the usual remote-control delivery shuttle. They had long since consumed the delicious grilled chicken and pesto pasta dish, but the extras were nice to nibble on while they were immersed in tracking this latest disturbance.

It had been a big one, the biggest one yet. The main disturbance had occurred, as nearly as they could tell, at 1330 in the afternoon. But its effects reached back nine years. That was a common characteristic of the disturbances caused by the institute: The origin was always present day; the effects sometime in the last twenty years. Also, they could always physically locate the origin within the institute grounds, and that sealed it.

From the time of the first disturbance, they'd been busy setting sensors, recording and analyzing data, and locating blips, both physically and chronologically. If they could find a blip that occurred chronologically after the origin event, it would give them an extraordinary opportunity to measure it.

"Doc? I'm catching a close one here. Present-time, over in Lower Queen Anne. Still causing ripples, and they are big ones."

The doctor came over to look. "If we can get a stable one that doesn't break down in a few hours, we can see how sensitive it is to outside influences. It would do a lot to help us determine what kind of causes we're looking at for these."

"If we can get a stable one," Lexil repeated, "I will go over there myself and find someone to interrogate. I will find out exactly what caused it."

"Not in the institute."

"These aren't in the institute. They're across Elliott Bay. I can still get there by tube, though."

"Look for details. Can you fine-tune it to a street and number? Find out what business or residence is at that address?"

"Yes, working on it."

They worked silently for a few minutes, with each man monitoring a half-dozen of the sensors. Each device consisted of two main parts. Half of it was surrounded by a chronetically-sealed enclosure, which blocked temporal quantum entanglements and would thus be impervious to changes in the timestream. The other half was left outside the enclosure, and fully subject to any changes. They were connected by thin strands of a chronetically sensitive alloy. The first device had been set up in 2199, the second and third at six-month intervals. All three were needed before any details about time and place could be determined.

Lexil remembered learning, as he worked with Doc in the early years, that the sensors resembled ancient seismographs, which had to be located some distance apart to be able to determine epicenters of earthquakes with any degree of accuracy. With the seismograph, the extra dimension had been depth. With chronic sensors, of course, the extra dimension was time.

He leaned back in his chair and stretched. It had already been a long night. They should start setting the automatic recorders to track changes while they slept, but neither of them wanted to leave the lab. All the other events they had had the good fortune to note from the origin were tiny drops compared to this one.

Finally the calculations were completed. "Here's the address, Doc."

The older man came over to look. "That looks familiar. Is it a residence?"

"Should be, in that neighborhood. Hang on, let me look it up."

A few more swipes with a finger, a few more taps on the screen, and Lexil displayed the names.

"Are you sure?"

Lexil was startled by the intensity in his mentor's voice. The names were unfamiliar to him. "Who are they? Do you know them?"

"Marak and Katella Wallace? I know them. I've known Marak for longer than Kat. He interviewed me once for story he was working on."

"A story? What is he, a journalist?"

"Yes, and a very thorough one. But one of the most honest and honorable ones I've met. He always checks his quotes, and he doesn't go searching for dirt. He hardly has to track a story any more. People come to him now, most of the time."

"What does Katella do?"

"I believe she organizes protesters outside our own favorite institute."

Lexil turned sharply to look at him. "She might not mind helping us with our research, then."

"No, although ..." he paused.

"Complication?"

"Kat's uncle has been involved with the institute since its beginning, when I was there. He's still marginally associated with it."

Lexil whistled. "I'll bet that makes for some interesting conversation at family gatherings."

Suddenly, Doc snapped his fingers. "I just remembered. You've met them too. You were with me the day Marak met Kat on her uncle's boat. It was back in 2208. You were eighteen. It was June 7. That's today, actually! Seven years ago today."

"Say that date again?"

"June 7, 2208."

"Doc, that's one of the first blips that appeared. That exact date."

Once more Doc came over to check his figures. "That is more than a coincidence. Has to be. Where was the blip located?"

"Elliott Bay Marina," Lexil answered.

"That was where they met. Definitely not a coincidence."

"But that would mean their meeting is a result of this disturbance. What then? They wouldn't have met otherwise?"

"Check it out. Look at the data from the enclosed devices."

Lexil combined the readings and ran the figures through some algorithms. "It's flat at June 7, 2208. So without the disturbance, there was no meeting that day. But look here. This was the first effect, the center of the first set of ripples, from this event."

"The characteristics are the same."

"Right, but on the other side, the inside, of the enclosure. Doc, I think in the original timestream, they met back in September of 2206. Is that what you see here?"

"I can't say for sure. We're scientists, and all that. But it's clear that something that happened in 2208 in our timestream occurred in 2206 in the original, and it could very well be the date they met."

"If that's the case, this would be an amazing opportunity. To be able to pinpoint the inciting event and be present when—if—the third force starts nudging things back into place ... wow!"

"I think we should plan some field work for you tomorrow."

"Should we call them first?" Lexil asked.

"That might corrupt our data. This contact will need to be under very controlled circumstances. You'll need to influence it only in certain very specific ways, if we want to follow through on the measurements before and after."

"Okay, so the first meeting should be mostly data gathering."

"Are you ready for this?" The older man eyed him carefully.

"I am so ready for this." An idea occurred to him. "Doc, there's that other thing I've been working on."

"The insertion experiment?"

"Yes. Could we use this as an opportunity to test that?"

Doc laughed. "You're getting ahead of yourself, Lexil. Let's see what we're facing first. Other plans can come later. Are your analysis programs set for the night?"

"All set."

"Then I think, young man, that we should get some sleep. It sounds cliché, but I'll say it anyway. We have a big day tomorrow. Especially you."

Lexil saw the sense in that. He excused himself to walk to the house. "Big day" was an understatement. It was not just a big day. It was like being present when the comet fragment hit the moon in 2116. Not just watching it from earth, but actually on the moon. A once-in-a-lifetime event, to use another cliché.

He wondered what tomorrow would hold. He couldn't wait to see.

16
DEDUCTIONS

WALLACE HOME, Lower Queen Anne, Seattle, WA. 2230, Wednesday, June 7, 2215.

Dani opened her eyes to see a circle of concerned faces, Kat's, Marak's, and a square-jawed one, trimmed at the top with a fringe of gray hair, belonging to an older man she didn't know. She didn't remember how she got on the sofa, but she remembered what came before that. Jored was gone. It was like he had never existed. And her best friends, his parents, didn't even know who he was.

That didn't feel as horrifying at the moment as it had earlier. It felt disturbing, but in a fuzzy and comfortable way. Had somebody—had they—

"We had to give you a sedative," Kat said. "Are you feeling any better?"

Dani considered. Yes, she felt better. But she didn't feel good that she felt better. It felt wrong and skewed and overwhelmingly off. Or maybe that was what the world felt like.

"I'm calmer. And a little giggly. But I'm still screaming inside," she finally managed.

Kat exchanged looks with the others. They had obviously been talking while she was out. "This is my uncle, Royce. He's a doctor."

"Nice to meet you, Dr. Royce," Dani mumbled.

He laughed. "Royce is my first name. Just call me Uncle Royce. From what Kat says, you're part of the family. I've heard a lot about you."

"We didn't know who else to call when you wouldn't stop screaming," said Marak. His eyes held only concern.

They seemed like the Kat and Marak she knew.

"Okay. I'm not screaming any more," she said.

"Do you feel up to talking about it, or will you get all worked up again?" Kat asked.

Dani tested herself, thinking about all the things that were different, reminding herself that Jored was gone. The panic stayed safely down in the fuzzy zone. "I think I can talk about it." She sat up, moving over to the left end of the sofa to make room, and also, she admitted to herself, to give her an armrest to lean on. Her head was woozy. She definitely didn't want to stand up yet.

"Can you tell me when you started feeling something was off?" asked Uncle Royce.

"Um, no. Well … I was over here last night. Played chess with Jored."

He turned to Kat and Marak. "What do you remember about last night?"

"She was over here last night. We talked about investigating RIACH, and suggested she make some friends in the institute," Marak offered.

Dani looked up, alarmed.

"Don't worry, Dani," Kat said. "He's on our side. One of the main reasons I started protesting and educating visitors."

She relaxed. Well, really, she was already relaxed. But she felt reassured by Kat's confidence.

"Do you remember that part, Dani?" Uncle Royce asked.

"Yes. And I brought some things to show you." She gestured toward her bag and looked at Kat and Marak. "I almost forgot."

"So when did this Jored come into the picture?" the older man persisted.

"Seven years ago," Dani blurted. "When he was born."

"But yesterday, he was here? Forgive me, my dear, but I'm trying to help you get to the bottom of this."

"Yes. Kat and Marak and I cut up meat and veggies for shish kebabs, and Jored put them on skewers. He had all that energy, and all the pure childhood joy, just like he always does ...." Her voice broke as she remembered. "We played a matching game, all of us together, and then he and I played chess, just before he went to bed," she finished lamely.

"Kat?" her uncle prompted her.

"Yes, we had shish kebabs. And yes, we played the matching game. But we don't even have a chess set in the house."

"You had to help him brush his teeth, because he always forgets when you don't!" Dani objected, almost accusingly.

"No." Kat shook her head.

"Nothing to correspond with that," Marak added.

Uncle Royce sat back, putting his fingertips together and tapping them on his mouth while he thought. "The way I see it, it can be only one of two things." He paused.

They looked at him expectantly.

"Either Dani had a very lucid dream last night, so vivid that it seems real ..."

"A dream that goes back seven years?" she protested.

"Well, it's a definite possibility, because of the way their memories of what is real are interwoven with your account."

"What's the other possibility?" Marak asked.

"There's been some sort of reality shift."

Marak snorted. But Kat's uncle wasn't laughing. Not, in fact, even smiling. "Wait, are you serious?" Marak asked.

"Dead serious. Dani, you work in the chronography laboratory in our reality. Do you in yours?"

"Yes." She grasped on to the possibility like a life raft. He made it sound perfectly reasonable, no matter how unbelievable it was.

"So let's just hypothesize, for a few minutes, that time has diverged somewhere. Two paths, both leading to a slightly different version of this moment. It would seem that our first order of business is to determine where they diverged, would you agree?"

"This all sounds wacko," said Marak frankly. "But in my line of work, I've heard all sorts of crazy stories, and sometimes you have to submit to what we call a 'willing suspension of disbelief' and see where it takes you."

Kat had been sitting back silently, thinking. Now she spoke. "Okay, let's go with this. If it diverged, it would have to be longer than seven years ago. Dani, in your reality, when did Marak and I meet?"

"September 17, 2206."

Uncle Royce pointed at her. "And that's what makes me believe this is possible. People who have had dreams, even detailed dreams, can't answer questions like that."

"We actually talked about this last night," Dani explained. "Well, not we exactly, but ..."

"Yes, we know what you mean," said Kat. "Go on."

"Marak—the other Marak—was wanting to go through a gate." Abruptly, she looked over at Uncle Royce. "A gate to your estate. Unless Kat has another uncle somewhere."

"No, he's the only one," said Kat.

"Interesting." Uncle Royce pondered this new information. "But I didn't know Marak in 2206."

"No, he didn't know you either. He wanted to interview you about something."

"I actually did go to your estate to interview you about something, back in 2206," Marak interrupted, "but I never found you. I can't remember the exact date. What happened, Dani? In your, uh, reality, I guess?"

"You tried the gate, but it was locked. You tried to climb the fence, with absolutely no success, and that was when Kat came by and saw you. She laughed, and that's when you met." Dani thought about mentioning that she saw Marak rattle the padlock in the lab, but decided that would just further complicate something already too complicated. The goal was to find where the realities diverged. She guessed, anyway. But Uncle Royce seemed to take this whole thing matter-of-factly, and it had gotten them a lot further than her panic had.

Uncle Royce turned to Kat. "Do you remember where you were on September 17 that year?"

She thought for a minute. "I was twenty. I would have been on a break between summer quarter and fall quarter at the University of Washington. I suppose it would have depended on the weather that day."

Dani flashed back to an image of a garden with a pleasant breeze on a sunny day. She knew what the weather was on September 17, but that was in her reality. It might not have been the same for Kat. For this Kat, anyway.

Marak stood, too intent on finding the answer to sit, Dani guessed, and starting piecing together clues. "I remember the day I was going to interview you, if that was the same day. It was a nice enough day that I decided to park several blocks away and walk. You had quite the garden back then; I remember flowers and even a few birds."

"My garden's still there."

"That's right. You had us out for a luncheon on the smaller patio last summer." Marak snapped his fingers suddenly. "Now I remember. I actually went through that gate to your estate. The reason I didn't interview you is because I happened on a private conversation taking place on that same patio, and I backed off as quickly as I could. Neither of the two people were you. But then I got stuck, because when I went back to the gate, it was locked. It must have had an automatic latch or something, because I couldn't get back out. I was literally trapped."

Kat started laughing. "You were actually trespassing?" she teased him.

Marak looked uncomfortable. "It was extremely awkward, to be honest. I couldn't go past the couple talking on the patio. I couldn't go out the gate. I finally worked my way around front and rang the bell. A maid answered and took pity on me. She buzzed me out the front gate, and I walked all the way around to get back to my helicar." He focused on some distant point, trying to remember the details.

"That would have been Randa. She was like a member of the family. She left us to get married in 2210. I still send her gifts on her birthday, and on her kids' birthdays," Uncle Royce said. "Curious, though. If you came to interview me, why didn't you just ask for me at the front door when the maid answered?"

Marak's gaze snapped back. "I remember now. I did ask for you. She said you were out on your boat. Which would probably be the same one I met Kat on seven years ago today, right?"

And that put the rest of the pieces together for Kat. "That's right. I remember now." She turned to Uncle Royce. "You had invited me to go sailing with you. I walked. I would have passed right by your side gate on the way to the marina."

Dani took a deep breath. "In my reality, after you met Kat, she invited you to come with her to meet her uncle on his boat."

A thick silence fell as they all processed the facts of the two different realities.

"I think," said Uncle Royce, "that we have found the time the two realities diverged. In one reality, Marak went through the gate. In the other reality, he didn't. But there's something else."

He paused. They all looked at him intently, waiting.

"The thing is, that gate did have a latch, about 2 meters up. Higher than usual for a lock, Marak, so you might not have seen it. But I always, always kept it locked."

There was another pause. This time, Dani broke the silence. "And you used a padlock, which you've since replaced, I'm guessing."

"I did! And I have! And I have to ask: How did you know?"

"Because the old padlock," she answered, "is in the object library at the institute. I scanned it two days ago myself."

"In *your* reality," Marak pointed out. "I wonder if it's there in our reality."

This "your reality, our reality" distinction was beginning to make Dani uncomfortable. She so wanted to think of these two as the friends she had met and become so close to over the last six months, but they didn't share her love for Jored, so how could they be the same? She would trust her Kat and Marak with her life. She had no reason to doubt the people that faced her across the room, but they had had almost nine years of different experiences. Different experiences could change you. Look what had happened to her in one day!

"I could check tomorrow," Dani offered.

"If it's there, it might be useful to see what it shows," Kat suggested.

"No," Uncle Royce said. "It is there. I donated it myself. I remember now. The institute had just determined that metal objects made the best sources, and I thought about all the people that had walked past that gate, along that street. It's a popular place to walk, on nice days, as scarce as helicar parking is down a little closer to the water."

Kat looked at him sharply. "You helped the institute?"

"Well, I am on the board of directors, you know. More of a figurehead now, but back then, I was involved to a fair degree. I was eager to further the science, not the privacy invasions." He patted her knee affectionately. "We didn't know as much then as we do now."

"You're on the board of directors?" This was news to Dani. The names of the board members were never published anywhere, as far as she knew. Wasn't there something she was supposed to find out about the board of directors? She tried to remember, but her brain was still fuzzy, and she suddenly realized she was really tired. She yawned.

"Yes, I am. I try to influence them in right directions. I've been working on the privacy issues from the inside," he said, "with little success, unfortunately. I still have some irons in the fire, however."

Dani yawned again. This time Kat noticed. "It's after eleven! I didn't realize it was getting so late. Dani, do you think you can get home by yourself, or do you want one of us to go with you?"

"I'll take her home," said Uncle Royce. "I have my helicar outside. Where do you live, Dani?"

She told him. She barely remembered getting in the helicar, arriving at her apartment, or stumbling from the elevator to her door. Just as she was dropping off, she remembered why she wanted to know about the board of directors.

"I never told them about the forty-three point six percent," she mumbled to herself as she fell asleep.

RIACH TUBE STOP, Alki Beach, Seattle, WA. 0740, Thursday, June 8, 2215.

When she got out of the tube car at the RIACH stop, Dani was surprised to see Anders getting out also, two cars down. She waited for him by the clock tower. She was still trying to wrap her brain around this two-different-realities concept. Had Anders done all that research in this reality, or was that the other reality? Or both?

That question led her to wonder about when she had made the actual switch. Last night, they had pretty well narrowed down the point of the reality stream divergence to that moment in 2206, but they hadn't talked at all about when her perceptions had changed. She reassured herself by remembering that she had looked over the data again on her way in this morning, and it had to have come from somewhere.

"I thought we weren't going to meet till lunch." Anders's tone was teasing, lighthearted.

Dani was preoccupied with marveling at how easily she had adapted to thinking in two realities, but she tried to match his mood.

"We do both take the blue line," she countered. "It's bound to happen sometime or another."

"We've probably passed each other a hundred times and not realized it."

"That's probably true. Maybe we should make it a regular thing." She smiled.

She decided to assume, for the time being, that either the switch came before her after-work meeting with Anders the day before, or the versions of Anders from both realities were similarly motivated. Either way, she felt she could trust him to still want to help.

He nodded happily. "So I'll be looking for hidden names of investors and contributors today, in my free moments. Anything else?"

As they set off walking for the security gate, she pondered. That sounded like he had the same memories she did of their last meeting. She took her cue from that, and mentally confirmed her assumption that the switch occurred before 5 P.M. It should be safe to share her questions with him. "Now that you mention it, yes. I was wondering last night where the extra money goes. Is it needed for operational expenses and salaries? Or is it being stored up somewhere?"

"Good question. I'll see what I can dig up."

"Also, do you know who sits on the board of directors for the institute? I don't remember anything ever being published. Nothing in the New Employee Handbook, anyway." She realized she felt more comfortable trusting the new Anders than she did trusting the new Kat and Marak. Maybe it was because she realized that at least half her shared experiences with him had come from this new reality. Whereas, with Kat and Marak, there were six months of potential differences. Or even more. In this reality, she might have met them earlier.

"Haven't run across that, but I'll look." He glanced up to gauge the distance to the security gate. "Shall we change the subject, just in case?"

"Yeah. We probably shouldn't talk about books either, right?" She teased, lowering her voice.

He made a face and muttered, "I'd prefer not, if it's the same to you." Then he said, more loudly, "So, what do you think the special of the day will be today, in the cafeteria?"

"I hardly ever eat there, you know. I don't suppose you'd care to make a recommendation? You could give me a gourmet review of the best of things and the worst of things."

"Sounds like the beginning of a novel I once read," he began. She could guess where he had read it. At the same moment, they looked at each other, snickered, and made the tacit decision to avoid that risky topic one more time. There were those gorgeous blue eyes again. Dani had never realized breaking the rules could be so fun. Or that clandestine behavior could be so addicting.

The irisscan confirmed their identities, and they walked together the remaining distance to the main entry in companionable silence, conscious of a blooming friendship. Dani toyed with the idea that it could be something more. The entry doors swung open and although the viewwall automatically split to show them each their daily schedules, neither of them paid it any attention.

RIACH TUBE STOP, Alki Beach, Seattle, WA. 0740, Thursday, June 8, 2215.

It wasn't until she reached the chronolab that Dani realized she hadn't seen the protesters outside. In the old reality, Kat's schedule was like clockwork; rain or shine, she was there. One more indication that she didn't really know this new Kat, no matter how much she seemed the same. She would be cautious until she knew more.

She skimmed her schedule. More time decay checks. She filled her tray with the first batch, then, on impulse, went to see if she could find the padlock. She remembered its number, 097113, so it would be a simple matter to check. Except she was automatically assuming its number hadn't changed, which, she admitted, it very well could have. But when she got to Case 097, there it was, and its number was the same. Feeling pleasantly furtive, she added it to the tray. Uncle Royce hadn't thought it necessary, but she was curious to see if the scan of the object would be the same as what she remembered from the other reality. She could easily sneak in one extra scan among the checks.

She worked quickly, until she was sufficiently ahead of schedule to justify an extra scan. Five minutes, if she remembered correctly. September 17, 2206, at 1144 and some seconds. She adjusted the settings for 114410, then started the scan. Immediately, she saw the garden she remembered, and now she noticed the patio that Marak had mentioned. Soon she should see Marak's hand shaking the padlock. But instead, right at 114417, the sensory images failed and the object blanked. She betrayed her surprise with a quick intake of breath. Time decay? That would mean that someone had made—and played—a recording of her scan. Well, unless it was an occurrence of random time decay.

Something clicked in her brain. What if the conclusions of her college paper weren't wrong after all? What if time decay was always linked to playing a converted recording? Her mind raced. That would mean that there were undocumented conversions being done, and undocumented holograms being used. And most likely, she noted to herself, they were being used for undocumented reasons.

And there was the privacy issue popping up again. Unbidden, an image of Joph, with his hasty scribbles and his astute analysis, sprang to mind. "If you're not looking for a particular person's secrets and you'd be satisfied with anybody's, the odds favor finding something worth some money out of a good proportion of the objects," his voice echoed in her head.

She wondered, with a growing conviction that she knew the answer already, if that proportion would match the rate of unexpected time decay. She went through the progression in her mind, to see if she could find any holes. Items yielded secrets. Secrets invited blackmail. Blackmail required proof. Producing proof caused time decay as an unfortunate side effect. Every time? So, maybe not so unfortunate, from her point of view. Time decay left a trail. Was there any way those trails could be linked to the anonymous contributions?

She began to look forward to lunch.

17
SUSPICION

HUNTER'S OFFICE. 1205, Thursday, June 8, 2215.

Finally, his secretary had left for lunch. Hunter didn't know what had kept the man today. He switched the monitoring equipment from his outer office to scan the corridors and usual gathering places. The freedom of thought he took pains to encourage was a ruse, of course, for the lower-level employees of the institute. Those at the upper level were carefully directed away from any potential for scientific breakthrough toward finding more efficient ways of carrying out what had evolved as the institute's main business. Nevertheless, the little people out there were unconstrained in conversation, and he had personally overheard as wide a range of topics as he might have found at a public gathering place. They were fools if they believed their calls on the nexus weren't monitored, if they believed the security cams were only there for their protection.

He had made the illusion of freedom into a useful tool. He frequently found fodder for his fund-raising activities. He'd learned to spot the telltale signs of secretive discussions. As he scanned, he made mental notes of the couple slipping off the main corridor to kiss in an underused hallway. Probably nothing, but perhaps an indication of an affair. He twitched a finger and an accommodating ID device scanned all identifiable features, identified the potential contributors, recorded their names, and awaited his next command. He didn't even have to see their faces. That would come later.

This was one of the most enjoyable portions of his job. Aside from acquiring large amounts of cash, of course.

There, in the courtyard, a young woman with her head bent over, covering her mouth. She may have thought bystanders wouldn't notice that she was speaking to someone on her connexion, but scanner knew. That was one of the benefits of a private nexus. She was saying something that she didn't want bystanders to hear. Perhaps domestic trouble? Was she making arrangements for purchasing something illegal? No matter. The device identified her and recorded her name as well, tagging and recording the conversation for later listening.

His system was efficient. The scans he made personally weren't really necessary. Hundreds of automatic devices noted anything out of the ordinary: routines abruptly changed, criminal charges inexplicably dismissed, large amounts of money exchanging hands. If a name appeared more than a few times from any of his sources, he'd be alerted. At first, he had kept it local; Seattle held its share of lawbreakers, and it was easier to obtain the objects that persuaded their ardent support. But he had found even more opportunities when he set up monitoring systems in New York and London.

He panned his monitors over the cafeteria crowd. Only about half the employees ate there; others chose the food court or coffee shops scattered around the institute grounds. Still others went off-campus, but he wasn't concerned about those.

What was this? A young couple with their heads together, whispering. He could barely see them at this distance, but it appeared that the young man had covered something up with a napkin. He kept glancing over his shoulder. He flicked his finger, and the ID device whirred.

This could be a fruitful day, indeed.

18
REALIZATION

RIACH CAFETERIA, Alki Beach, Seattle, WA. 1230, Thursday, June 8, 2215.

Anders dimmed his worktablet screen. "I have dates, but no names. But if your idea is correct, we could try to find a way to figure out when the recordings are being converted. If the dates are a bit before the dates the contributions came in, that would show us something definite." Anders scratched his head.

Dani nodded slowly. "But how would it help? When there's time decay, I can't look at what was recorded any more."

"Could you look at the part right before or after the blank part?"

Dani opened her eyes wide. "I can't believe I didn't think of that! I'm doing time decay checks all day today. If I find one, I'll see if I can determine who is involved."

She could think of one object right now: the padlock. But she hadn't told Anders about the two realities, and she hadn't mentioned Kat or Marak. She repeatedly had to remind herself that she had only met him yesterday. She'd check out the padlock, for sure, but she wouldn't tell him about its significance. Not yet.

In her original reality, she was working on assignments from Kat and Marak, and Anders was a means to complete them. In this reality, she found herself teaming up with Anders and doubting Kat. And then there was Kat's Uncle Royce. Which reminded her of the other question she was going to ask.

"Did you find out anything about the board of directors?"

"Not a lot. I found out we have offices reserved for their use when they come in for the day. Not anywhere close to me or to you, though. It would be hard to keep an eye on them to see who uses them."

"Is it strange that their names aren't published anywhere?" Dani asked.

"Not necessarily, for a privately owned organization. If they were publicly owned, the stockholders would want to know all those details."

"Frustrating."

"Yeah. Well, I can poke around a bit more. You follow the time decay lead. That was a real breakthrough you got on that idea, by the way."

"Only if it's true. It could be way off base."

"I'm betting it's true," he said. "And if it isn't—well, this is the most fun I've had for months."

Dani smiled. She would think it was fun, too, if she knew Jored was safe and sound in his classroom, or at home with his mom and dad. But for now, the most she could manage was the smile.

He winked at her and added, in the voice of some holostar that she couldn't quite place, "You're the best thing that's happened to me in forever, darlin'." He put his hand over hers for just a second.

Just a second. She was surprised at how good that felt.

She cleared her throat. "Time for work."

"Well, you're right!" He stood. "Tube station?"

"See you there."

RIACH LABS, Alki Beach, Seattle, WA. 1300, Thursday, June 8, 2215.

Dani went to fill her tray in the object library. More time decay checks, but now she was on the hunt for something that could give them some answers. For the second time that day, she stopped by

Case 097 to borrow the padlock. She was beginning to know every rust spot and groove.

She started on her list. She'd have to get a little ahead on her time schedule to be able to fit the padlock in, and she wanted to see if there were any blank objects so she could have some news for Anders. Plus, she would need a good ten minutes to explore the before-and-after parts of the padlock scan.

While she worked, she went down her mental list of questions she would need to follow up on. First, how did Kat and Marak know Dr. Seebak? That was true in both realities. She remembered also that they had mentioned his son, in this new reality. She didn't remember that he had ever been married. She considered that. He could have married after he withdrew from the scientific community. So that could also be true in both realities, but she wouldn't know until she got back.

Dani caught her breath. She hadn't actually allowed herself to think about it, but she realized she had been counting, all along, on being able to put things back in place, get her Jored back. That was her real goal, not just figuring out what had happened. That goal was going to ultimately determine who she could ally herself with and who she couldn't. It occurred to her that nobody in this reality might want their world dissolved, any more than she would hers. Actually, until she knew what caused the shift, she had no idea whether this world would dissolve or continue on, after the problem was fixed. And, she admitted honestly, she might not know even then.

Was it just a few days ago that she'd been griping about how boring her job was? Her head spun with all these new questions. Not the least of which was whether she'd ever see Jored again, play chess with him, chase him down the hall to tickle him, give him a good night hug. She tried to swallow the lump in her throat, and her eyes stung with impending tears.

She hadn't allowed herself to think about him. She hadn't allowed herself to cry. But this was real grief, just as real as if he'd been killed or kidnapped. Actually, it felt more like a kidnapping. She had to believe that he was out there somewhere, and she didn't know if he was cold or hungry or scared. His parents should be with him, to take care of him, but they were here, and not at all inclined to go look for him. If only they could see him! They'd love him and want him back too.

She remembered the demonstration at Alki Elementary. She wished she had made a recording of Jored so she could show Kat and Marak a glimpse of their adorable, engaging, astonishing little boy. Dani loved him with all her heart, but she'd only known him six months. Kat and Marak had—well, in the other reality, they had—known him all his wonderful little life.

Now the tears were flowing freely. She sat down and sobbed. Her schedule was forgotten. For now, she just needed to cry. The ache in her heart overwhelmed her, and she had no one, absolutely no one, to share it with. Who would understand this grief for a boy that, to them, had never existed?

She reached into the pocket of her lab coat for a tissue, not really expecting to find one, but hoping all the same. Instead, she found a plastic leaf, a scrap of leather, a stone, and a metal disk. With a pang of nostalgia, she remembered how Jored had quickly figured out which were the best sources. A thought crossed her mind, so brief she almost missed it, but there it was.

Those objects had been with her all this time. If she could remember Jored, would these objects still have their chronetic imprints intact? Could she, if she scanned the leather or stone or metal disk, see him one more time?

She fumbled for an object and found the leather scrap. She placed it in the chamber, taking out the object she had just scanned before her meltdown, and tuned into 22150606:180000, scanning forward quickly.

At first, all she saw in the filtered light was pocket lint and glimpses of the other three objects. About five minutes in, she saw her own hand reach in and surround the objects. A room emerged, a familiar room. Kat and Marak's house. A shelf materialized under her viewpoint. Still, all these things could have happened in this new reality as well as the old. She kept watching. As the Dani in the image stepped back from the shelf, her throat tightened. There was Jored's dear, smiling little face. Her hand shot out to hit the pause button, and she gazed at him hungrily. Her integration with the machine made it seem absolutely, completely, real. She wanted to reach out and touch his face. Her arms ached to hug him. If only Kat and Marak could see this!

Suddenly, she knew what she had to do. But that was a plan that would have to wait until tomorrow.

For now, she would need to finish her assigned—and self-assigned—tasks. She sped through the time decay checks without finding any blanks. She had just enough time to check the padlock before leaving for the day.

By now, she had all the settings memorized. She put it on full circle to catch every possible clue and backed it up two minutes for a first try. If she saw something interesting, she could always back it up more.

Dani was used to ignoring most of the sensory inputs from the scanner when she did her daily tasks, but now she absorbed the details and ignored her own surroundings. It helped to close her eyes.

In front of her was the garden with the empty patio. Behind her was a street scene. People passed her along the sidewalk, some in pairs or groups, chatting cheerfully, others alone, intent on their destinations or a connexion call. She listened attentively, looking for anyone that might be a blackmail target.

"... never have enough games at a party. My daughter can recommend ..."

"...would be a mistake. Finally, he listened, and everything ..."

"... going to want to reschedule that meeting. When's a good time for ..."

"... got home and the kids had cleaned their rooms. I felt like I was ..."

She hit the blank without finding anything. No words that sounded suspicious or guilty. No potential for blackmail here. Of course, she couldn't tell what conversations might have passed the padlock during the blanked out time, but she remembered that the original investigation had been directed toward the patio. If it was the blackmailer who had commissioned the recording, it would make sense that the focal point of his interest was there.

She adjusted the settings for the time after the blank and turned the scanner on again, ready to absorb every detail.

There! There were people on the patio. This must be the couple Marak talked about, the people he avoided by sneaking around the front. A distinguished-looking middle-aged man with graying hair, dressed comfortably but professionally in a short-sleeved button-up shirt, was standing near a seated woman, bent over with her face in her hands. She was crying quietly. He reached over for her awkwardly, then seemed to think better of it.

The man had his back to Dani, and she couldn't see the woman's face. Maybe if she kept watching, she would catch a glimpse.

"Are you sure?" the man asked.

The woman looked up, and Dani caught her breath. She knew this woman, with her dark hair and soft eyes. It was Dr. Brant, nine years younger. "Why else would I have this lapse of memory, Mitch?"

Mitch. Dani tried to think who that might be.

"Could you have fallen asleep? It was late at night."

"I don't think so. And I was so groggy when I got home. I hardly remember anything from after the accident, until the next morning." She thought for a minute. "And I remember absolutely nothing from before the accident."

"Still, you haven't had anything to drink for months. Do you remember going to a bar? Did you find a bottle out at home the next day?"

"No, but ..." She stopped, ashamed.

"What is it?"

"I do have a bottle at home, that I tucked away for, well, you know, emergencies?" She looked up apologetically, then continued, "I took that out the morning after, and nearly half the bottle was gone. It wasn't that big a bottle, but it was enough. I'm so glad Royce was there to take me home before they tested my alcohol level!"

Royce! That had to be Kat's Uncle Royce! Then that would make Mitch ... Dr. Mitchum Seebak!

At that moment, he sat back down, with his face where she could see him. "If he hadn't, you'd be in jail now."

"Do you think I'm worried about that? I'm worried about the family. What will happen to Lexil if Elena doesn't wake up? This is all my fault."

"Lexil is okay, for now. Well, physically, anyway. He's with me. He misses his mom and dad, of course. But he's sixteen, and he doesn't like to let it show. I've known him practically all his life, and he used to talk to me all the time. But this will take a while, I think. The only thing I get from him, other than small talk, is to ask me every day if I've heard anything new. He spends all day on Saturdays at her bedside. He used to be there even more often, every waking hour of every day, until we convinced him he needed to go back to school."

Dr. Brant groaned again. *So much guilt to bear!* Dani thought. But Dr. Brant regained her composure in a few seconds. "He's a smart kid. I hope, for his sake, that she does wake up. He was so close to both of them."

"I hope so too, but it's not looking good."

"We can always pray for miracles."

"Yes, we can always do that."

She had recovered enough to stand. He put an arm around her shoulders in a fatherly gesture and walked with her off the range of the scanner.

Dani was so absorbed, she almost forgot to turn it off.

She was a little shocked to find out that Dr. Brant had been involved in the accident that ultimately killed Dr. Howe. That was a piece of information that had not made the news or the textbooks. She was certain, now, that she'd learned what the blackmailer knew. But who would want to blackmail Dr. Brant? What would the blackmailer gain? Was it for money or for something else?

Dani decided she would try, one more time, to talk to the scientist. Only this time, she would do it somewhere she wouldn't be seen. It was likely that the blackmailer was part of the institute in some way, and until she knew who it was, she would need to hide her investigations from everybody except Anders. She supposed she could add Dr. Brant to that list now. The victim was not likely to also be the blackmailer.

She glanced at her worktablet. Time to go.

Time to talk to Anders.

RIACH TUBE STOP, Alki Beach, Seattle, WA. 1710, Thursday, June 8, 2215.

"Going my way?" Anders was waiting at the tube station already, sitting on a bench. He flashed a broad grin.

"Thought I might!" She smiled. That grin lifted her spirits, even though she knew they would be talking about serious—and possibly dangerous—things. In this world where she had to consider everybody a brand new acquaintance, he was fast becoming one of her favorites.

He hopped up to join her. As they moved together toward the back of the platform, away from the pressing crowds. Dani had a vague sense that something was different here. Was the clock tower shorter than it used to be? Or its face shaped differently? She couldn't remember exactly. Oh well. She shrugged slightly.

Anders interrupted her momentary puzzlement and asked her quietly, "Find out anything?"

"Yes, actually." She, too, lowered her voice. "Something pretty big. Did you?"

"I looked into the question of where the money is going. If your theory is correct about the anonymous money being blackmail money—"

"I think we can be sure of that, after what I found today," Dani interjected.

"Yeah?"

She nodded. A string of tube cars pulled into the station. She watched to the right while Anders watched to the left for one they could claim for just the two of them. Not this time. There would be another in a few minutes.

"So where is the money going?" she prompted him.

"Well, it isn't necessary for the general operating expenses of the institute. It's being shuffled aside into a Research and Development account."

Dani felt an unexpected sense of relief. She hadn't realized it, but she had had a nagging worry that her job was only possible because of illicit gains. "So we're not minions of a criminal mastermind?"

"Oh, I don't know. A criminal mastermind might still be running the place." He grinned at her. "Do you want to work for a criminal mastermind?"

"Not particularly. Criminal masterminds aren't my type."

"No? What is your type, out of curiosity?" His tone was light, but his eyes avoided hers when she glanced over at him. Was there the hint of another question beneath the teasing inquiry? She couldn't be sure. She decided to ignore it.

"For an employer?" She matched his tone. "Why? Do you know someplace I can put in an order and get one ready-made?"

"If I did, would I be working in a place that barely acknowledges my existence?"

"You might, if you had reasons for wanting to go unnoticed!" Dani countered.

"Speaking of that, what did you find?"

She glanced around to be sure no one was in earshot. "I found an object with a blank."

"And you checked the before-and-after parts?"

"Yes. The before part was nothing. Just people walking by, snippets of conversation. But the after part was definitely blackmail material, and I can only assume the missing part was too." She wasn't sure if she wanted to share the details with him. Dr. Brant was no anonymous victim. She was someone they both knew.

He nodded. "So your idea was solid. Is the blackmail material anything we should report to someone?"

She considered, then shook her head. "No, I don't think so. Not until we know more about what's going on here, anyway. We don't even know who we could report it to safely."

"Then don't tell me any of the details." He paused and looked at her carefully. "Unless you need to, you know, for yourself."

She laughed, a little startled. "Is it that obvious?"

He had looked down at his worktablet, but she caught the noncommittal smile before it shifted to a slight frown. "But here's another question. Can you tell me when the blank might have been made? Give me a date for a scan that worked and one that didn't?"

"Actually, yes. It was intact on Monday, when I scanned it the first time. The first time it could have been converted and used was Monday evening."

He skimmed quickly through his figures. "Nothing. The last deposit was early Monday."

"Well, the thing is ..." she paused.

"What?" he prompted.

"This person might not be being blackmailed for money."

"No? What else? Control?"

"I think so."

He had come to the same conclusion she had, without even having seen the specifics. She thought through what she had witnessed in the observation box that afternoon. Every time she saw Dr. Brant at the institute, she was subdued and distant. But in the garden she seemed vulnerable and open. Granted, she was with a good friend. But was her daily resistance to any kind of casual conversation a real preference? Dani had always thought so. But now she wondered. Was it a byproduct of tight control?

A new set of tube cars slid into the station, whooshing almost silently into place. The platform had almost cleared with the previous set, so it was a simple matter to claim one.

"I have a little experiment I'm going to try, tomorrow," she told him after they got settled in. "I might be able to find out more."

"Sounds good. Listen, I've been meaning to ask you: Have you given any thought to what we should do with this information, assuming we find something really conclusive?"

She hesitated. Was it time to introduce Anders to Kat and Marak?

"I'm really not sure what to do about it. But I've got a couple of friends that would have some ideas. What are you doing tonight?"

"Nothing I can't cancel."

"I'll try to set up a meeting, if you're willing. How do I reach you if it works out?" she asked.

He gave her his contact information just as the tube slid into place at his stop. "See you tomorrow!"

"Or later tonight!" she called after him. Then she sat back to think.

19
RECOLLECTION

SEEBAK LABORATORY, Vashon Island, WA. 1720, Thursday, June 8, 2215.

"Okay, Lexil. Are you ready? The disturbance is on the move again." Doc had superimposed a map on the time disturbance graphic and was studying the screen intently. For the moment, all other research was forgotten.

"Where is it?" Lexil reminded himself that what they called a "disturbance" was, in this case, almost certainly a person. A person whose actions were changed as a result of the unusually large original disturbance they had noted the day before.

"Departing from the institute, heading across the bay."

"On the tube, then. Can you tell which line?"

"The blue line, I think. Heading toward First Hill."

"I'll catch the green line and head that direction. The disturbance will get there first, I'm sure." Lex grabbed a hip bag and his worktablet and walked with long, easy strides toward the door.

"We'll keep in contact, and if it moves again, I'll direct you to intercept it. "

Lexil hesitated. "You're sure you have no specific instructions for me? I feel pretty blind, going out there without a plan."

"First order of the day is just to investigate. You're a scientist. Observe with as little interaction as possible."

"I'd still like to try the insertion experiment, if we get a chance."

"We'll see how it looks, after you make contact with it. Him? Her? Well, you'll find out the gender of this 'disturbance' soon enough." Doc grinned. "Enjoy yourself."

"Yeah, right. Here I go!" Lexil left, muttering to himself. Doc was getting a little too much enjoyment out of his discomfort, he thought. Granted, he'd been eager to get out and do some real field work for a long time, and he'd even asked for this opportunity last night. But he really felt that anybody would be a little tentative given the totally untested nature of this whole deal. Being on the cutting edge of research had its definite disadvantages.

Then he smiled. It was an adventure. What he might discover today! He let out a whoop, grateful that the road to the nearest tube station was mostly deserted. A hundred years ago, there'd have been ground cars along this road and he'd have garnered some questioning looks.

Vashon Island was one of the few places left in the Seattle area where a person could still find towering fir trees, flourishing madronas, and gentle streams. While the urgent need for housing in the more urban areas had stacked apartments high and squeezed homes together, the quirky community on Vashon had continued to hold out.

It wasn't just the Seebak house and lab combo that nestled among the trees. Most homes, except those along the shore or close to the main highway along the length of the island, still had a green belt buffer to separate them.

Lexil remembered the West Seattle neighborhood he had come from, over ten years earlier. Houses were spaced no more than seven meters apart. Side windows were always tinted, to give a measure of privacy, both upstairs and downstairs. Some of the older homes had been divided into quaint, multi-level apartment units. His parents, both professionals, had been wealthy enough to afford a house without an upstairs apartment.

What a different life that had been! His mother was the consummate hostess, gracious and caring. His dad was a little more reserved, but appreciated his mother's social ease. He had come to know all his neighbors at a very young age because they were frequent dinner guests and often joined his family for afternoon barbecues on the weekends in fair weather.

In contrast, on Vashon, he interacted with none of the neighbors. He knew other people on the island, of course, because he had enrolled in Vashon High School for his last two years. Most of his studies there had been through the telestudy program, because it was more convenient to his work with Doc in the lab, but there were the mandatory group sessions and lots of online interaction. He probably knew a hundred or so other kids—now young adults—his age. There had even been a girlfriend for a while. Their relationship had ended on a friendly note, but he had completely lost touch with her in the intervening years. He had heard she was married and had a little girl and another on the way.

Funny that she came to mind just now. Well, she was his only serious relationship. He didn't count the casual flings he had enjoyed during his college years. By that time, his work had become so interesting he hadn't invested the kind of time or attention that a strong relationship had needed. To be honest, he had probably been an irritation to those girls, and he didn't blame them at all for breaking it off after just a few weeks. He wasn't a very good relationship risk. He missed it, though, he had to admit. What he really needed was a partner, someone he could share his work with.

Lexil laughed at himself. That was a dream unlikely to happen any time soon.

He spotted the tube station, and sprinted the remaining distance. Green line to Alki Point, blue line to First Hill. Then the adventure would begin.

After an uneventful ride in a tube car with two people staring off into space—evidently absorbed in something on their eyescreens—

and a man taking a quick nap on the way home, Lexil transferred to the blue line at the Alki Point substation. The tube cars to First Hill were crowded, even at this time of night. Eventually, he arrived. He was grateful he didn't have to commute every day to work.

He put through a call to the lab. "Doc? Any movement?"

"Yes, I'm afraid you'll have to travel a bit more. Head over to Lower Queen Anne. It looks like the disturbance is heading back to the Wallace home, or something nearby. It—she? he?—is moving that direction."

Lexil checked the schedule. He'd have to wait about ten minutes for the shoreline tube to arrive from the south. He found a bench and tapped into his calculations for the insertion experiment.

About three months earlier, he'd started toying with the idea of a program that could cancel the effects of time decay, which was a continuing annoyance in their research, and, he imagined, any research at the institute as well. First, he had had to investigate what caused the time decay in the first place. He had come to a tentative conclusion, but he wouldn't be able to be sure until he was able to test out his hypothesis. Perhaps this would be the opportunity he was waiting for.

20
INTRODUCTION

DANI'S APARTMENT, First Hill, Seattle, WA. 1740, Thursday, June 8, 2215.

Dani disconnected. Maybe a connexion call hadn't been the best way to talk to Kat about bringing Anders over to meet them. She had to admit, Kat had been right about all the things they had to address between the three of them before bringing Anders into the equation. He didn't even know about Jored yet. At least Kat and Marak knew that, from her perspective, they were part of an alternate reality.

Although, Dani reminded herself, they might not have realized that she fervently wanted to reduce them from the "real" to the merely "possible" in the process of getting her own Kat and Marak back, the Kat and Marak who were the parents of a very appealing little boy named Jored.

So she had agreed, reluctantly at first, then in complete accord, that the meeting with Anders should be postponed. It might be possible later in the evening, but Kat had suggested waiting until the next day. Friday was the day before the weekend, and they would all feel more relaxed. That was one of Kat's strengths, being able to step back and see a bigger perspective. In that, at least—and really, in almost every other way she could think of—Kat was her Kat. She just wasn't Jored's mom.

She glanced at the time and was startled to realize that she'd have to hurry to catch the next shoreline tube train to the Wallace house. They still hadn't increased the frequency on that line, and she didn't want the fifteen-minute wait between trains. She grabbed her bag and rushed out the door, almost hitting her shin on the edge of the chair on the way. Who had moved that? She could have sworn it wasn't there just a few minutes ago. She wasn't old enough to be getting this forgetful.

No time to worry about it. She owed Anders a call to explain the delay, but she could make that once she got settled in the tube car.

WALLACE HOME, Lower Queen Anne, Seattle, WA. 1755, Thursday, June 8, 2215.

This time, it was Kat who opened the door after the irisscan announced her arrival. She greeted her with a warm hug and a question. "How was your day?"

"Good, I think. I came up with an idea that I think you'll like."

"Meeting Anders, you mean?"

"No, that was just an impulsive thought in the tube car home. This is better."

"So then, what?"

"I want you and Marak to meet Jored."

Kat opened her mouth to answer, and then closed it. Then opened it again. Finally, she got out a feeble, "How, exactly, do you want us to do that? Describe him to us really well?"

Dani tried not to laugh at her flustered friend. If this worked out the way she hoped, Kat would be going through a lot of other emotions as she saw herself and her son interacting. There was so much love in their family! She found herself longing for just one more taste of that. But she wanted Kat and Marak there too.

"No, I have a different idea. But I have to figure out a way around a difficulty, first. That's part of what I want to talk to you about." She looked around. "Where's Marak?"

"He's in his office. Has a story deadline. Said he'd be out in a few minutes." Kat walked toward the kitchen. "Do you want something to drink? I assume you're staying for dinner."

"Yes. What do you have?"

"Iced tea, frapple, beer, Italian berry vanilla blast-of-caff lemon-lime cola supreme?" Kat made out-of-breath noises at the end of the last option, exaggerating them comically for Dani's benefit.

Dani laughed. She couldn't help it. "My grandfather used to call those 'graveyards.' He'd probably never believe we actually buy that stuff now."

"I'm convinced we'll buy anything, if it's packaged attractively. So what'll it be?"

"Iced tea is fine. It's hot outside, for June. It'll feel good to cool off."

"Want to take them outside? Or would that be too hot for you?"

"No, you've got shade out there. It looks nice." The back yard did look nice. She was used to seeing it scattered with baseball bats, riding toys, and a swing set. This new back yard was nicely manicured, with flowering shrubs and annuals arranged around the outer border and a raised vegetable garden near the back. A fountain just off the patio offered soothing sounds. It was very calming.

The two women sat down at the table with their drinks and sipped companionably for a few minutes. Kat waved at the glass door to remove the tint for a moment. "I was checking to see if Marak was coming," she explained. "I wanted to ask you what you found out about the finances at the institute. Last night was so crazy, we didn't get a chance to talk about that. But I keep thinking we should wait until Marak gets done and can listen too."

"Until Marak gets done and can listen to what?" asked Marak, as he slid the door open and waved at it to tint it again.

"Those questions she was digging into about the institute's finances."

"I *would* like to hear about that." He turned to Dani, and his friendly grin dropped for an instant, to be replaced by a look of concern. "You are keeping safe, though, aren't you? Not taking any risks, inviting unnecessary attention?"

"I'm pretty sure nobody knows that I exist there," she reassured him. "Except Anders."

"Who's Anders again?" he asked, pulling up another chair to join them at the table.

"She's managed to cultivate a confidential informant already," Kat explained. "Minus the compensation, of course."

"Whoa. Moving up into big time investigations already. You learn fast!" He was teasing, but she could tell he really was somewhat impressed.

"Anders works in Financial Services. He's an intern too, and they pay about as much attention to him as they do to me. He was eager to help, and he's really good at covering his tracks on the system."

"Could be useful. What has he discovered?" Marak asked.

"More than forty percent of the money that comes into the institute is from unidentified contributors and donors. He said that wasn't including the donors that choose to remain anonymous. These are just unexplained sums of money."

Marak whistled. "Any idea where they come from?"

"Well, yes. But this part comes from my own investigation. And it ties in to Kat's main gripe with the institution."

"Privacy." Kat interrupted.

Dani nodded. "What do you guys know about time decay?"

"It happens to objects you used to be able to scan? And you can't scan them any more?" Marak asked.

"Yes. I helped write a graduate paper at the university. It showed that time decay was caused when—and only when—the video, audio, and/or olfactory recordings of an object were played on an independent projector for the first time. Later, at the institute, I was told that some objects decay without that, but now I'm not so sure."

"Ah. You're talking about blackmail." Marak had already leaped to the end.

"Wait. How do you get from what she said to what you said?" Kat asked.

"Scan and record a crime. Play recording. Demand money. Blackmail!" he said, succinctly. "And time decay, seemingly with no explanation for why it is happening."

Dani nodded again. "I hate the idea that the institute is doing that. And I'm sure that some of the commissioned scans they have me do are helping to give them more evidence," she added, miserably.

"You're also researching history," Kat said, reassuringly. "The goal is to put a stop to the bad stuff so the good stuff can go on."

"How did you come to the blackmail conclusion, Dani?" Marak asked. Always the journalist, confirming each source.

"I went back to the padlock. It had decayed. But right after the blank part in the scan was another that showed me, pretty clearly, what had gone before."

"And it was the kind of material that could be used to threaten someone?" he asked.

"Yes, except it's someone at the institute, so I'm not sure if they're getting money from that person."

"Control then." Marak got it again. "That puts an interesting spin on things. If you've got someone at the institute under that kind of control, you might find someone who could answer a lot of your questions."

Dani sat up. "That's what I was thinking."

"Whoa, girl. Don't go there. That person is also a person who is being closely watched. He might feel threatened if he knows you know something damaging to him. And he might be under some kind of pressure to report on other people there. You'd be waving your hands and asking for attention."

Dani didn't bother to correct the mistaken gender words. It wasn't her intention to expose Dr. Brant and further complicate her life. She'd just let Marak go on thinking that the blackmail victim was a man, for now. Maybe forever.

But she wasn't ready to give up her idea of trying to get the scientist alone to talk to her, either. With Marak's warning ringing in her ears, she'd just take extra steps to be cautious.

"None of this surprises me," said Kat. "It would be good to get some specific evidence and shut the whole thing down, of course. But Dani, don't you dare think that we expect you to do this."

"I'd like to do what I can."

"I know." Kat took a sip of her iced tea. "But hey, what was that idea you were going to talk to us about?"

Dani brightened. She turned to include Marak in what she'd already told Kat. "I want you both to meet Jored."

Marak looked puzzled. "How would we do that?"

Dani pulled the four items out of her pocket and set them on the table between them. She had meant to put them back into the supplies closet, but not any more. They were her only link with her old reality. "These objects have traveled with me since before I experienced the shift."

"Have you figured out when the shift occurred now?" asked Kat.

"Not exactly. I know it had to be between Tuesday evening here, when I last saw Jored, and yesterday evening here, when I discovered he was missing." Her voice caught a little, and she swallowed. "But beyond that, I'm thinking it was sometime yesterday afternoon. I did two scanning sessions, and when I stepped out of the observation box between the first and the second, I remember feeling dizzy, like the room was spinning around me. It took me a few seconds to get my balance."

Marak leaned in. He had that look on his face that Dani had learned to recognize: the journalist on the scent of a story. "And everything else fits with that as a dividing point?"

"Yeah, as far as I can figure out. Things that happen at the institute don't really seem to be affected, except for the time decay."

"Dani," Kat began slowly, "I know this has all been really strange and heart-wrenching for you, and we're trying to talk about it matter-of-factly to make it easier for you to adjust. We know you, and we know that a rational discussion of the facts helps you deal with emotional upheavals. But I'd be keeping secrets I shouldn't keep if I didn't tell you that it's a little weird for me too."

"Because you feel like you don't know me really?"

"Actually, not that at all. You seem the same. As far as I'm concerned, you are our own Dani, and we love you very much."

"What, then?" But Dani thought she knew. They would want to keep their own reality, just like she wanted to keep hers.

"I am happy—we are happy—to help you try to figure out what happened. But if we meet Jored, and I'm still waiting for you to tell us how, I have to admit I'll be experiencing some difficult emotions also." She stopped, searching for words.

Marak took over the story. "Dani, I don't know if you know this or not, but Kat got sick a little less than a year after we were married, and it did some damage to her body. We've tried to have kids, but the doctors have told us we can't. We got the final word just last year."

Kat nodded. "If we do this, I will see this little boy, and I know I will want to love him and hold him, but don't you see? If that other reality could be restored somehow—and I realize that is what you are hoping for—it won't be me. It will be another Kat, without nine years of my memories. I feel like I'd be ceasing to exist myself. It would be like agreeing to commit suicide. I don't know if I'm that unselfish."

Dani didn't know what to say. Finally, she offered a wholly unsatisfying response, only because she couldn't think of anything else to say. "I hadn't thought of it that way. I won't ask you to help. I don't even know if it's possible. I guess...I guess I just wanted someone else to mourn him with me. But that's being selfish. I don't need for you to grieve too. You've already done that."

"How would we do it, if we did decide to meet him?" asked Marak. "Would we just be watching? He couldn't see us, right?"

Dani picked up the objects again and passed them from one hand to another, one at a time. "I can use these to show you the last evening I spent with him. I checked them out; they still have the chronetic energies from the other reality. If I could get you in the lab, you could see it too."

"How could we get in the lab?" asked Marak.

"You'd have to get permission, and a temporary visitor's pass. I'm not sure how to go about that."

"My uncle might be able to pull some strings," said Kat, "but can we think about it? I really don't know if I want to do this. And I don't know how I feel about Marak doing it without me either."

"I wouldn't do it without you, babe. It's both of us or neither of us."

She smiled at him, gratefully.

Dani felt really bad for even bringing it up. It had seemed like such a good idea at the time, but she hadn't had any idea of their struggles. She wondered if that was another change from her reality, or if her Kat and Marak had faced those struggles too.

INTERCEPTION

OUTSIDE WALLACE HOME, Lower Queen Anne, Seattle, WA. 1930, Thursday, June 8, 2215.

Lexil wished he had come in a helicar so he could be waiting inside it instead of standing out here on the street. He was sure it looked suspicious, even a little creepy. He expected sirens any time. At least it was a nice evening. It would be so much worse with a steady dose of Seattle rain.

Maybe if he walked back and forth a half block it would look like he was a neighbor out for a stroll. Except this would be the fourth time he had gone for the same stroll. He sighed, and paced in a tight circle.

He called Doc again. "You're sure the center of the disturbance is still in this house?"

"Yes. And it's still sending out ripples. I'll let you know if it moves."

"And I'll let you know if someone leaves."

At first, he had considered walking right up and introducing himself to everybody in the house, but the Wallaces had an irisscan, and they might not even open the door. Besides, they had agreed before he left to influence events as little as possible. He needed to narrow down the source of the disturbance first.

Looking between houses on one of his neighborly strolls, he had caught a glimpse of three people on the back porch. He supposed the man was Marak Wallace. One of the women would be Kat, but he didn't know which one.

It was most likely that the visitor (whoever she was) was the source of the disturbance, since it had traveled from First Hill to here just before he arrived. He wished he had been standing outside then, so he could have intercepted her. This visit could go on all evening.

He was just about to start off on another neighborhood stroll when he heard the door open. Voices with goodbye tones leaked through the opening. He couldn't make out more than a few words, but those few were promising also. "... morning?" "... hug for me?" "... let you know ..."

Now the door was opening wider. He looked around quickly for a shrub to hide behind. He didn't want to be seen and make her go back inside. He needed her to separate herself from the two in the house so that Doc could let him know whether the disturbance was leaving with her or staying in the house. He stooped behind a hedge, hoping the neighbors wouldn't happen to look in his direction any time soon.

He called Doc on his connexion and whispered, "The visitor is getting ready to leave. Tell me if the disturbance moves, so I don't miss another chance to make contact."

The two waited in tense silence on opposite ends of the connexion, Doc monitoring his sensor reports, Lexil stooping awkwardly just out of visual contact with the door. Finally, finally, the visitor stepped onto the slidewalk.

In the fading evening light, Lexil could see that she had blond hair, swept casually behind her shoulders. A light jacket covered her sundress, and she moved purposefully as she shifted her position on the slidewalk. She was deep in thought. She had the expression of someone trying to solve a puzzle, a slight frown while she bit her lower lip, flickering glances skyward. Suddenly, she smiled, and her face lit up.

Lexil inhaled sharply. He wasn't sure if it was the intelligence he saw in her expression, or the purposeful way she walked, or the genuineness of her smile, but he suddenly found himself hoping his next move would be in her direction rather than toward the house.

"Doc, is it the visitor or the Wallaces?" he whispered. "She's about fifteen meters in front of the house, almost to the street."

"Definitely the visitor," Doc answered. "There's a smaller disturbance in the house, but the main source is on the move. Go find out what you can. But remember, you're an observer, not a participant!"

"I'll try to remember that," Lexil whispered. But as he hung up, he was already trying to forget. He considered the best way to introduce himself as he waited for her to reach the street. She'd be most open to the simple truth, he decided.

She turned away from him to make her way to the tube station. He followed, quickening his pace. She glanced behind her, curious.

"Hey," he said. "You look like a person who could use some answers."

"I do?" Good. She wasn't running. She was waiting for him to catch up.

"You do. And I think I might be the only person who can help you find them."

She stopped abruptly. "And who might you be? How would you know anything about my questions?"

"Lexil Myles." He held out his hand, hoping she would respond.

She took it. "Danarin Adams."

He liked her handshake. Firm, confident, totally competent. Or maybe that was his imagination.

"You haven't answered me yet," she prompted, waiting patiently. "How would you know anything about my questions?"

"Let me try to describe them. You can let me know how I do."

She nodded.

"You've recently—let's say 1:30 yesterday afternoon?—experienced a kind of time disturbance. Something huge has changed in your world. You might be the only one who knows it has happened. Besides me," he added as an afterthought. And Doc, he thought silently.

Her astonishment made her even more attractive. Whoa there, he chided himself. This is field work, not a social event.

"Tell me." It wasn't so much an invitation as a command. "Tell me what you know."

"Is there someplace we can talk? I'm not from the neighborhood," he apologized.

"There are benches in the tube station," she said. "We can sit there, if we need to. But start now."

So he did.

22
EXPLANATION

OUTSIDE WALLACE HOME, Lower Queen Anne, Seattle, WA. 1945, Thursday, June 8, 2215.

Dani was happy for the hugs as she left Kat and Marak's house. She felt a little less alone. She was resigned, though, to walking this road by herself now. Tomorrow, at work, she would take one last look at the little boy she used to call "bud," put the objects back with the others like them, and adapt to living in this new reality. It hurt more than she could say, but she had to trust that time would help her heal. Whether it did or not, she realized now that there wasn't going to be any going back. This was it.

No, the problem to solve now was the blackmail issue. She thought about places in the institute where she might find Dr. Brant alone, and came to the conclusion that there were none. She would have to leave her a note in a place where she could read it without being observed, and arrange to meet her later somewhere. Leaving a note was risky, she realized. It could be kept and given to someone else, or it could be found by someone else before Dr. Brant ever saw it. Perhaps she shouldn't sign her name, just in case. She could be "wellwisher" or maybe come up with a code name like "bud."

She smiled at a sudden clear memory of the day she had first started calling Jored by his nickname. Most people thought it was short for "buddy," but she and Jored knew the truth. They had been looking at the flowering shrubs that were starting to produce the beginnings of new leaves and flowers, with Jored up on a chair so he could see the ones up high. He had swatted at an branch that had tickled the top of his head, and she had said, "Don't hit that; you'll knock off the bud!" But as she said it, she had turned and knocked him off the chair. He had landed on his feet, giggling, asking her if he was the "bud" and whether she should be careful too, so as not to knock off the "bud," and the name had stuck.

Still smiling, she considered whether she really wanted to let those objects get mixed in with the others in the supply room. Maybe not. If she was going to walk this road alone, she might as well have a place to find a little comfort.

Dani had just turned right at the street to walk toward the tube station when she heard the footsteps, walking almost fast enough to be a jog. She turned, curiously.

"Hey," said a strange voice in the fading light. "You look like a person who could use some answers."

Well, he was right about that. But she wondered how he would know. "I do?" She waited for him to catch up. He slowed as he neared her and flashed a very appealing smile. And big brown puppy dog eyes. She always fell for the eyes first. Stop that, Dani, she told herself firmly.

"You do. And I think I might be the only person who can help you find them."

That was pretty arrogant. "And who might you be? How would you know anything about my questions?" She might have snapped at him a little. She wasn't sure.

"Lexil Myles." He held out his hand, oblivious to her irritation.

She couldn't resist checking out his handshake. You could tell a lot about someone by the way he shook hands. "Danarin Adams."

He had a great handshake. Firm, but not the kind that tried to take control of everything. She decided she'd give him another chance.

"You haven't answered me yet," she reminded him. "How would you know anything about my questions?"

"Let me try to describe them. You can let me know how I do."

She agreed. He had a nice voice, too, she had to admit. Rich in timbre and, even when she was being so pushy, it held more than a hint of humor and happiness.

"You've recently—let's say 1:30 yesterday afternoon?—experienced a kind of time disturbance. Something huge has changed in your world. You might be the only one who knows it has happened. Besides me," he added.

Okay, this was either really creepy, like he'd been watching her for over twenty-four hours, or something she desperately needed to hear. She was hungry to know what had happened to her. How could he know the time when she hadn't figured it out herself? She realized she was gaping at him. "Tell me what you know," she said.

"Is there someplace we can talk? I'm not from the neighborhood."

That meant he had traveled to find her. She was wary. She wasn't about to take him to her house. On the other hand, what were the chances that the one person who knew the answers to her questions would actually live in this neighborhood? She decided to compromise.

"There are benches in the tube station," she said. "We can sit there, if we need to. But start now."

"You're probably wondering how I found you," he began. "We have time sensors running constantly, looking for disturbances. We can tell where they are and when they are, but we can't tell who they are without coming to look."

"Wait. You said 'we.' Who, besides you?" Was he part of some organization? Was he part of the institute, some secret branch that had found out that she was scanning things that weren't on her assignment list? Did they already have Anders?

"Doc."

"Doc who?"

"Okay, listen. When I first saw you, I was worried you were going to run away from me. The truth is, we need you as much as you need us. We have data. You have the experiences that can help us match blips on a screen to actual occurrences."

"Blips on a screen?" she repeated. She was mystified. Nothing at the institute showed up as blips on a screen. Then she realized how stupid that sounded. "What do they represent?"

He smiled. A great, big, beautiful smile. "Want to help us find out?"

"I have no idea who you are, other than your name and that you seem to have some mysterious source of information. You're asking me if I want to help you with something that, apparently, is really important to you! But I don't have a clue about who you're working for, or if your purposes are for good or not. Could you give me a little background? Who's Doc, for starters?"

He hesitated. "What do you know about the science of chronography?"

Dani started laughing. She couldn't help it. The incongruity of being asked the same question she had asked the school kids just two days earlier, plus the relief at realizing he didn't know all that much about her after all, melted her defenses.

After a few seconds of looking baffled, Lexil started laughing too. He had a funny laugh, and that made her laugh harder. Between snorts and guffaws, he finally got out, "What's ... so funny?"

"I work for RIACH," she answered, still snickering. "I give presentations on chronography." Then she started laughing again. "For a man with the answers to my most puzzling questions, you don't seem to know a lot about me."

"No," he said, with a comical look, "I guess I don't. But," he added in a much softer voice, so soft that she almost didn't hear it, "I'd like to, very much."

The strained atmosphere was gone. In its place was a comfortable warmth that started seeping into all her worries and tensions. She wanted to melt into that. But first she had to get some of those answers he had promised.

"So ... Doc who? Given my background, will I recognize his name?"

"Dr. Mitchum Seebak. He's my employer and mentor. Used to be my guardian, when I was young enough to need one."

Something clicked. Lexil, he had said. Suddenly, she was hearing again the conversation from the padlock scan, hearing Marielle Brant's voice asking, *What will happen to Lexil if Elena doesn't wake up?*

"You're ... you're Dr. Howe's son!" she blurted.

It was his turn to look startled. "Well. It seems you know more about me than I know about you," he said pointedly.

She suddenly remembered, too late, that she wasn't supposed to know that Elena Howe had a son, that his name was Lexil, that he lived with Dr. Seebak. She wasn't ever supposed to have heard that conversation. Involuntarily, she clapped her hand over her mouth.

"There are exactly four people in the world who know that." His eyes narrowed. "And you're not one of them."

"There ... there might be more than that who know," she said, humbly, desperately wanting that warm comfort back. "Um. Maybe I do owe you some help."

His connexion signaled an incoming call. He answered, still looking steadily at her, willing her with his eyes to stay put, not move, wait for him to be done.

"Doc," he said succinctly, then listened. "Yes, I made contact. Yes, she's *quite* willing to help." He continued looking at her, daring her to contradict him.

She just nodded, mutely. All her reasons for distrusting him had vanished when she found out he was involved in Dr. Seebak's research. Unfortunately, he now had a whole lot more reasons to distrust her.

"To the lab?" Lexil sounded surprised. "Are you sure?" He looked over at her doubtfully. He listened some more and then hung up. Then he stared at her for a few moments. Finally, he spoke, but the warmth was gone.

"Ms. Adams," he said formally, "Would you accompany me to our laboratory? It seems my mentor would like to meet you."

Numbly, she said, "I'll go."

SEEBAK LABORATORY, Vashon Island, WA. 2030, Thursday, June 8, 2215.

"Welcome!" Dr. Seebak's smile was genuine and friendly, Dani noted with relief.

"This is Danarin Adams, Doc. Turns out she works at the institute, and knows rather more than she should."

"I hope those extra things you know will end up explaining some things for us, and we'll all benefit! Do you have coat? No? Would you like some refreshment? Wine? Tea? Something fizzy?"

"Just a glass of water, if it's not too much trouble."

"Not at all. I have a dispenser in the break room over there. Filters and cools. Let me show you where, and then you'll be able to get your own refills later." Dr. Seebak turned to Lexil. "Lexil, while I show Ms. Adams around, will you check the sensor readings to see what they are doing now that she is here?"

Dani followed him to the break room. "Call me Dani, please. Everyone does. Wow! This looks more like a studio apartment than a break room!"

"Sometimes we have to sleep here, to monitor the equipment. We're a two-man operation. A lot different from what you're used to, isn't it?" He smiled at her, with a fatherly look, then gestured toward the back corner by the sink. "There's the water."

He brought her a glass, and she thanked him. But as she turned to go, he said, in a much quieter voice, "What have you said to Lexil to get him so huffy?"

Startled, she almost spilled her water, but steadied herself quickly. She realized suddenly that she could tell Dr. Seebak everything. She wasn't sure what Lexil knew and what he didn't, but Dr. Seebak had been there.

"I recognized that he was Dr. Howe's son."

His eyes widened. "And how do you know that, exactly?"

"I scanned an object that showed you talking to Dr. Brant in a garden patio, back in September of 2206. Dr. Howe was unconscious. You talked about her. I heard Dr. Brant refer to Lexil. She was worried about him. You reassured her."

"I see," he said slowly. "I remember that conversation. I remember that there were some other things said that day too. Did you hear those as well?"

"Yes," she said, miserably. "I know Dr. Brant's secret."

"Did you tell Lexil?"

"No! I haven't told anyone!"

"Make sure you don't. Actually, I have my doubts about her assessment of her condition that night. But that's a topic for a later time." He resumed his cheerful, fatherly expression, and turned to go.

"Dr. Seebak! Wait!"

He looked at her quizzically.

"Some of that conversation had been blanked. I only saw the later part."

"Blanked? Ah. That explains a lot. Someone else has seen the first part, yes?" He didn't wait for her answer. "Come back out to the lab now, please. Let's get this mess straightened out."

Lexil was waiting for them. He avoided her eyes completely. Dani could tell he was still upset.

Dr. Seebak invited them both to sit. "Here's what we need to do. We need to put everything on the table, so we can all see where we stand. I think Dani has the missing pieces to a lot of our puzzles, and I think we can help her understand some things as well."

They sat, with Lexil and Dani on opposite sides of a square table.

"We can take weeks, getting to know each other, becoming friends, deciding to trust," said the doctor. "But we have a situation here, and we don't know how much damage to the timestream it could cause in weeks. We need to learn everything we can in the next few days—hours, if possible. So." He paused to make sure they were looking. "We're going to choose to trust, right now. All three of us. Do either of you feel you can't do that?"

"I can do that. But I don't think we can ignore that she knew something no one is supposed to know," said Lexil.

"You say that? You? Who was it again who interrupted my evening walk to tell me something nobody should know? Let's see, how did that go again? Oh yes: 'Something huge has changed in your world. You might be the only one who knows it has happened. Besides me.' I would think you would be the first person to acknowledge that sometimes people know things through legitimate means!" Dani was not doing very well in the "becoming friends" department.

Lexil looked a little ashamed. "You're right. I didn't really give you a chance to explain."

"And she has already explained to me, at least partially. I'm eager to hear more, later. But I can assure you, she hasn't been spying on you. Can we get past this?"

"Yes," they both said at the same time. "For now," also in unison. Then they both smiled; they couldn't help it.

"Let's do it," said Dr. Seebak. "Lexil, you first. Dani, as you hear a date and time, tell us anything you know that happened then. The disturbance we see on our sensors has been following you around."

They compared notes. Wednesday, 1:30. Dani was in the observation box at the institute, but she didn't know what changed. September 17, 2206. Kat and Marak didn't meet when they should have. March 6, 2207. Kat and Marak didn't get married when they should have. June 7, 2208. Kat and Marak did meet, when they should have already been married. There were some other dates that Dani couldn't help with. She guessed that Kat and Marak must have been doing different things than they had done in the old reality, but she didn't know them then and couldn't be sure.

"You've been talking about disturbances," she said, while Lexil was gathering more dates. "What is a disturbance, exactly? What triggers your sensors?"

"Anything that produces a difference in a timestream from what it was originally," said Lexil.

"How can you know what happened originally, after everything is changed? I'm apparently the only one who remembers what the old reality was like."

"How do you know that? Who else have you discussed this with?" asked Lexil.

"Just Kat and Marak Wallace, and Uncle Royce."

"Uncle Royce. Would that be Kat's uncle?" Dr. Seebak was taking notes, she noticed.

"Yes. Also he's on the board of directors of the institute. But you probably already know that."

"I do. He has been on the board since I was at the institute. Most of the other members have been changed, though, in recent years. Lexil, will you answer her earlier question, about how we find disturbances?"

"We have dual sensors; half of each pair is in an observation box. Both halves record simultaneously, and any difference is recorded."

Dani stopped him. "So you're saying that anything in an observation box is protected from the change? And I was in an observation box when it happened, so I remember the other reality? I'm like a human sensor?"

Lexil nodded. "Yes. The observation box was one of the first developments in the science of chronography. When Dr. Seeback and my mother made the first pair of them, we had a timestream sensor. We had sensors before we ever had scanners. This disturbance made a bigger difference than any we've seen previously—I already told you about that—and we have a couple of ideas as to why. The first main factor is because you were aware of the change. Every decision you made differently because of your awareness is a blip, and every blip causes ripples that can cause more blips.

"So I'm causing more damage?"

"That's not necessarily true," said Dr. Seebak. "Some of the things you do may be moving the timestream back toward its original course. We see blips in both directions. Also, in addition to the original timestream disturbance and the responses of the timestream to the original change, Lexil has detected a third factor, a force that works to put the timestream back in order. We are still learning."

She turned toward Lexil, "You say my responses are the first main factor. What is the other one?"

"We have a hypothesis—supported in every test we've done—that the disturbances are caused by objects being physically removed from the timestream. If that's the case, then the more significant disturbances are the ones where more significant objects have been removed."

"That's where we were hoping you could help us," the doctor interjected. "We would like to find out what might have been removed, in this case."

Dani thought about that. This was the first time she had heard the idea that something could be removed from the past, and she still wasn't clear on how that was done. But the question was what might have been removed to make the difference. There was only one object that could be. "It was the padlock," she said.

"How can you be sure?" asked Lexil.

"First of all, I scanned it. I know the institute is working on it. Secondly, it made a big difference in the events that followed." She thought about Marak being able to go inside the garden, not meeting Kat that day, not being married when Jored was supposed to be born. "Thirdly, it resulted, finally, in someone not being born."

Both men looked up at that statement. "An entire person was removed from the timestream?" asked Dr. Seebak.

"Yes." Dani blinked back tears.

"Someone you knew, evidently," Lexil said, gently.

Dani could only nod.

Dr. Seebak had turned to move some numbers around on the viewwall, constructing equations with a practiced hand. "How old would this person be today?"

"He would be seven. He was supposed to be Kat and Marak's son, but they didn't meet—in this reality—until after he was born." She was trying to be objective, emotionless, but it wasn't working. Her voice dropped to a whisper. "I miss him so much."

Lexil reached over and put his hand on hers. "I'm sorry. I didn't know."

They sat in silence for a few minutes. Dani wished someone would talk, because she was fighting back tears again. She was getting so tired. It was much easier when she wasn't thinking about him, when she could distract herself.

Dr. Seebak cleared his throat. "Well, that would certainly fit the parameters for a significant disturbance: the removal of a whole person."

"You make it sound clinical, Doc. Can't you see she's hurting?"

"Our whole existence is hurting, Lexil. Dani is strong. She will have ample time to grieve later, and do it right. As hard and unfeeling as it seems, we need to act now, or the effects will amplify. Can you help us, Dani?"

Dani nodded. Strange, she thought, that Lexil should be so angry on her behalf. "Can you show me how you found out that objects were vanishing?"

"Come with me," Lexil said. "Doc, excuse us for a minute?"

"Of course. Going to the library?"

"You guessed it."

SEEBAK HOME, Vashon Island, WA. 2230, Thursday, June 8, 2215.

The walk to the library took them outdoors. Dani inhaled the fragrance of fir trees and madronas. She was amazed at the persistence of natural surroundings on the island. The demonstration hologram she used in school presentations could have been recorded here, with no need to go back a hundred years.

"Peaceful, isn't it?" Lexil asked.

"It really is. If I lived here, I don't think I'd ever want to leave."

"I don't, not often. Hey, about the way I was acting ..."

"It's okay. I was suspicious of you, too."

"The thing is, we know there is a person at the institute who is getting private information and blackmailing people with it. Or a group of people," he added as an afterthought.

She caught her breath. "You know about that too?"

"What do you know about it?"

So she told him about Anders, and what the two of them had found in the financial records, and how she had linked it to the blanks in the scanned objects. He asked intelligent questions, and seemed to have a knack for getting to the heart of the matter effortlessly.

She skimmed over the specifics of the scene she had witnessed, but mentioned that it concerned one of the main three scientists.

"Dr. Brant," Lexil said, and it wasn't a question.

"Yes!" Dani was startled that he knew. Hadn't Dr. Seebak told her not to tell him anything? "How did you know?"

"She came to see us; told us she was being blackmailed. I really want to get her free of those crooks. She's constantly monitored, afraid to even send messages to us because she can't trust anybody there to be a messenger."

At the same time, they both stopped and looked at each other. It was obvious they were thinking of the same thing. "I could do that," said Dani.

"Yes. You could do that," said Lexil.

They discussed the details. Dani would have to find a place to contact Dr. Brant that wouldn't be seen. She would need a code word to tell her that the message came from them, and that Dani could be trusted. They dare not use their names, but the institute wasn't aware of the location of their lab, so the word "Vashon" would tell her all she needed to know. They had covered a lot of ground, both physically and metaphorically, by the time they got to the house.

"The library is around the corner there, to the left," he said as he opened the door.

Dani found it easily. She was astonished at the number of old-fashioned books that lined the shelves. "Anders would love this," she said.

"This Anders guy. He's important to you?"

She glanced at him, wondering at his interest. "He's important to the investigation," she said, noncommittally.

"And to you too?"

"Does it matter?" she countered.

"It might. I was just wondering." He looked at her steadily.

Those puppy dog eyes again. She wished he would just say it, if he was interested. But then she realized she didn't wish that at all. This was not the time to think about romantic entanglements. She needed to change the subject. Refocusing her attention, she examined the books on the shelf in front of her and asked, "So, did you have something to show me?"

"Yes, I did. Remember that outfielder who caught the ball back in the 2089 World Series? His name was Ansell Buckton, and he wrote about that moment years later. I read his account a while back. I was just curious; those photos have always fascinated me, and I wanted to know more. But when I read it, I noticed something. Here's what I want to show you." Lexil reached over to the bookshelf on the wall and took down a thin hardbound volume.

By the careful way he turned the old pages, Dani knew this book was no recent reprint. "How old is that book?" she asked.

"It's the real thing," Lexil answered, "and you can't find this volume anywhere any more. Here, look at this passage."

She skimmed two paragraphs, then caught her breath. It couldn't be, but there it was. Why hadn't anyone noticed this earlier?

He smashed the ball deep into the outfield, going up, up, up and to my right. I raced toward left field, running desperately to cut off the ball high above my head. Suddenly, it grew eerily silent. I knew the crowd was yelling, but I couldn't hear it. I ran, just keeping my eye on that ball, and letting my feet find their own way.

At exactly the right moment, I leapt high into the air, reaching up, and I could tell it was going to hit the webbing of my glove. For a moment—no more than a fraction of a second—I couldn't see the ball, and I thought I had misjudged it. But then there it was, just where it was supposed to be, and I squeezed my glove around it. My momentum carried me to the wall. And then I heard the crowd again.

"So it's true."

"Yes. For some objects, some recordings, things simply stop existing for those moments when they were used as a source. They pop back into being immediately afterward, of course, and usually their absence isn't noticed. Usually their absence has no effect on anything. Buckton still caught the ball. Chef Solveig still made her blueberry sauce. The anonymous fiddler continued fiddling. Who looks at a floor tile when there's a fiddler playing? In fact, it's very rare that we notice a disturbance, indicating something, however subtle, has changed. That's how we found this old book. Ansell Buckton wouldn't have written those words if the ball hadn't disappeared for 1/200 of a second—the shutter speed on the camera that snapped the photo."

"You monitor everything?"

"Well, our timestream sensors monitor everything. There's too much, way too much, data for us to put eyeballs on all of it. But the reports point us in the right direction, and we look at the things we need to."

Dani thought that through. "So this—this meeting we are having right now—will show up on your reports?"

Lexil laughed. "You're quick. Yes, this meeting would never have taken place if Buckton hadn't written those words."

"Or if Jored hadn't disappeared." She suddenly realized that the missing padlock was her fault. It was her recording, converted to a form that could be played, that had stolen Jored.

His smile gone, Lexil nodded solemnly. "That was the biggest disturbance we've seen. I had to come myself."

"But why come? What can you do, once the damage is ... done?" Dani had some trouble getting the words out. It still hurt, so much, missing him and being the only one to mourn. And now she felt like a murderer, only worse. Murderers take what is left of a lifespan. She had taken the whole thing, all of it, from the moment of his conception to the end, whenever that might have been. It barely touched the surface of her grief to remind herself that she hadn't meant to. That she was just following through on an assignment.

Lexil didn't answer. She wasn't really expecting an answer.

Preoccupied with her thoughts, it took her a few minutes before she looked up at Lexil and found him studying her carefully. His expression wasn't the resigned, sympathetic look she would have expected. It was more contemplative, as if he were trying to make a decision. "Why are you looking at me like that?" she asked.

He cleared his throat. "It might be possible ..." he started.

"What might be possible?"

"We have a method—and you have to understand it is completely untested—that might let us replace objects that have been removed."

She caught her breath. "Like the padlock?"

He nodded. "It would take some time to prepare. We'd need to test it out here; remove an object, replace it, see if it is stable. We'd need exact parameters for the padlock. The location will be relative to where the padlock was, so as long as we have the current padlock, setting the time and duration will be enough. Our scanners here are little portable ones. They can only reach back a few days. They'll work for testing, but not for the actual procedure."

"So we would need to use the scanners at the institute."

"Exactly. But Doc can't go back there; it's part of his *agreement*." His tone of voice made it obvious what he thought of the agreement.

"I don't want anybody else knowing who I am, so I can't go there either. It would be up to you."

"I can do that."

"Yes, but you don't know how to set it, and the settings have to be exact. We're going to have to give you something you can plug in there at the institute, after you get to a scanner and retrieve the padlock. Is there any difficulty getting things inside?"

She thought about the bag check at the security gate. "It would depend on what it looked like, I guess."

"It's just a memory rod."

"I should be able to get that past security okay. How long will it take?"

"Most of the day tomorrow, I'm guessing. We'll only get one chance at this. We have to make sure it will work correctly the first time. I'd send a program with you tonight, except there's a little boy's life at stake."

"Lexil?"

"Yes?"

"Thank you."

23
PREPARATION

SEEBAK LABORATORY, Vashon Island, WA. 0730, Friday, June 9, 2215.

"So I think it would be an ideal platform for an experiment, besides helping put the timestream back into place." Lexil was hoping Doc would see the benefits. He was already realizing he might have been a little premature in his conversation with Dani the night before.

She had cast a lure and was reeling him in. Everything had been fine while he was mad at her, but as soon as Doc had reassured him on that count, he was hooked again. The walk to the tube station in the evening moonlight had just made it worse.

He must have sounded stupid, asking about that Anders guy. But she'd made it pretty plain it was none of his business, and hadn't given any indication of any kind of return interest when he'd hinted so broadly. He had pretty much told her he was smitten. And now he felt foolish for it.

"How certain are you of your procedures?"

He'd almost forgotten he was talking to Doc. "I know the procedure. I've just never tested it. That's why I want to use our scanner today. Also, our VAO converter."

"Tell me again exactly what you plan to do." Doc was rubbing his eyebrow, which was both a bad sign and a good sign. It meant he was worried about the results, but at least he was considering it.

Actually, the worry was good too. Doc would question anything he might not have thought of, and Lexil had to admit that he wanted this to work so badly, he hadn't allowed himself to believe it wouldn't. Ever since he first spotted her on the road outside the Wallace house, he had wanted to do something to bring her some resolution. Even more so, when he saw how much she cared for the little boy.

"First, I'll have to deliberately make an object vanish. I'll have to leave evidence that it has, and then attempt to replace it and see if the evidence vanishes."

"Have you thought about what kind of evidence you will want to leave?"

"I've got some options. I can set up a video camera to film it, but that adds a layer of complexity. We don't know for sure if the image would be removed when the object is removed, although my research so far favors that."

"I agree. Something more straightforward would be preferable."

"So I thought I might just spray paint an object against a background, so the spray leaves an outline, then go back and remove the object."

"So the entire background would be painted, without the object there to block it."

"Yes, well, also, the object itself won't be painted if it's not there when the paint hits it."

Doc nodded. "I like this idea better."

"Can you think of anything I've missed?"

"You have the means of recording your time very precisely?"

"Yes. I'm only going to do a short burst of paint, and I'll be removing the object for at least ten seconds on either side of the spray, to give a little leeway for when I replace it."

Doc stopped rubbing his eyebrow and nodded slowly. "I'll assist."

The testing procedure took most of the morning. He made

frequent reference to the paper generally acknowledged to offer the best specific information on the subject, "A Study of Chronography Blanks and Their Causes." He looked up settings, checked angles and durations, fine-tuned the VAO converter output, projected the hologram to match the experimental settings in the paper.

It wasn't until halfway through the morning that he glanced at the authors' names while awaiting a result. There was her name among the others: "D. Adams." The paper was published in early 2213, which meant the research had been completed when she was only twenty or twenty-one. She must have been an undergraduate at the time, doing impressive work! What he wouldn't give to have her work with them on the timestream disturbances! He'd wait for a good time to broach the subject to Doc.

The first experiment was a failure. He spray painted a rock, and was able to successfully remove it from its time frame, but when he tried to implement the reversal program, it didn't work. He knew the rock should vanish from the current time frame for the same amount of time it was restored to the target time frame. By the time he determined what had gone wrong, they had exceeded their planned time window. That wouldn't have been a problem at RIACH, with its dozens of scanners and the ability to have multiple experiments going at once, but for his purposes, it meant starting the experiment over. Nothing like operating on a shoestring budget, he thought ruefully.

The second experiment was a little better. It was a triumphant moment when the object disappeared from the chamber, but both Lexil and Doc suddenly had memories of a small explosion during the spray paint process, right toward the end, and of having to smother the resulting flames before they licked out and consumed the paint can. That was an exciting moment, in retrospect. They carefully compared the times and realized there was a bit of lag before the object actually appeared and disappeared. When the insertion caused the object to fill the same space twice in the same time frame, the increased pressure caused an explosion. At least, that was the theory. Better just to have a built-in buffer to leave room for the lag. How much lag, exactly, was going to be critical.

They decided to film it while they were doing the spray paint, to see if the recording would catch the object's disappearance, to allow them to bypass the paint can and give them the ability to fine-tune the timing a little more. It succeeded, and that ability proved to be a breakthrough in their experimental methods. Lexil was glad he was keeping careful records. This would be the material he needed for his own paper on the subject.

So then it was film, remove, restore; film, remove, restore, at both extremes of the time window available to them, plus readings in between. After multiple iterations, they were able to reproduce the same results every time.

But they would need to test their equation for the lag time. They could only conjecture what would happen when their interval increased from a few hours to nine years. It became obvious that they would need an experiment of at least twelve hours to determine whether the lag time increased at a linear or exponential rate as they went further back in time.

Lexil called Dani to let her know he wouldn't have an answer for her today. He was disappointed when he didn't get her directly and had to leave a message. He kept it cryptic, "Hey, going to have to reschedule for some time tomorrow!" and hoped she would recognize his voice. He certainly didn't want to leave his name and risk someone at the institute happening to overhear and being able to identify him.

He was also disappointed, he realized, that he wouldn't see her again until the next day.

When they had done all they could to set up several experimental stations, he returned to his study of the time disturbances. It was odd to see so many of them clustered around the lab on Vashon Island. He watched a little trail of them follow him out to the tube station on the display of the data from the night before. Soon he was remembering the delights of her quick mind and her sense of humor. Conversations and expressions replayed in his mind and he berated himself for not being more obvious about his interest in her. Then he shook his head. She would have rejected that as quickly as she had his pointed question about whether she was in a relationship with Anders.

"Lexil!" He realized Doc had said his name more than once. He shook his head to clear away the vision he'd been savoring.

"Here!" he answered, guiltily.

"It's six o'clock. Are you so buried in that that you can't break away for dinner? Time to call it a night anyway, I think." Then Doc looked at him more closely, with one of those too-discerning looks Lexil had come to know well. "Where are your thoughts, son? Are you immersed in your experiment, or are you falling in love?"

Might as well admit it. "Both, Doc. Is it that obvious?"

"You've been tracing the path of your walk last night on the disturbance graph, so, yes, pretty obvious."

"Okay, I'm coming in. Need help with anything dinner-wise?" The two walked to the house in comfortable companionship. He was so grateful that this man had stepped forward to take him in after his father had died and while his mother's life was fading.

Later, while Lexil was drifting off to sleep, it suddenly occurred to him what the little trail of disturbance ripples meant. Disturbances were events that differed from the original timestream. Every interaction he had had with Dani was a disturbance. That meant every moment they had shared was an anomaly, and shouldn't have happened. If their efforts to restore the timestream were successful, all those moments, every smile, every gaze, every contact, would be gone.

He wouldn't remember her at all.

24
DECISION

RIACH CAMPUS, Alki Beach, Seattle, WA. 0745, Friday, June 9, 2215.

When Dani emerged from the tube car, she looked around for Anders, but couldn't spot him among the crowd of people milling about. She shrugged. She could catch him at lunch. She remembered her fear from the night before that "they" were after her and might already have Anders. She smiled now at her baseless apprehensions.

She was pleasantly surprised to see Kat with her holosign walking back and forth near the security gate. She waved and moved to intercept her. Kat seemed to be doing better than she had last night. Dani still felt bad about how she had pushed for Kat to see Jored. If Lexil's experiment worked, it wouldn't matter whether this Kat had seen the scan or not. This Kat would return to being her Kat, happily enjoying her son.

When she got to her, Dani gave her a hug, gladly accepting a little awkwardness avoiding the sign post between them in exchange for the genuine warmth she felt. "How did you sleep?" she asked her friend.

"Not well, at first," Kat admitted. "It was the first time I'd allowed myself to think of having a child since last year. I thought I had adjusted to it, but I guess not."

"I'm so sorry."

"It wasn't your fault. It was something I had to work out on my own, and Marak did too, although he didn't make it as evident as I did. When I couldn't get to sleep, I went out to the kitchen for some tea, and he followed me. We talked for a long time. Didn't get to bed until after midnight. I thought about calling you, but I was pretty sure you'd be asleep."

"Actually, I was still up."

"That's unusual for you, isn't it? Anyway, we talked, and we figured something out. We really, really want to see that scan. If only for a moment, we want to see who our son would have been."

Dani was surprised. That was the last thing she would have expected. At the same time, she felt a little leap of joy. It would be so nice to share that with Kat and Marak. "Did you talk to your uncle?"

"Yes, and he will have a security escort ready to take us to you sometime later this morning. He's going to let me know what time, so I can't tell yet. He said he was pretty sure it would be okay for you to escort us out again after we see it. After we see him."

Dani pictured the scene in her mind: this erstwhile protest organizer, avowed enemy of the institute, being escorted by a security guard into its big open mouth. She giggled. "Do you know what that's going to look like, with the security guard?"

Kat looked puzzled, and then she got it and started laughing too. "It'll probably help with my reputation," she said. "They all think I'm too tame anyway. Should I let you know what time we're coming?"

"No, they'll put it on my schedule. I'll see it."

"Okay. Thanks for doing this."

"No problem! Just be sure you really want to."

"I'm already sure." Kat turned to go, and then turned back. "Dani?"

"Yeah?"

"What kept you up till after midnight?"

Dani smiled. "Well, I didn't get home until around eleven thirty."

"What? How could it have taken that long?"

"I took a little detour to Vashon Island. Saw a secret laboratory.

Walked in the moonlight with a really good-looking guy. But it's too much to talk about now. Time for me to be at work!"

"You can't leave me like this!"

"Have to. I'll tell you more later."

As she cleared security and walked to the institute doors, she heard Kat calling after her: "I want to hear about the moonlit walk first!"

Yeah. Because secret island laboratories were so passé. Dani smiled to herself, although she had to admit that there were some memories from that evening walk that made her inexplicably happy.

RIACH OFFICES, Alki Beach, Seattle, WA. 0810, Friday, June 9, 2215.

The morning's assignments were all things she could do quickly, so Dani reviewed her personal list of things to do. She wanted to leave the coded note for Dr. Brant, reaching out to make a contact, but cautiously. She had written the note at home before she left. "Let's talk about Vashon. Tube station bench 1715." She wanted to find Anders and reschedule his meeting with Kat and Marak. Perhaps, if they arrived close to lunch, she could take them to the cafeteria and happen to run into him, but she didn't want to draw any attention to him while he was still digging into the finances of the place.

Most importantly, of course, she had an institute-approved slot in her schedule to see Jored again, and show her friends their son. She hoped it would make them happy, and not cause them more pain.

She had to walk past the researchers' conference area to get to the lab. Occasionally, she saw Dr. Brant there in meetings, but that was usually on Mondays. Still, she checked to see who was there today, just in case. The conference area was empty, with a few research fellows at the work areas that ringed it on the outside. No sign of the doctor. No sign of any of the doctors, for that matter. She wondered if she should make a little detour through the hallway where the offices were.

Dani glanced around. No one was paying any particular attention to her. She wandered down the hall with a vague idea that if Dr. Tasman happened to ask her where she should be at that particular moment, she would tell him she was heading for the garbage can at the end of the hall. She wouldn't actually stop at Dr. Brant's office, but if she was there, she would make eye contact.

Dr. Brant was in her office. She looked up as Dani passed by. Instead of glancing then turning away, Dani made a point of locking eyes with the doctor and nodding, almost imperceptibly. Then she continued down the hall, nonchalantly dropping the crumpled note in the can at the end of the hall. Then she turned and retraced her steps, back toward the lab. She hoped this was not a wasted trip. But she didn't know how else to catch the doctor's attention.

Unnoticed, the camera behind her pivoted to watch her go.

But so did Dr. Brant.

RIACH LABS, Alki Beach, Seattle, WA. 0830, Friday, June 9, 2215.

When Dani got to the lab, she started working her way down the list of scans on her schedule. Everything went smoothly, so she had time to scan the stone and preview the scenes she was going to show Kat and Marak. She didn't know how much time they'd have, and she wanted to know the exact settings to use before they started.

That was probably a mistake, though, because soon she was fighting tears as she watched herself chase Jored down the hall, just out of sight, and heard his giggles. She loved the whole family feeling when they all played the matching game. To be able to have a meal like that, one more time, with all of them together!

She was still absorbing every detail of his wonderful little voice and contagious joy when she was startled by a tap on her observation box window. The boxes were clear from the waist up; it was easy to spot which ones were in use. But the doors couldn't be opened while the scanners were hooked up. The young woman standing outside her box was a stranger to her. She was dressed like a security guard, though, and for the first time, Dani felt uneasy. Had she made her extracurricular activities too obvious?

She carefully disconnected and opened the door. "Yes?"

"You have visitors in the lobby. I was asked to give you a message."

Relief flooded her. Of course! It was Kat and Marak. "Oh, thank you. I'll go meet them."

She headed out of the lab, toward the lobby, chiding herself for being so nervous. Kat and Marak were waiting for her, and soon she would see Jored again.

RIACH LOBBY, Alki Beach, Seattle, WA. 1105, Friday, June 9, 2215.

Kat was peering down the long hallway, waiting for her to come. Marak was gazing at the massive doors. The viewwall that usually showed Dani's schedule when she entered simply read, "Welcome!"—a message left over from when visitors were the norm rather than the exception. Kat and Marak would have been irisscanned on their way in, and permitted only because Uncle Royce had made the arrangements. Since they were inside the building, they had obviously been pre-approved.

It seemed so odd, seeing them at the institute, but Dani was very happy they were there.

"Which way is the lab?" Marak asked.

Dani led the way down the hall, waiting when they paused at the displays, giving them time to look around. To anyone watching, she was a tour guide. But she wouldn't mind at all if her friends managed to see something they could use later to help her gather information they needed.

As they walked, she played her role well, pointing out areas as they passed. "These areas are where the researchers work. I pass right by this area every day. There are the scientists' offices, down that hall back there. Financial services and the directors' offices are on the second floor. The coffee shop and supplies room are in the other wing on this floor. The cafeteria is in the basement."

Kat and Marak nodded, smiling at anyone who noticed them. Dani could tell that Marak was making mental notes, not missing a thing.

Finally, they got to the lab. Dani led them to the scanner she had been using that morning. Only one person could use the observation box at a time, but Dani had two objects she could use to show them: the rock and the metal disk. She could borrow the adjacent scanner for this.

"I'm going to put one of these in each chamber," she told them, "and close the chamber door. When you step into the observation box and close the door, you'll feel a tickling sensation in your brain as the scanner hooks up directly to your sensory nerves. It will look as if you are there, with the rock or the disk, able to see and hear what is going on at the times I've set."

"Will we still know we're here?" Kat was a little nervous.

Dani reassured her, "You won't be all that aware of your surroundings here in the lab, but you can choose to see and hear what is here instead of there, if you want. It's under your control. If I tap on the window, for example, you'll hear it."

She adjusted the settings for each machine. "Okay, who wants to be able to smell the shish kebabs? Only one of you gets to do that. This machine has the metal disk, so you get the full experience here."

Marak stepped back to let Kat have that spot. Dani hoped Kat wouldn't be too overwhelmed by it.

"I've already set the time frames. All you'll have to do is tap 'start' and it will take over. There are thirty-eight minutes I've framed for you, so get comfortable. Sit or stand; the machine doesn't care. If you need to take a break, for whatever reason, the 'start' button will have become a 'pause.'" You can resume right where you left off when you are ready to go on.

"Can we replay if we want to?" asked Marak?

"That's a little more complicated. I'd have to give you a short training session first. Just live it like you were there, for now."

They both nodded.

"Ready? Then step in, get comfortable, close the door, and tap 'start.'"

Dani pulled a chair over to wait. She remembered the first time she had experienced a scan. She had scanned a stone from a public fountain on a chilly winter day. A commonplace item in an insignificant setting. Still, she had been awed by the whole thing, with the water splashing down around her and the occasional passerby walking swiftly to get out of the cold weather. Kat and Marak were probably equally awed, but their experience would be so much more intense. They would be seeing themselves.

She watched their faces change and imagined what scenes they were seeing. That slightly squirmy look as they saw themselves doing things they knew they hadn't done. That look of amazement at their first glimpse of the little boy that looked so much like both of them. A taste of joy at his squeals and giggles. Wistful yearning at his hugs. Tears as they reached the end, when Dani had pocketed the items again as she prepared to leave. She could see the viewscreens signaling the end of the session, and still they sat, remembering. She respectfully gave them time to recover before she tapped on their windows. It was almost lunchtime, and the labs needed to be cleared by noon.

Kat emerged from her box and went straight into Marak's waiting arms. They cried together and Dani found herself crying with them. She passed out tissues, which they gratefully accepted. She hoped they didn't hate her for putting them through this.

When she had regained a little of her usual composure, Kat turned to Dani and said simply, "Thank you." Marak nodded in agreement.

That didn't surprise Dani at all. What surprised her was what came next.

Taking Marak's hand to give her strength, Kat said, "Do it. Do whatever it takes. Get him back."

RIACH CAFETERIA, Alki Beach, Seattle, WA. 1230, Friday, June 9, 2215.

Once she found out Kat and Marak's visitor badges entitled them to a free lunch in the employee cafeteria, she continued her tour by showing them the basement level.

They got to the cafeteria for lunch a little late. Dani looked around for Anders. He should have arrived and bought lunch already. She was puzzled when she didn't see him. But maybe it was better this way. The three of them had so much to discuss. She thought about sitting at the table where they'd eaten before, but when she started toward it, she saw it wasn't there. That was odd. Had someone moved it? She glanced around the rest of the cafeteria. Were there other differences? She didn't eat here often enough to enable her to be sure, but it seemed as if the walls were a different color. Maybe that was due to the timestream change.

Kat interrupted her puzzled inspection of the cafeteria. "Dani, what actually changed everything to this reality? I know it had something to do with that padlock. Marak and I were talking after you left, and he couldn't remember having seen it at all on the day he got into the garden."

Dani nodded. "You've heard our slogan, 'It's not just seen,' and all that?"

"It's heard, it's smelled, and so on," Marak supplied.

"It's PastPerfect!" added Kat.

"That's right. Well, it turns out that it's not just seen and heard and smelled. It's used. And the worst thing about that is that it's used up. Not just for PastPerfect purposes, but for everybody. For those moments of its existence within the time frame in question, it's just not there any more. It's erased."

"We suspected something like that," said Marak.

"The moments are usually so brief, it doesn't matter. If someone notices, they'd look again, and it would be there, and they'd wonder about it, but nothing really changes. Sometimes, though, it does matter. It matters a lot. If we erase a key object at the moment it plays a part in an event, major or minor, the ripples begin. And this is not merely an alternate timeline. The object at that moment in time is erased throughout all potential timelines. That's what I meant when I said used up."

"What do you mean when you say ripples?" Marak's eyes had narrowed. He was honing in on everything she said.

"Well, there's a story behind that word," said Dani. "I have a lot of things to share with you guys, actually, not the least of which is where I was last night and what I learned there."

"The moonlit walk?" asked Kat, smiling.

"The moonlit walk, yes." Dani laughed. "But not just that. The most important thing I want to tell you about is that it might be possible to do exactly what you told me you wanted, back in the lab. Put the world right again. But how do you really feel about that?"

Kat answered slowly. "I said before that it would feel like giving up my memories so some other Kat could have her son back. But as wonderful as those memories are"—she squeezed Marak's hand—"I watched that other Kat, and she felt like me. This world has felt wrong to me for a long time, in ways that I couldn't put my finger on. I thought it was just that we really wanted a baby and couldn't have one, even though we tried so hard. But other people go through that too, and I'd be stupid to think that everybody else's difficulties were because of some time disturbance somewhere."

Dani interrupted. "And they aren't. This is the only one that has occurred of this significance."

"You can tell that?" asked Marak.

"Yes. I'll tell you more later. Go on, Kat."

"When I sat there in that observation box, the things I saw felt right in the same way some of the things I've lived feel *wrong*. Not you, Marak. Being with you has always felt right." She smiled at her husband.

"Likewise, babe. But Dani, I felt the same thing. I wouldn't feel like I was sacrificing myself for another version of me. I'd feel like I was going back to a life that I was meant to live all along."

"So I have your blessing to pursue this, both of you?"

"Absolutely," said Kat.

"You bet," said Marak.

Just then, Dani looked up and saw Anders at a table across the room. He had probably seen her with company and hadn't wanted to interrupt. She gestured toward him. "That's Anders. I want you two to meet him. Finished eating?"

They were, so they picked up their trays and dropped them off on their way over to his table. Kat and Marak hung back to let Dani go first.

Anders looked up, then quickly dropped his eyes back down to his food.

"Anders? Are you okay?"

"Dani, I can't talk to you," he muttered.

"What?" she dropped her voice. "Why?"

"Just leave, please. They're watching me. They have something on my brother, and I can't let them ruin his life. I wouldn't care if it was me. You understand?" He looked up at her, just for a second, but she could read the agony in his eyes.

She nodded, then moved away quickly.

She was fuming when she got to Kat and Marak. Kat knew her too well to ask why. Dani would talk when she got some semblance of control back.

Dani was expected to see them past the security gate before she went back to work. They walked through the big doors and let the irisscan check them and open the exit gate.

Finally, Dani spoke. "They got to him."

"How?" asked Kat.

"They're blackmailing him with something they have on his older brother. He and his brother are really close. We have to stop this!" She almost growled as she said the last sentence.

"If the time disturbance can be repaired, will that stop it?" asked

Marak. "I'm guessing this blackmailing existed in your reality too?"

Dani pondered that. "I can't say for sure. I know that before everything changed, there were high school kids clamoring to have their privacy protected, Anders willing to dig to see what he could find, and you, Kat, demonstrating outside the institute every weekday, rain or shine. So I think there was some concern, yes. But I don't know how far it went."

"Then we have two possibilities," Marak continued. "Either it didn't exist, and reality fixed means no more blackmail, or it did exist, and fixing it here won't have any effect on the correct reality. Either way, whatever we do here won't help us there. Am I right?"

He was making perfect sense. Dani nodded.

"I have another question, in that case," said Marak. "Will we remember anything from this reality's last nine years, and more specifically, from these last three days, if the timestream is repaired?"

"No, not unless you are in the observation box when it happens."

"So everything we find out here has no effect there."

He was right. The three of them looked at each other, speechless, and feeling completely powerless to do anything to help.

RIACH TUBE STOP, Alki Beach, Seattle, WA. 1710, Friday, June 9, 2215.

Dani had finished her afternoon assignments as quickly as she could so she could be out at the tube station early. If anyone was watching her, she wanted to know before Dr. Brant came out—assuming she got the note and made it to the meeting. Dani really didn't know what kind of limitations they had placed on her movements. Perhaps a walk to the tube station would be seen as different enough to get her in trouble. If she didn't see the doctor in another fifteen minutes, she would just go home.

In the first fifteen minutes, the time since she had first sat down, there had been no sign of anyone watching or paying any attention to her. Everyone who had been waiting for the tube when she first got there had left. She even saw Anders, and he had walked right past her to get on his tube car. Their eyes had met only once, and that was enough to know he wouldn't be stopping to talk. She hated the hurt she saw in his eyes. There had to be some way to help him!

Two minutes before Dani was going to leave, she saw Dr. Brant, walking purposefully toward the bench behind Dani's, carefully avoiding any kind of eye contact that might give her away. They sat, back-to-back, two casual travelers waiting for a tube car.

"I got your note," Dr. Brant said quietly. Her enunciation was indistinct. Dani suspected she was trying not to move her lips.

Dani pretended to tap her temple to call someone on the nexus. That would disguise her own lip movements. "I'm glad you got it. I wasn't sure how to pass you a message."

"How do you know about Vashon?"

"We have mutual friends on Vashon who wanted me to help you communicate more easily with them."

"I think you are too obvious when you walk down that hallway. There's a camera there. But this is a good place to meet."

"Not daily, though," Dani said, and gestured as if to pull an image up on her eyescreen to show to her caller. She laughed to cover up her nervousness. She had a lot to learn about this espionage stuff.

"No, not daily. We should have a signal. That laugh sounded almost convincing." Dr. Brant was almost laughing herself.

"What do we both see every day? Someplace with no cameras."

"We both go in and out of the main entrance. If I need to see you, I'll place a tiny bit of red tape on the right edge of the viewwall border. If you see it, remove the tape."

"If I can't meet for some reason, I'll leave the tape there."

"That's fine."

"And if I need to see you to pass on a message from Vashon, I'll leave a piece of blue tape."

"That will work. I'll watch for it."

"Dr. Brant? May I ask you a question?"

"You may ask, but I don't know if I can answer."

"Don't you have any friends at the institute you can go to for help?"

"Friends." Her tone of voice took on a slightly bitter tone. "My old friends are gone, and I've been advised that it would be in my best interests not to have any personal relationships with any of the current employees."

"Not even Dr. Calegari or Dr. Tasman?"

"They are so guarded with me that they may well have been advised the same way I was. Sometimes a new intern or someone on the support staff will stop to try to chat with me…" She stopped abruptly. "You did that, I think."

"Yes, I did. More than once."

"But I never know who might have been hired to spy on me and report back."

"That sounds awful."

"It is. And they won't let us do any real research any more."

"Why don't you just leave? Work with…" Dani stopped herself before she said any names. "I mean, work on Vashon?"

"I can't. The blackmailers know…they would tell…" She struggled for words. "It would hurt someone I love, very badly. I can't explain. I know you don't understand. I'm sorry."

But Dani did understand. "Please, don't apologize."

They sat in silence for a few minutes, then Dani had an idea. "I know someone on the board of directors. I could ask him to help you."

Dr. Brant laughed, but it was a hopeless, hollow sound. "Oh, I know board members too, and I don't need their kind of help. Trust me. I'd stay away from the board of directors if I were you."

Dani understood. It was almost certain the blackmailers were associated in some way with the board of directors. She reminded herself that Uncle Royce had said he was mostly a figurehead. Even if he was, as he said, trying to have some influence on the rest of them, he was probably as helpless as she was. Well, at least he had been able to get Kat and Marak visitors' passes. That was something!

"Watch for my signal. I have to leave now or they'll be wondering where I am." Dr. Brant was standing. "I want to tell you, though: It's nice to have someone to talk to."

Dani nodded, then pretended to continue her connexion. After a minute, she told the imaginary person on the other end, "I do too! Bye! Later!" and pretended to disconnect.

She waited for a while until she felt it was safe to turn. Dr. Brant was almost at the entrance to the parking garage, thirty meters away. A tube car was coming, and Dani was ready to go.

It wasn't until she was inside the car, speeding away, that she realized she hadn't seen the clock tower—taller, shorter, or whatever—at all. Was she that oblivious to her surroundings?

25
NEUTRALIZATION

HUNTER'S OFFICE. 1800, Friday, June 9, 2215.

The institute was quiet. The employees had gone home. It had been a good day, with many secrets learned and used effectively. He put on a lightweight overcoat and waved his hand at the controls to fade the lights.

As he walked out the door, he made mental notes about his progress. Four payments of various sizes had been received, totaling 600 million credits. Three new possible sources had been identified, and eight suitable objects retrieved for scanning on Monday.

It was good to have successfully taken the young man, Peerson, out of the picture. There would be no more digging into the financial business of the institute. He hadn't even known about his brother's teenage indiscretions, but he certainly knew now. What a surprise it had been!

At first, Peerson hadn't believed it. "I know my brother, and my brother would never do that." The boy had been defiant. So he had described the dog and the car in great detail, and revealed the specifics of how the dog had died, and identified precisely what his brother had been carrying in the back seat. He had told him the two people, a girl and a boy, who were with his brother and what his brother had said. He had described what his brother was wearing:

the color, the fabric, the cut, and how he wore it with rolled up sleeves.

He had provided such specific detail that the young man had grown pale and silent; the defiance had melted away. He had pointed out that any kind of trouble over making and marketing illegal substances would not be good for a new pharmacist and his young family. But Peerson's mind had already reached that conclusion. Finally, when he was done, the young man had said, "What do you want?"

He had been quick to reassure Peerson, of course, that he would guard the evidence carefully, and his brother would never know he had it, as long as Peerson's own equally illegal, unauthorized accesses to company records ceased immediately. The young man was bright. He had agreed to cooperate. And given enough time, and enough regular reminders of his brother's vulnerability, he would come around and learn to tolerate the intolerable. Managed properly, he might even prove to be a valuable asset.

He had passed his first test. Asked about the young woman whom he had eaten with, he readily revealed the extent of her involvement. It had turned out that his association with her had been nothing more than a harmless flirtation. She knew nothing about the financial reports. Nevertheless, he would continue to keep an eye on her. Perhaps she too could be useful.

26
INFORMATION

WEST SEATTLE HIGH SCHOOL, Seattle, WA. 1000, Saturday, June 10, 2215.

As Dani stepped onto the slidewalk in front of the high school, she considered how much to share with the Political Action Club members. She really only had knowledge of one specific person being blackmailed, and she wasn't going to mention Dr. Brant by name. She wondered if she should talk about what she and Anders had discovered. Would that be considered corporate espionage? She couldn't recall anything in her contract that said she couldn't talk about what went on at the institute; in fact, part of her job description had been to be a mouthpiece. She was supposed to talk.

Of course, she was pretty sure the intent was to promote good will, not to expose criminal behavior. Some ambassador she had turned out to be. But the momentary feelings of guilt were swept away by indignation. She wasn't the one who had chosen to turn this amazing new technology into an instrument of greed! And she was still just stubborn enough to believe that most of the employees at the institute were there for the good they could do. Some could be victims, like Dr. Brant and now Anders. A very few people could be running this whole scheme themselves from the top of the org chart.

Ms. Harris came to the door to admit her. "It's locked on the weekends," she explained.

"Who all is here today?" Dani was a little cautious. Since the change had removed Jored, she had no idea whether the club members were made up of the same people or not. Lexil had assured her that the timestream had a tendency to repair itself, so most things should be the same. He was just guessing, though, and had been honest enough to admit it. She glanced around the school to get her bearings. The posters looked familiar, with a couple of exceptions. She wondered whether she had just missed those before, or if they were timestream changes. It was also possible that the students had put up some new ones in the last four days.

The principal led her down the hall toward the same room where they had met before. "Two of the club members, Meredin and Beck, couldn't make it because next week is exam week. They have a chemistry final first thing Monday morning, and they are meeting with a study group this morning. Alanya is on a weekend trip with her family. The rest are here, though. Joph, Jazz, Shard, Lora, and Ronny. Oh, and Ronny asked his grandfather to join us today."

"His grandfather?" Dani vaguely remembered that he had talked about his grandfather, but she couldn't remember what he had said.

Ms. Harris nodded. "Yes, the detective grandfather. You remember? The one who says to follow the money?"

"Oh, yes. I remember now."

"He's quite a character. He comes along with Ronny about once a month. Tells us stories, some of which even have something to do with politics."

"Nothing like keeping on topic!"

"Exactly. Here he is now. Detective Tom Rayes, this is Dani Adams."

The detective's broad, good-humored smile faded abruptly. "Adams? Danarin Adams?" At her nod, he reached back for something—she had no idea what. Handcuffs? Gun? "Young lady, I'm afraid you'll have to come with me. You are under arrest for—"

Dani couldn't say anything. Her mind raced. What had she done?

Was the digging she had done with Anders illegal? Was the Dani from this timestream involved in something else?

At her shocked expression, he laughed and smacked her on the shoulder. "I'm just kidding. Never fails to get a reaction! Pleased to meet you!" He stuck out his hand.

She smiled back, a little uncertainly, and shook his hand. "And you. Um, I think," she added doubtfully.

The kids were all grinning, even though they tried to hide it by pretending interest in the fruit and cheese on the refreshments table.

"Don't worry, Dani." Lora comforted her. "He does that to all of us, or something like it."

"You get used to it." Jazz had taken her plate and was already sprawled over the arms of the chair at the end of the table, which was automatically attempting to adjust to her awkward position.

That girl really put demands on her chairs, Dani thought. She must wear them out once a month.

"He'd better not try to arrest me," said Ms. Harris.

"Already tried that, when you and my daughter were study partners, back in your younger days, if I recall correctly." The detective shook his head ruefully. "Won't try it again."

Ronny laughed. "My mom has told me about that story."

The others looked at them expectantly, shifting their gaze from one to the next to see who would spill the details first.

"And that," said Ms. Harris firmly, "will be enough of that. Dani, did you have anything new to share with us?"

"Yes, actually." Dani was quite willing to change the subject. "It might be good that you're here, Detective Rayes. We've found some evidence—well, not evidence, exactly; more like indications—that there could be some illegal activities going on over at the institute."

"That would be the chronography institute?"

"Yeah." She took a deep breath. "I work there. A friend found some unnamed sources of income, referenced only as 'investment' or 'contribution'—and they aren't anonymous donors; he checked. I've got a record of them here."

She pulled out her worktablet to show him. She had summarized the files Anders had given her, not wanting to reveal the names of legitimate donors and investors. The kids clustered around to look too, but quickly moved away at the masses of figures. Only Joph stuck it out; Dani could have predicted that, based on his fascination with numbers.

Joph whistled. "That is a lot of extra funding! Must be almost half of the total."

Detective Rayes nodded. "I'm not nearly as quick at the totals as you are, Joph. But it's a large percentage, pretty clearly. And the institute has no official accounting for these amounts, you say, Dani?"

"Nothing published. And I found out something else." She hesitated, gathering her thoughts, then continued, "I personally know of two instances where people are being threatened with something unless they keep silent about something going on in the company. One of them is the friend who got this information for me."

"So he won't testify, if it comes to that?" asked the detective.

"No, I don't think so. He looked pretty scared."

"You said two instances," said Ronny. "Has anyone threatened you?"

"No, not me. If anyone had, I'd know who it was, and I could testify."

Jazz sat forward abruptly, and the chair whirred to keep up. "I'm assuming the blackmailer's material comes from what we talked about? Using objects and chronography searches to dig up dirt?"

"We're pretty sure that's the case."

"Is there a record of scans? Can you match the deposits to objects and get a clue that way?"

Dani shook her head. "There are too many scans going on daily. And the demands for money may come weeks after the initial scan. The blackmailer would have to have a second scan done—we call those investigative scans, when we're doing them for historical purposes—and once the specific time frame was established, he'd have to convert the chronic information into a VAO hologram—oh!"

She was vaguely aware of puzzled looks on the faces of all the club members except for Shard, whose face reflected Dani's own look of dawning realization. He spoke up for the first time. "You use another machine for that step, don't you?"

"Yes! And there is only one of those."

"Are there records of what that machine has been used on?" asked Lora.

"There are! I can look those up and find out which objects were scanned for periods within the last twenty or thirty years. That could definitely help. And I could look at the dates and times they were converted to VAO holograms and match those with the..." she trailed off, thinking about dates and data.

"Is there any way you could get some names from that?" Detective Rayes was intrigued. "If so, I can get warrants to see if I can find withdrawals to match the unidentified contributions in your data." He winked. "Might as well be the one person in this room who won't be arrested for something. Although I'm not sure they would let me arrest myself anyway!"

Dani smiled, then frowned as she considered his request. "It's possible. It would take a lot of work. After I get the list of objects—which will take a while, just from the volumes of data I'll have to go through—I'll have to look at each one and view the parts before and after to see if I can see any people who might have done something in the part I can't see that they'd pay to hide. It's going to be a hit-or-miss thing."

"Will people have a record of what you have done?" asked Shard.

"They could get one, but they'd have to be specifically interested in the scanner I usually use, and go look at the records for that scanner. I think I'll be okay." *Unless they are already watching me*, she thought. *And they might be, since they got to Anders.* She decided not to think about that. "I have a certain amount of leeway about sharing things outside of the institute, because I'm a sort of ambassador to the public."

"You need anyone to help you go through data?" Joph waved his hand in an if-so-I-volunteer type of gesture.

Dani gnawed on her lip, considering. "I don't think that would be revealing anything secret. I could send you the activity list from the VAO converter and show you what numbers are important. Let's swap connexions."

"You'll need mine too," the detective said.

While they did the swap, Lora moved over next to Joph. "I'll help you, when you get the data. We can get together Monday or Tuesday afternoon, after exams are over for the day," Lora said.

"Monday works best for me. I've got a study group Tuesday afternoon."

"Okay, I'll try to get that to you by noon on Monday." Dani made a note on her worktablet to remind herself.

"We'll send back a filtered list, as far as we get, by Monday evening." Lora was already taking charge, and Joph didn't seem to mind at all.

"Thanks." Dani swept the group with her glance. "I really appreciate all of you. You got me started in the right direction."

WALLACE HOME, Lower Queen Anne, Seattle, WA. 1200, Saturday, June 10, 2215.

Dani sidestepped the slidewalk, lifting the laden branches of the lilacs to walk around the right side of the house to the Wallace's back yard. By next week, the purple profusion of blooms would be over. She sniffed appreciatively as she spotted Kat and Marak sitting at their patio table and waved to them.

"Thanks for inviting me!"

"Hi, Dani! How was your morning?" asked Kat. "Do you want some iced tea?"

"Yes, thanks. It was good. I met with a group of high schoolers in a political action club. They're concerned about the privacy invasions, and they're going to help me go through the data. Don't worry," she added, seeing their expressions. She could tell that Marak, in particular, was envisioning all kinds of legal difficulties for her. "I won't give them anything that will get them—or me—in trouble."

"How can you be sure?" Marak pulled out a chair for her to join them.

"It'll just be a sample printout from one of our machines, something I'm allowed to do for presentations. I have a lot of leeway for things like that. Besides, now that I don't have Anders working on the data for me, they'll be a big help."

"So what do you expect to find, exactly?" Kat poured tea into three tall glasses filled with ice cubes and sat down.

Dani explained about the date matching, and the possibility of the detective tracking down the victims and using their testimony to reach the blackmailers.

"This is amazing, Dani," said Kat. "We've demonstrated outside that big building for years, and never really had a chance at making a difference like this."

"There was never a clear indication of wrongdoing," said Marak. "You only had the possibility of it before, babe."

"I know, and I have mixed feelings about that. I never wanted there to be wrongdoing. I wanted to prevent that." Kat was such an idealist, and Dani loved her for it. Loved them both. But then she remembered that whatever difference they made wouldn't be a real one, if they got Jored back. It would only apply to the altered timestream.

"I hate to point it out, but remember what you said, Marak?" asked Dani. "If our timestream fix works, none of us will remember anything that we've done."

"I've been thinking about that," he answered. "What if you stayed in the observation box while it was happening? Wouldn't that mean you'd remember all this? That's why you remembered before, right?"

Dani considered that. "I'd be missing the memories from these last few days, and the transition might not be as smooth as it was this time. Well, not smooth exactly," she added, remembering her meltdown when she found out about Jored. "But at least I was among friends. I'm not sure what it would be like if I'm at the institute."

"That's risky," said Marak.

Wasn't it a risk worth taking, though? She could think pretty well on her feet. She'd dealt with the hostility at the high school. Why not try it? "On the other hand," she said, "it may be, when the timestream gets restored, that I will have done all of this there, too. This whole investigation, talking with you, working with Anders, scheduling a meeting with the high school kids, started before the switch. Events tend to match up. Lexil says a lot of the disturbances repair themselves. I could ask him what he thinks."

"Who's Lexil?" Kat asked.

"He works with Dr. Seebak."

"Dr. Seebak?" Kat was startled. "How do you know him? Just a few days ago, you had no idea he was still working in chronography."

"Yes, well." Dani stopped, embarrassed. Oops. She had forgotten to fill Kat in on those details. "Remember the moonlit walk and the secret lab?"

"Oh! But how did you meet them?"

"It turns out that that Dr. Seebak and Lexil have a device that can spot disturbances in the timestream. Jored's disappearance showed up as a big one, and everything I did because of it left a trail they could see. Lexil tracked me down. Found me outside your house that night."

"And took you to their lab?"

Dani nodded.

A funny look crossed Kat's face. "You didn't walk in the moonlight with Dr. Seebak, did you?"

"No! Lexil walked me to the tube station." Dani laughed at Kat's expression. "It was a nice walk."

"Sounds like it." Kat kept her tone very neutral, but Dani knew she'd be wanting more details later.

She steered the topic back on track. "The work they are doing is groundbreaking. It's what I thought chronography would be, when I started my studies. They can see the timestream disturbances, and if the timestream is going to be restored, it will be Lexil who has figured out how to make it happen."

"When would that be?" Marak asked.

"I don't know. He said he'd let me know. Could be hours. Could be weeks or months. He's got some testing to do. We'll only have one chance at it, so it has to work the first time."

Marak nodded. "So back to the memory issue. If Lexil thinks it would be safe for you to stay in the box, we'll have to arm you with facts and evidence that will convince the rest of the world in that timestream. Either that, or the knowledge of where to find that evidence so you can build a case there too."

"That would be good," said Kat. "Even if we—the other we—have been helping you in that timestream, even if you have some evidence gathered there, and Anders and the West Seattle kids are helping, we may have some facts from here that you wouldn't have been able to get there."

"I think passing that along is vital," said Marak. He grinned. "It's what my other self would want."

Kat snickered at his expression. "All this talking about convincing ourselves is getting kind of weird."

"Oh, hey! I talk myself into things all the time. Cheesecake, another baked potato, a night out with my wife…"

"You have to talk yourself into a night out with me? I'm hurt."

"She didn't see the pattern, I guess." Marak winked at Dani. "These are all good things, babe."

"Speaking of baked potatoes," Kat said, "our dinner should be about done now, shouldn't it?"

Marak hopped up and opened the barbecue with a flourish. "Perfect! Nice timing! I knew it was a good idea when I talked myself into marrying you."

Kat started throwing potholders at him.

"Hey! Watch it! The barbecue's open! You want to burn something?"

Dani laughed. "You two need to get off the patio. Take it over there. I'll get the burgers off the grill."

Marak took her up on her offer and zoomed around the side of the house. In a few seconds, he came back, dragging a hose with a spray nozzle. "I warn you! This thing is on!"

Kat raised her hands in a gesture of surrender. "I yield," she said, then muttered so only Dani could hear, "for now."

Dani cleared her throat and, in an exaggeratedly bright tone of voice, said to no one in particular, "Hey, what about these hamburgers? They look great! And look! The condiments are already on the table. It must be dinner time!"

Marak and Kat laughed, put down their playful weapons, and sat down with Dani at the table.

"Please pass the mustard," Kat asked Dani, "and tell me all about this Lexil guy while you're at it."

SEEBAK LABORATORY, Vashon Island, WA. 1000, Sunday, June 11, 2215.

"Found my way here all by myself this time," Dani said, with just a trace of smugness.

"We can't have that. Now we're going to have to erase your memory," Lexil teased. "Secret lab, you know."

"Okay, but can it wait till after I find my way home? I'd be really puzzled if I suddenly woke up here, with no idea why."

"Yeah, that's reasonable, I guess." He stepped aside to let her enter the lab. "Doc! We have a visitor!"

Dr. Seebak's head emerged from a workstation. "Oh, hi, Dani! What brings you here today?"

Dani considered. What actually had brought her here? Most of what she had to ask them about or share with them could have been done over a connexion. It was mostly whim that had urged her to board the tube car this morning and make the trip to the island. She realized, with a start, that the main reason she had come had a lot to do with the smiling young man who had opened the door at her approach. "It must be your magnetic personalities," she said.

With a disbelieving chuckle, Dr. Seebak suggested, "Probably more like the magnetic science research we do here. But you are always welcome."

"Thanks. I feel welcome."

"Where did we leave off, last time you were here? Oh, I remember. Were you able to talk with Marielle Brant?"

"Oh, yeah. We met after work and talked really quietly on back-to-back benches." She paused, remembering her impression of the missing clock tower. Should she mention that? Maybe later. "I don't think anyone observing could have told we were having a conversation. You were right, the word 'Vashon' was enough to let her know I was contacting her on your behalf."

"Good. I thought it would be."

"We also figured out a way for her to signal me if she had something to share, or vice versa. I offered to talk to someone on her behalf—I was thinking Royce—but she implied that he couldn't help. I'm still wondering if I should go to him anyway, though."

"I think she's probably right. He most likely has very little influence, and if word got back to the blackmailer that he knows about her troubles, it could cause her more difficulties. She's been told not to talk to anybody."

"It might not be a good thing for Royce either," suggested Lexil.

Dr. Seeback agreed. "You're right. It might hurt Royce's ability to be useful there. I think he's had to back off a lot to be able to keep his position on the board. He plays the part of a benign, grandfatherly adviser, respected mostly because he seldom offers an opinion."

"So I won't go to him." Too bad, she thought. There really was nothing she could do to ease the pressure on Dr. Brant.

"You can still help her by passing messages to us," said Lexil. "But remember, anything we do together here will probably not have been done at all once we fix the timestream. That applies to any contact you have with her, also, because you wouldn't have met with her if you hadn't talked to us first."

"I was talking to Kat and Marak about that just yesterday," Dani said. "We had some ideas, but I said I'd ask you about them first."

"What did you tell them about me?"

"Just that you worked with Dr. Seebak. I wasn't sure what they knew about, well, about whose son you are."

"They don't know anything about that, unless Royce told them. I don't know what he's mentioned," said Dr. Seebak.

"Thanks for being cautious, Dani," said Lexil. "I really appreciate it."

His smile was so warm, it was almost tangible. It felt like a hug, and Dani fought a sudden impulse to hug him back, to hold onto him and tell him he mattered to her. She wondered at herself. She barely knew him. Why was she drawn to him this way?

Lexil was oblivious to her inner conversation. "What did you want to ask me?"

Dani gestured to a chair, asking wordlessly if she could sit, and Lexil picked up a notebook from the seat to make room for her. Focus, girl, she told herself. She cleared her throat. "We were talking about all the evidence we're gathering on the blackmail activity at the institute. It's pretty pointless if we can't access it in the restored timestream, so we were wondering whether some of the investigations might have been done there too."

"Nothing will have been done that would depend on us meeting you; we know that. I wouldn't have gone to find you if you hadn't been trailing time disturbance ripples wherever you went. In the restored timestream, we...won't have met." He held her gaze for a few seconds, then glanced down at the notebook with an attempt at nonchalance that didn't quite ring true. "This notebook, for example."

"What's in the notebook?" She decided to ignore the hidden emotion, whatever that was about. It was too much to think that he was drawn to her too, despite Kat's teasing about the moonlit walk. She had no illusions of romance here. Lexil was fascinated by Dani-the-time-disturbance, and nothing more.

He was flipping through the notebook. It looked ordinary enough on the outside. Among all the other notebooks visible in the lab—most of them in a pile around Lexil'—this one wasn't anything special. It was a nondescript gray with a black binding. The only thing that marked it was his name on the front cover, and the words, "Timestream Data."

"Most of what is in here is about the ripples and blips that have occurred since your event. A few pages in the beginning are about things that stemmed from other disturbances, but almost everything you see here will not exist in the original, 'right' timestream. I presume that the other Lexil will have done other research in the meantime—he's pretty obsessed with research, to be honest—but it won't be the same stuff that's in here."

"What all have you discovered directly as a result of 'my event,' as you call it?"

"The biggest thing is that the VAO converters can actually remove objects from the timestream. Evidence that it needs to be stopped." He laughed wryly. "I've got all that really vital stuff boxed in red penstrokes, for all the good it will do when it's gone."

"So none of that will be available after we fix it."

"Right. Remove the original disturbance, and you don't have the evidence that it causes any damage, so there's nothing to write in my notebook."

"Okay, so we lose that. What won't be lost?"

He thought about it. "We will still have our sensors, and much of the evidence from past ripples. Kat and Marak's non-meeting wasn't the first incident; it was just the one that caused the biggest changes."

"And the Dani that hasn't been alarmed by Jored's absence will still have data files from Anders, ideas from talking with Kat and Marak, and the research the high school kids are going to be doing tomorrow. I think all that would have happened even if I hadn't met you two."

"We could check some of those events to see," Lexil said.

Dr. Seebak had been listening quietly to their conversation. "You young people work on that. I'll get back to my research over here." He dove back down among his screens and notebooks.

"I can't check on your meetings with Kat and Marak. Whenever you meet with them, there are ripples."

"Because I always played with Jored when I saw them."

"That would do it. So we can't assume or confirm any information you might have gained from those visits. But let's try the meeting with the high schoolers. When did it happen?" He sat down opposite the viewwall, waving at it to bring up the time ripples view. A few quick strokes and he had zeroed in on the school.

"I met with them yesterday, from 10 o'clock till a little before noon."

Lexil narrowed the third axis to that interval. There were no blips, only a very faint green shimmer. "Looks good. That meeting would have happened anyway."

"Okay, so, if my other-timestream self would know some of this, I'll know it when I get there too, right?"

"Yes, you should."

"But anything I've learned from you and anything I've researched because of conversations we've had, I won't remember. Which brings me to the idea Kat and Marak and I had. We were thinking that when we do the restoration, I could stay inside the observation box with some key pieces of information and…"

Lexil was shaking his head, but it was Dr. Seebak who stood up and spoke. "You must not!" he said, urgently.

Dani blinked. "Why not?"

"While we were experimenting yesterday, something a little unexpected happened." Lexil gestured toward the opposite corner of the lab. "I should show you our setup later. We were working on replacing objects that had been removed from the timestream. At first, we kept the environment exactly the same, whether the object was there or not. The only things we changed were the time settings: the beginning of the replacement and the duration. But when we got that part figured out—"

"You solved it? Does that mean we can definitely repair the timestream?" Dani caught her breath, wanting to make sure she had heard correctly. Yesterday, she'd been talking with Kat and Marak, tossing around ideas about how to make the investigation move forward after the timestream repair. They'd kept it matter-of-fact, casually accepting the possibility of a miracle. Given that, it was hard to explain the lump she now felt in her chest. As she realized it would actually happen, an unexpected feeling of yearning flooded over her. She would get to see Jored again, hear his giggles, hold him in her arms.

Dr. Seebak had walked over to join them. He put a hand on her shoulder. "He found a way to make it happen, Dani."

Lexil nodded. "The only thing left is to automate it, so it can be done on your machines with a simple installation program."

She closed her eyes, overwhelmed with gratitude.

They gave her a moment to recover. That was nice of them, but she wanted to know more. Lexil had said something unusual happened. Would it interfere with getting Jored back? Would it complicate things? "Lexil, what were you saying? What was the unexpected thing you going to tell me about before?"

"Well, we started making changes to the environment, keyed to whether the object was there or not. We wanted to simulate the circumstances that surrounded our real problem. Let's go back there so I can show you."

As they walked back to the corner of the lab, he continued. "I set up a mechanism that would eject a marble through a slot, but only if the object was resting on this plate during the time interval I had specified in the program. It worked."

They had reached the experimental set up. Dani was amused by the multiple spray paint patterns on the panels arranged against the wall. They almost looked artistic. There were several dozen, some with full spray patterns, some with empty spots in the center. One had a scorched area, with parts if it burned completely through the panel. She pointed to it. "Is this the unexpected one? It looks a little alarming."

"No, we solved that one. Good thing, or it would have been alarming indeed. You'd have had a burned padlock, and maybe a burned gate as well! That only happens when the object is sent back to a time where it already exists."

"What's the concern, then?"

"The concern is with the time ripples. We wanted to find out what happened to a secondary object—or person, but we didn't try that—that had been displaced because of the first object's existence or non-existence. We placed the object on this plate." As he talked, he pointed. "Its weight triggered this mechanism here, and the marble was released through this slot, to fall into this cup."

"Okay." Dani was following fine, so far.

"We left it there, then used your technique"—he handed her a copy of the research paper she had helped with—"to blank it from the timestream."

As she took the paper, she noticed that it was heavily underlined and highlighted. "Glad I could be of some assistance!" she said.

"Oh, no doubt! Excellent work, by the way. Not sure what part of the research was yours, but it's pretty impressive to have your name on a paper like this as an undergrad."

"I was right in there, in the thick of it."

"Good job! Anyway, the marble was in the cup when the object was there. Later, when we blanked the object, the marble was up above, unreleased from its initial position. After I restored the object, the marble was back in the cup again."

"Sounds good, so far. What's the catch?"

"Just to change things up a bit, we moved the release mechanism over here, so the marble would be released into the chronetic shielding of the time sensor device—same environment as your observation boxes, at the institute."

"And?"

"Initially, the marble was in the cup, inside the shielding. After the blank, it was up above, behind the slot. But when we replaced the object, we found two marbles, one in the cup, and one up above."

"Oh! Because the marble inside the shielding wasn't affected by the change you made when you replaced the object."

"Exactly. And it turned out that both marbles were altered in their basic structure, although we aren't exactly sure how. Something to do with the Law of Conservation of Matter. They each only half-existed, in a sense. When we measured their masses, each was only half as massive and half as dense as it had been before." He looked at her earnestly, and he spoke very deliberately. "If that were a person in the box, we have no idea what could come of the duplication. We wouldn't want that to happen to you."

"Probably not a good way to lose weight?" She made an attempt at levity.

"Dani, don't."

"Not funny?" She looked at him sheepishly.

"Look," he said. "I'm just going to be blunt with you, no matter how you may feel about it. You can't take this lightly. You're going to be doing something that could be dangerous, and a lot depends on it. Jored's existence. The integrity of the whole timestream. It's a big deal, okay?"

"I know that!" She wasn't trying to make it seem less important.

What had made him so sensitive all of a sudden? Wait. What was this he was saying?

"...already fighting this sense of loss because I won't know you—won't remember even meeting you!—after we do this thing. I know you feel nothing for me, but I keep hoping, if you keep yourself alive, we might encounter each other in the other timestream too. We might have time to get to know each other, to see if...if..." He stopped suddenly, looking uncomfortable. "I really didn't mean to say all that."

"Uh...I don't know how to respond to that." A sense of loss? Apparently, she had been wrong about him being attracted! But here he was, saying anything they found here was bound to end, and in the same breath saying he didn't want it to.

"You don't have to respond at all, other than to promise to be careful."

"No, I know, and I will. But I mean..." Spit it out, Dani, she told herself. Just say it. Don't run from it like you have every other relationship since Jhon dumped you. "I mean, you're wrong about the other part."

"Which other part?"

"The part about my feelings for you."

"Oh." His eyes brightened. "Really?"

That right there—that look of surprised delight—that would have been enough to charm her. The realization that it was Dani herself who caused the delight put it right over the top. "You doing anything important? Want to go for a walk?" she asked.

They both knew he was, in fact, doing something very important. But for the moment it didn't really matter.

She was vaguely aware of an amused and not at all surprised Dr. Seebak watching them go, but all her attention was on Lexil.

27
REVELATION

SEEBAK LABORATORY, Vashon Island, WA. 1130, Sunday, June 11, 2215.

Outside the lab, Lexil noted that the clouds were clearing. The day promised to be a warm one, another in a string of sunny days. In the Pacific Northwest, a day was considered "clear" if the cloud cover burned off for part of the day. Completely cloudless days might occur for a day or two during the summer months, but not usually in mid-June. Summer had not yet arrived in the Pacific Northwest, but the sunlight filtering through the leaves of the madrona trees held promise.

As Lexil and Dani walked along the trail through the woods, the branches brushed their sides, gently coaxing them closer together. So far, they hadn't said anything. He assumed that she, like he, needed a little time to process this new possibility. His thoughts had already run the same course several times. He pictured them together, working side by side, excited by new discoveries, laughing unself-consciously just as they had that first day. Could it be that it was only three days ago? He shook his head, marveling how quickly he'd abandoned his practical decision to avoid relationships. Three times since they had left the lab, he had indulged in thoughts of companionship and tenderness, and three times, he had stopped himself abruptly with the realization that this relationship, more certainly than any other in history, was bound to end. It had to, if they were to rescue the timestream.

And each time he came to that realization, he slipped right back into wondering what could develop between them if this were the true timestream and they didn't have to worry about all that. Where would it lead? Where could it lead?

Dani spoke first. "We can't just ignore this, can we?"

"I know I can't. I've been trying, actually." He realized that might sound as if he didn't want to be with her, which was exactly the opposite of what he thought. He felt the need to explain. "I didn't want you to think I didn't care about Jored. I was worried it would trivialize what we were doing to help him, if I told you how I felt about you. But no, we can't ignore it. And I don't want to."

Almost unconsciously, they found their hands connecting, first with a brush, and then with a feeling of belonging together. They walked along in silence for a few more moments. He hoped she felt the same way. He worried a little about her silence.

He stopped in the middle of the path. She looked over at him questioningly. How could he put this? He struggled for the right words. He had to know. "Dani, if this whole timestream mess weren't an issue, if we were just two people who met and found a common interest in science, who went outside to enjoy a pleasant walk on a sunny day, who discovered.... Would you let me kiss you?"

The suddenness of his request took them both by surprise, but he saw his answer in her smile and tenderly, hesitantly, brushed her hair back from her face. As he leaned in closer, she closed her eyes and tilted up her chin. The first touch of their lips was like electricity finding ground, like atoms bonding covalently. He went back for more, and all at once it was her seeking him, her arms across his broad shoulders, her palms gripping the back of his head, pulling him toward her. His fantasies about a perfect partner for his life's work gave way to other, stronger yearnings.

Abruptly, she pulled back. "If!" she said, in a frustrated tone. "If we had no worries, no obligations, if you weren't working on solving a problem that has stolen a little boy and threatens the whole timestream, if we were actually two people who could decide things based on our feelings and nothing more. If."

"What?" He shook his head, trying to clear it.

"In another world, without so much depending on us...yeah. But don't you see? We can't. And it wouldn't last anyway."

He felt miserable, frustrated. More than he wanted her, he wanted their relationship to be founded in honesty, not this false set of circumstances and events. He knew, without going back into the lab to look on the viewwall, that there were time disturbance ripples surrounding them, there in the filtered sunlight, with the tingle of her lips still fresh on his.

They stood for a few moments, avoiding each other's gaze. He hated the thought of returning to the lab to work on the one thing driving a wedge between them, but there was no question that it had to be done. Nobody else in the world was even aware of it. Nobody else in the world could fix it. He wrestled through conflicting emotions, but ended up where he had known he would. He looked up at Dani just as she looked up at him, and their eyes met.

Lexil nodded and gestured toward the lab. "Shall we get back to work?"

Back inside, he was pleased to see how quickly Dani caught on. Soon she was setting up separate trials and recording the results alongside his own efforts. It doubled their speed, but the automation process was challenging enough that it took several hours to begin working properly.

Doc hadn't said a word when they came back to the lab in a much different frame of mind than when they left it. He noticed their intensity, though, and when they started running into complications, he pitched in and monitored the sensors as they ran each trial. They didn't even take time for lunch; Doc brought out a tray of fruit and cheese, and they snacked while they worked.

Finally, with repeated successes, assuring them the timing of the automation process was correct to the millisecond, it was time to make the device that would alter the settings on Dani's scanner at the institute. "Do you know the file structure on the scanning stations?" Lexil asked her.

"Do you need the specific file structure?" She looked worried. "I've never been able to get to that from my control screens. I mean, I can give you a rough idea, but not the specific path names."

He pondered that. If he could figure out a way to be there when she inserted the device, he could find his way to the right path, but he dare not let anyone at the institute see his name. Entering through the security gate would pretty much ensure that they would make the connection between Lexil Myles and Nicah Myles, his father, who had died in the same accident that put his mother into a coma. But perhaps there was a way around that difficulty. "I will need it, but I might be able to give you something to extract that information for me. It will mean another day's delay, though."

"Can we afford that?"

"We'll have to hope so." He stretched. "Help me with this extraction program, and then we'll take a break."

Later, after the work was done, he invited her into the house.

"Is it okay if I look through your lab notebook?" she asked. "I know I won't remember any of it any more than you will, but I'm curious about how you first began analyzing this, and how you arrived at your conclusions. What were you thinking?"

"Sure, you can look. Actually, I can do more than that. I can make you a copy."

"Really? How do you do that?"

He had to laugh at her astonishment. He was aware that outside the Vashon lab, paper records were almost unheard of. "We keep a lot of notes, and sometimes we have to look at each other's numbers."

"Why don't you just make the notes in digital form?"

"That would be more efficient, I know, and that's what Doc usually does, but there's a kind of energy you get from having papers piled around you, being able to scribble notes in the margins, emphasizing things by pressing harder on the pen."

"Okay, I guess I can see that. Can't really imagine doing it myself, but okay."

"Anyway, if Doc wants to study my results or we want to pass information without leaving an electronic trail, we make a copy on this machine over here. We built it ourselves. It was one of the first projects we worked on together."

He remembered when they started, those first mornings after his mom had died, when he was feeling the need for something to fill his empty days after spending so much time at the hospital. Doc had told him that if he wanted to handwrite things, they needed a way to share. Many hours of research later, they had some diagrams and schematics, and they began building the copier, the same way Doc had built most of the other instruments and machines in the lab.

Dani was fascinated, more interested in the way it worked than in the copies themselves. After she told him which pages she wanted to look at, he left the door open to the innards of the machine. She watched, absorbed in the workings of all the gears, drums, and multi-colored inks, while he made the copies.

When he was done, he handed it to her with a flourish. "And just like that, it's done."

"They're warm!"

He laughed. "Yes, the machine has baked the ink into the paper so it won't smudge."

She flipped through the papers. It was amusing to watch her check each page, as if she thought it was some sort of illusion. "It's amazing. Every page is here."

She tucked the papers away in the back pocket on her worktablet. "One more blip, I suppose. You would never have made a copy if we hadn't met."

He didn't even have to go look at the monitor to answer. "True. Those copies only exist here. In the other reality, they'd be blank paper. I'm sure there's a blip. But what's one more?"

28
DISTRACTION

SEEBAK LABORATORY, Vashon Island, WA. 1730, Sunday, June 11, 2215.

"Thank you for making the copies," Dani said. "Is there anything else I can help you with before I head home?"

"You've been amazing!" Lexil's smile was genuinely appreciative, without a trace of his earlier passion, and she was grateful. She had been worried that their relationship would get even more awkward after the moment in the woods, but instead, the decision had helped them turn back to their real focus and work. They had made a good team, and it felt nice to be productive. Tomorrow, she would find an opportunity to run the extract program, and soon—oh, so soon!—she would be hugging Jored again, without any memory of the last few days.

For just a moment, she let herself visit the corner of her mind where she had stuffed all her feelings for Lexil. It would have been nice if they had been free to explore that possibility further. If they'd met in the real timestream, she had no doubt she'd be hugging him goodbye, leaving reluctantly if at all, instead of merely asking if their work was done. Part of her still wanted that, but she made the conscious choice to ignore its muffled voice.

"Would you like to see the rest of the house before you go?" Lexil broke into her reverie.

"You mean there's more than a library and a kitchen?" She smiled.

"Let's go see." He led her around the side of the house so they could enter through the front door. The entry way featured a tile floor. An umbrella stand, a shoe rack, and a simple bench sat against the left wall. On the right, a staircase led up to the second floor. "If we go straight back, we'll get to the part of the house you've already seen. But here's the living room on the left."

In the living room, a couch and two comfortable-looking chairs flanked a fireplace in the center of the far wall. To Dani, it looked rustic and old-fashioned, an effect lessened only slightly by a couple of ergonomically-correct, modern plastic chairs on the right near a small gaming center. She knew the plastic chairs would automatically provide the exact support needed for anyone who sat down in them, but these other chairs, the upholstered ones, looked strangely inviting, and she wondered what it would feel like to sit in one of them. Her move to try them out was cut short by Lexil ushering her out of the room.

As they passed the gaming center, he commented, "Doc got me started on these games when I moved in."

"Doc got *you* started?"

"Oh yeah, he loves them. He's way better than I am, too, but I have fun playing. He says they remind him of scientific experiments. You try one thing, and if it doesn't work, you get do-overs. And he likes that there is guaranteed to be at least one solution."

"That's always nice."

They moved on. "We have a guest room down here. Doc had an extra-wide doorway put in for wheelchair access when we thought my mom might recover." He paused. "Back in the beginning, we had a lot more hope."

"I'm sorry, Lexil."

"No, I'm fine. I'm happy here. I like it a lot. I miss her sometimes still, that's all."

Judging from his expression, she doubted that he was telling the full truth. But she didn't really expect that kind of familiarity, not after just a few days. And a few days was all she would ever get; she would never have a chance to get to know him well enough for any real trust.

He was leading her upstairs. By island standards, the house was neither large nor small. Its upper floor included one more guest room and the two bedrooms for Lexil and Dr. Seebak. The bedrooms were furnished neatly but sparely. Each had its own viewwall. Doc's was set on a jungle scene and Lexil's was set on "translucent" to let the natural sunlight in.

"What's your favorite so far?" he asked.

"Oh, the library. I'd love to browse that more. I only really looked at that one shelf."

"I think you'll like this next part even better! Come see." He opened a door at the end of the short hall between his room and the doctor's. It led out onto a wide deck on the west side of the house, which wrapped around to the south. Four deck chairs and a round table were arranged so that their occupants could absorb the view.

The view was amazing.

Firs and madrona trees painted the landscape with lush greenery. She could see from here that the house was set on a hillside, which hadn't been evident on either the path from the lab to the house or from the lab to the tube station. In the distance, looking down the hillside, she had a clear view of the Olympic Mountains.

"It's peaceful out here," she said, standing at the railing. "What's the water I hear? Is that a stream?"

"Well, there is a stream, but you're hearing the waterfall." He gestured out to the left, and Dani saw it, water cascading down a bank, tumbling over piles of stones and ending in a pool with a flat stone patio around it. She inhaled the scent of the fresh-water spray.

"You can't see them from here, but we have fish in the pool."

They stood quietly for a few moments, letting the soothing sound drain away the stresses of the day.

"Sometimes we eat up here." Lexil said softly. "Would you like to stay for dinner?"

Dani realized that she would, very much.

"Dinner" turned out to be salmon and green beans, with boiled red potatoes.

"Fresh off the boat," Dr. Seebak said, as he took the herbed salmon fillets off the grill.

"Did you actually go fishing?" With these two, anything was possible.

The doctor laughed. "No, I have an old friend who delivers them. He helps manage permits for a small fleet, and we get tube deliveries when they're in season."

"We grew the beans and potatoes ourselves, though," Lexil said, straight-faced, as he took a bite of beans.

"Don't let him tell you that, Dani. We are nowhere near that self-sufficient. We depend on deliveries, same as everyone else."

Dani scowled at Lexil, then she smiled at his wink. "Regardless, they're really good. No stories needed. The flavor speaks for itself."

At first, it felt a little awkward, eating with these people she'd only known for a few days. The memory of the kiss made it worse. But within minutes, their light-hearted banter had relaxed her. By the time they were finished with the meal, the topic of conversation came back to their research.

"Your notes talk about three forces. Hang on, let me look at those again, because I had a question," Dani said. Where were those pages he had made for her? She knew she had brought them up here with her. Aha! Under her chair. She brought them up to the table, pushing her plate back a bit, flipping through until she found the spot she was thinking of. "Here. You mention the disturbances, the natural damping force, and then a third force that seems to erase blips. We know what causes the disturbances, or some of them anyway, but have you discovered what causes the other two forces?"

Lexil shook his head and moved her plate out of the way, stacking it with the others. "Not for sure."

Dr. Seeback added, "We have some ideas, though." He pushed their beverage glasses together to make them easier to pick up.

"I'd love to hear what you've been thinking." Her childhood training kicked in. "Can I help you carry stuff down?"

"We weren't going to take it down yet, but you can grab the silverware, if you want to. Might as well take care of it now. Can you carry the papers too?"

"No problem."

As the three of them walked down the stairs, Lexil continued, "We see the second force as a natural force, something akin to the tendency of an object at rest or in motion to remain so."

"Newton's First Law." Dani recognized it. "So the timestream has inertia and momentum?"

Lexil nodded. "That's what we're thinking. That would mean the second force is simply the timestream's resistance to change."

"But the blips have overcome that resistance, somehow."

"Well, considering that the blips are human responses to the timestream change, that's easy to explain." Dr. Seebak chuckled. "You're a walking blip, Dani. Humans make choices that can be stronger than the inertia of the timestream."

"But sometimes the universe pushes back, and repairs the timestream? Is that the third force?" Dani wasn't sure she completely understood, but it was fascinating to try.

"You can call it a force of the universe if you like, but I think it's something different." Lexil glanced over at his mentor. "Doc and I talked it through the other day, and we keep coming up against the obvious intentionality of that third force. It's like there's a consciousness making deliberate choices to repair the timestream."

The doctor nodded. "And it would have to be a consciousness that knew precisely what kind of action to take to exactly offset the changes that caused each blip. Nobody knows that much about this science."

"Not yet," said Lexil. "So we narrowed it down to two possibilities. It could be people in the future who have developed the science of chronography to such an extent that they can make intentional changes like this. We're planning one such intentional change, but we had the unusual advantage of your knowledge of what had caused the change."

"Because I was in the observation box, and happened to know Jored personally."

"A slim chance, by anyone's standards," said Dr. Seebak. "How likely is it that someone from the future can come up with a way to restore these blips we've been noticing?"

"Not very likely at all," said Dani.

"In addition to that, there's another complication." Dr. Seebak rinsed the dishes and silverware and placed them into the self-cleaning cupboards and drawers. "Shall we go back to the library?"

Lexil led the way. "Dani's second-favorite part of the house."

"After the deck." Dani confirmed it.

"Right, after the deck."

When they were settled in the library chairs, Dr. Seebak spoke again. "If a person from the future changed the past to restore a blip, the absence of a blip would make it so he would have no reason to initiate the change. Would that make the blip come back?"

"Possibly?" Dani guessed.

Lexil leaned forward. "And if it did, we'd have a repeating cycle. We wouldn't see those blips smoothed out at all. Which is why I think that the agency that restores the blips has to be outside of the timestream."

She was startled. That was not where she expected him to go, not at all. "What could be outside of the timestream? That doesn't make sense."

"It would have to be a being who wasn't bound by time, who wasn't affected by the timestream changes." He was watching her carefully.

Suddenly, her mind made the leap. "Never ending, never beginning. Eternal."

Lexil nodded, gratified. "I thought you'd get it."

But that would mean— "Are you saying what I think you're saying?"

"What do you think I'm saying? That there is a God after all? That somehow, for reasons I don't know, he concerns himself with our affairs?"

"Is that what you're saying?"

He nodded again. "I've seen too many things inexplicably put back together."

"Like Kat and Marak meeting anyway."

"Yes, exactly."

She pondered that. It would explain a lot, but it wouldn't explain one thing. "Why didn't he fix Jored's unbirth, then? Where's the third force in the whole problem of his existence or non-existence?"

Dr. Seebak had been silent, but now he spoke. "I think I have the answer to that one."

They looked at him.

"Judging from the ripples at that moment, I think it was arranged that you would be in the observation box at the precise moment the padlock hologram was played, protected from the timestream switch. I think the third force has been directing us on this all along."

RIACH TUBE STOP, Alki Beach, Seattle, WA. 1710, Monday, June 12, 2215.

The signal had worked perfectly, and now Dani sat on the bench at the tube station, facing away from the tube cars, ready to fake a connexion call to cover her anticipated conversation with Dr. Brant. She checked for the clock tower, and chided herself for worrying when she found it exactly where it had always been.

Early that morning, in between doing the day's assigned tasks, she had extracted the object records from the VAO converter. Some were tagged with identifiers associated with interns, some were simply labeled "Administrative." She thought about using just the "Administrative" ones, but quickly realized that might take her in a wrong direction. Her own task list had included scanning the padlock in preparation for the blackmailer's needs, so she knew interns were used for some of the illegal data gathering. Instead, she filtered the list by recent time frames. Joph and Lora should be able to get through all of them, and she wanted to be sure not to leave out anything that might hold the clues they needed.

The conversation from the night before echoed in her thoughts as she worked. She wondered how many of her actions might be directed by this third force. Was it really something—or someone—sentient? Lexil had used the word "intentional": a force that acted toward some intended purpose. She tried to detect any hint of being nudged as she worked, in subtle or not-so-subtle ways, and then laughed at herself. She supposed that as long as she was working to restore the timestream, she wouldn't have to be nudged anyway. Still, it would be interesting to isolate and identify the effects of the force in her own life, since she seemed to be something of an epicenter right now.

Perhaps she could talk to Lexil about it when she saw him at Kat's tonight. They had agreed to meet there, so they could talk with Kat and Marak about their plans for tomorrow.

At noon, she had left the institute to go for a walk. Once off the institute grounds, she had sent the filtered list to Joph. He and Lora had promised to send her back a list of times that seemed to coincide with the unidentified contributions. By this evening, she would have a much smaller list of objects to scan, and tomorrow she would look for the blackmailer's possible victims.

In the afternoon, she had used Lexil's device to extract the file structure he'd asked for. She had been so busy, she almost hadn't had time to think what that meant. That had almost been a necessity at work. She had never stopped missing Jored, and now, in less than a day, or two at the most, she would say goodbye to this timestream and be casually looking forward to the next time she spent an evening with him, or watched one of his games on a weekend. Her other self wouldn't even know he had been gone.

And her other self wouldn't know what she had left behind to return, either. A new, unexpected sense of loss gripped her suddenly. Unconsciously, she touched her lips, closing her eyes, remembering a kiss on a forest pathway.

When she opened them, she was so involved with her memories, she was almost surprised to see Dr. Brant walking toward her. The doctor was looking at the passengers waiting for tube cars, looking at the time, looking at the distant tube entrance to see if another car was coming, looking anywhere but at Dani. Finally, she sat on the bench behind Dani with an exasperated sigh and took out her worktablet to fill her time while she pretended to wait for the next car.

Dani pressed her temple so that anyone who heard her talking would assume a connexion and look away. "Do you have the list of the board members?" she asked.

"Yes, both the old members and the new ones, with the dates their appointments ended or began. I didn't dare put it on my worktablet, though. I believe they are monitoring its transmissions. I hand-copied them onto a sheet of paper."

Dani had never before in her life met so many people who used paper! "Okay. Um. Do you want to let it slide through the slats in the bench, and then later I'll drop my bag and grab the paper at the same time I retrieve it?"

After a few seconds, Dr. Brant said, "There, it's done. I folded it a few times first. Dani, be careful with this. I don't know who among these names is responsible for the blackmailing. I suspect they all are involved to some degree. Don't take any risks that would hurt you or hurt people you love."

"I'll be careful. And I'll pass that message on to Vashon too." She tapped her temple and stood up, dropping her bag to the pavement.

She leaned down, reached under the double bench, and retrieved the bag and the folded paper. Then she got up and, without looking back, joined the waiting passengers on the platform. No Anders tonight. She wondered idly whether he had left early or stayed late.

No matter. She wasn't traveling to First Hill anyway. The car to Lower Queen Anne was pulling up, and soon she'd be talking with Kat, Marak, and Lexil. She caught herself whistling a fiddle tune for the first time in days. She almost didn't hear the sound from her connexion implant, alerting her to incoming data. She opened it on her worktablet, glanced at it, and smiled.

Joph and Lora had come through. She was eager to see what they had found.

WALLACE HOME, Lower Queen Anne, Seattle, WA. 1745, Monday, June 12, 2215.

Lexil was waiting outside when Dani arrived at the Wallace home. Lounging against a tree trunk, looking cheerful, with his cap at an angle, he grinned as he saw her.

"Waiting for me?" she asked. "Or are you just too timid to brave the irisscan?"

"Aw, you figured it out. I was trying to pull off a casual stance here. What gave me away?"

"The fact that you were outside instead of inside, maybe?"

"Maybe. Should we fix that?"

She laughed. "Sure. We can get scanned together."

They paused at the irisscan, and started up the slidewalk. Without any conscious intention, her hand found his, their fingers catching a few times before resolve caught hold and they curled away. Dani steeled herself. She knew where this would go if she weakened even for a moment. Enjoy the friendship, just the friendship, she told herself sternly.

Fortunately, Marak threw open the door enthusiastically when they were halfway to the house, providing a welcome distraction.

"Hi, Dani! Who've you got with you? Must be Lexil." He turned without waiting for her response to shout inside, "Kat! Dani's here—with friend."

Lexil's hand was soon involved in a vigorous handshake, temptations forgotten. Good. Better not to have to deal with that. She shook off the wistful thoughts and focused on the tasks that had brought them here.

"Drinks, anyone?" Marak took their orders and excused himself to the kitchen to whip up some fruity concoctions. Kat invited them into the living room. Dani noticed the furniture was rearranged, and asked about it.

"I know! It's different, isn't it? I got home today and found it this way. Marak must have found some time to get creative while he was working from home today. He didn't say a word, though, just let me find it myself. Silly man, probably waiting for my response. I'm not going to give him the satisfaction of commenting on it."

"I like it, I think," said Dani.

"Me too."

As they got settled, Marak came back with the drinks.

"We need a name for this group," he suggested. "How about the Ephemeral Ones? Or the Ephemerists?"

"What does that even mean?" Kat frowned at him, but the corner of her mouth twitched upward into a smile.

"Oh, you know. Lasting only a day? We're going to be this version of ourselves for what, a day or two more? We should live it up, right? No possibility of regrets? We can quit our jobs, go crazy! You up for it, babe?"

"Oh yeah, always. Whatever you say." She rolled her eyes at Dani and Lexil, and they laughed.

"Let's hope we don't have to do anything too drastic," Dani said. "We've got to stay alive to see this through."

"No diving out of helicars in mid-air?" Marak pretended to pout. "I had my heart set on it."

"Maybe later, hon." Kat patted his arm. "After these guys leave, we can talk about your fantasies."

"Yes, please, wait till we leave," Dani interrupted. Who knew where he might be going on this train of thought! "Please."

"Well, okay." Marak relented. "What have you two brought, and how can we help?"

Dani pulled out the little recorder Lexil had sent with her the day before. "First I need to get this back to you. It worked; I got the file structure."

"Excellent! This little treasure," he said, showing it to Kat and Marak, "will let me put that padlock back in place and introduce you two when you were supposed to have met."

"You're going to the institute?" Kat asked.

"No, I won't need to. Dani will be able to plug this in, after I incorporate the correct file pointers, and use her scanner to reintroduce the padlock to the timestream. I'll give it to her tomorrow."

"So we're looking at Wednesday for our Last Day Here on Earth?" Marak asked. "We'd definitely better get planning some crazy stuff."

"Hush, Marak. Lexil will think you're never serious," Kat chided him.

"What do you mean?" Marak put on a hurt expression. "This is me, being serious. Right, Dani?"

"Pretty much," she said, then added for Lexil's benefit, "but he settles down eventually and offers useful stuff."

"Well, I'd expect that." He turned to Marak, "I've heard you are an incisive, quick-witted investigative reporter."

"You've heard that? So now I have to live up to my reputation." He sighed. "Okay, I'll behave. What do you guys need from us?"

"Remember your question about whether I could stay in the observation box while the timestream was being fixed?" Dani asked. "That won't work, it turns out."

Marak frowned. "So all of our investigations here are going to be lost?"

"Unless they also happened—" Lexil paused. "I never know what tense to use with things that haven't occurred in this timestream! But you know what I mean."

They nodded. "Go on," said Kat.

"Unless they would also have happened in the original timestream, which is unlikely in your case, but possible—even likely—in the investigations Dani has been doing with that Anders guy and the high school kids."

"I've been trying not to mention anything that I got from you guys when I'm working with them," Dani confirmed. "I sent all the data to Detective Rayes while I was on my way here. I'm hoping the other Dani would have done the same."

"Why can't she stay in the observation box?" Kat asked.

"Without being too dramatic, I'll just say it this way: It might threaten her life," said Lexil. "If she is outside the box at that moment when it switches back to the original timestream, her body would exist in two places, with half the substance in each, and each version of her would have two different sets of memories. It would be messy, and I'd kind of like her to survive, if possible."

Dani laughed. "I'd agree with you on that one. Although I suppose I wouldn't be alive to worry about it, if not." Then a thought occurred to her. "What about the other interns?"

"Other interns?" asked Lexil. "What about them?"

"We have four labs, each of which has several scanners. At any given time, there might be three or four interns using a scanner somewhere. If it's a threat to me, it might be a threat to them too."

"Possibly. I think their actions would be the same in either timestream, but we don't really know how far the ripples might have reached at the institute. Is there any time when the scanners would be sure to be unused?"

"Lunchtime, on most days. Or after hours." Dani considered his question. She would have to be sure, if it might risk someone's existence. This timestream stuff could be touchy, she was realizing. "But that's not guaranteed. Sometimes, if there are special projects, interns work through lunch."

"You never have, not as long as I've known you," said Kat.

"No, they try to chase us out of the labs for lunch. Something about pleasant work environments and opportunities for socialization. Not that that actually happens much. Which brings up another concern."

"What's that?" asked Marak.

"They actually take the scanners offline at lunchtime to encourage us to take breaks, unless we need one for an officially sanctioned purpose. I can't do what we need to do at lunchtime."

"Is there any way you could clear the labs during a time when the scanners are up and running?" Lexil asked.

"Not unless there was an emergency evacuation for some reason. An earthquake, maybe. Or a fire drill. But I can't personally schedule anything." She frowned.

"How about a bomb threat?" asked Kat.

"That would work. If someone called one in, you mean?"

"Yes, and I might be able to help with that. I have someone who's been wanting to do something like that for a while." She made a face. "I think he'd rather plant a real bomb, but he'll be thrilled just to be able to make a threat."

"That guy I saw you arguing with the other morning?"

"Yes, that's the guy. Neferyn James."

"I don't know, Kat. I don't really trust him," said Marak.

"I can manage him. He might be prone to theatrics, but he's harmless."

"Any objections?" With a glance, Lexil surveyed the room. "No? Okay, Kat, can you schedule it for sometime Wednesday?"

"I'm pretty sure that won't be a problem. I'll meet Dani tomorrow for lunch and confirm it."

"Good. And Dani, do you want to come to the island tomorrow

night to get the program?"

Dani nodded. The whole idea of a fake bomb threat, while initially horrifying to her as a really irresponsible action, faded into insignificance when she thought about Marak's comment about having only days left of this timestream. Nothing they did in this existence would count. People could die, even, and they'd still be alive in the original timestream. What really mattered was the fix. And she was the only one who could put it in place.

RIACH LABORATORIES, Alki Beach, Seattle. 1000, Tuesday, June 13, 2215.

The next morning, it took Dani several hours to get far enough ahead on her assigned tasks to make time for the investigations she needed to do for Detective Rayes. Gradually, as she selected the objects needed for her daily assignments, she began adding the extra items. Joph and Lora had eliminated irrelevant entries from the VAO list. All the remaining objects would need to be investigated.

She added them a few at a time to her tray. Working without a lot of interaction from her superiors had its advantages, she realized. She wasn't sure whether they left her mostly alone because they recognized how efficient and productive she was or because her assignments were so tedious (she suspected the latter), but she made full use of the freedom now.

As she scanned them, she began to notice a pattern. All the objects with blackmail potential had been converted during lunchtime or after the workday ended. In addition, they were all tagged with the "Administrative" ID. Once she had a pattern, she became more efficient at isolating the objects. Unfortunately, knowing which objects had probably been used for blackmail, and even seeing enough to figure out what secrets the blackmailer had targeted, wasn't enough to get the list of names Detective Rayes had requested. She had dozens of faces, but faces weren't names.

While she was working, her mind raced, trying to find a way to identify the victims. The faces could be run through identification programs, but to get the images, she'd have to use the VAO converter herself. Her activities would suddenly become a lot more noticeable. She didn't dare risk it. So she started to pay attention to tiny details, visual and audio clues. Out of the fifty or so objects the blackmailer had probably used, three of them gave her enough information about the blackmail victims to identify them with a name or an address. She hoped that would be enough.

BATELLI'S DELI, West Seattle. 1200, Tuesday, June 13, 2215.

At noon, when she went off campus to meet Kat for lunch at the retro place, she sent the information she had gathered to the detective. She looked up when the waiter arrived to take their order, and realized Kat hadn't said a word to her, after their initial greeting. Instead, she was studying her, her expression communicating a thoughtful concern.

"What's worrying you?" Dani asked, then laughed. "I mean, besides everything?"

Kat frowned. "I'm trying to figure that out. In just a few words, I'm worried about you."

"Me? Why?"

"You've changed in so many ways in just a few days." Kat ticked them off on her fingers. "You're falling in love—no, don't try to deny it! You're participating in, and even arranging, clandestine meetings. You're working to take down a scarily dangerous person, and there might be more than one, and you're not showing any real signs of fear. You're engaging in corporate espionage and agreeing to bomb threats. Are you okay with all this? You almost seem like a different person!"

Dani looked around a little nervously, reassuring herself that no one had heard Kat's words. "Not so different that I'd toss around all those incriminating words!" She smiled ruefully. "Maybe you're the one who has changed?"

"No, I've always been an activist. Peaceful, yes, but still an activist.

You're the one who usually does everything she can to avoid making waves."

Dani considered. "Well, in a way, I am a different person than the one you've known. Your Dani has never invested herself in the life of a little boy, for example. But I acknowledge that all these things are new even for the Dani of my timestream. I think I like the changes, though. Are they too terribly shocking?"

"Not to me. I just want to be sure you're not getting sucked into something you're not ready for."

"What difference does it make? All the changes will be erased—tomorrow! Except maybe the investigations, and we don't know about those. Besides, they really need to be done."

"You're sure."

"Very sure."

Kat studied her for a moment, then nodded. "Okay. Then I'll call my guy back. I told him to be ready, on my confirmation, to call in his threat just as the afternoon shift is starting. I figured that would make sure that everything is up and running, but the interns would just be setting up, so they'd be able to leave easily. Was I right? Will that be okay for you?"

"That's good timing," Dani answered. "I can hide while everyone else is leaving."

The waiter stepped out from behind the counter. He made his way through the tables toward them.

"Looks like our order," said Kat. "Shall we forget about this, and enjoy this last lunch?"

Dani nodded as the waiter served them their sandwiches.

"I wonder if you'd do me a favor," Kat said.

"Of course. What do you want?"

"Will you tell me more about my son?"

SEEBAK LABORATORY, Vashon Island, WA. 1735, Tuesday, June 13, 2215.

After work, Dani called to confirm that Lexil had the device ready, then went straight to the tube stop. The rush hour crush of riders there ensured that her car would be filled on the trip to Vashon. Seven of them boarded with her.

Wait, seven? She frowned. Tube cars only held six people. When had they put this larger car into the rotation? It didn't look all that new.

Maybe she was just being more observant than she usually was. Her senses were heightened by the realization that this timestream had only hours left before it dissolved into the other. She noticed little things that would normally escape her. Quick glances between fellow travelers communicated in seconds. The precise duration before breaking eye contact and the way they sat at angles to avoid facing each other spoke volumes without words. The ride, they all knew, would be a silent one. One of her companions wore a faint scent of a perfume that smelled of spring bouquets. Another had a scuff on his right shoe. A third tapped his knee nervously to some internal rhythm.

Would any of these things have been true in the real timestream? Would any have been different?

By the time she got to the lab, the evening felt surreal.

Lexil felt it too; she could tell. When he opened the door, his usual smile was replaced by a solemn expression. With a nod and a gesture, he invited her in and they walked back toward his work area.

Doc looked up to acknowledge her arrival, but remained silent. A common awareness left their thoughts unexpressed, but nevertheless understood. Their sense of the magnitude of this thing they were doing fought words and invited only silence.

The truth that none of them would say was that nothing they did tonight, aside from acquiring the device, could have any real significance. It would all be erased in less than twenty-four hours. There was no point to experiencing relationship, furthering friendship, or—as much as two of them might want it—encouraging intimacy. Nothing mattered except this work they were engaged in.

She hated that part.

Then she remembered Jored, and felt ashamed. In just a few days, she had gone from thinking about him constantly to being almost willing to relegate him to warm memories, memories that she shared with no other person in the world. Her conversation with Kat at lunch had helped her feel his loss again. Truly, she would do anything to save her little bud.

All these thoughts tumbled through her head as she followed Lexil through the lab, no more than a few steps behind him. Suddenly, she hit her knee on a small table that inexplicably sat where he had walked seconds before. She stumbled and dropped her worktablet and all her papers.

"Ow!" she said involuntarily, breaking the silence and rubbing her knee.

Lexil turned. "What happened?"

She picked up her things and gestured toward the table. "Was that there a moment ago?"

"No! I would have had to walk right through it."

Suddenly, Dani remembered the way the furniture was moved in her apartment, the changes she thought she had seen in the clock tower, the extra seats in the tube car.

Lexil was already checking the monitors. "It's accelerating. The disturbances are small, but they are happening much more frequently. And when they are noticed, as this one was, they cause more ripples." He made some quick projections. "This could become unstable. The damping forces aren't powerful enough to keep up."

"Unstable? What would that mean?"

"Causality could be completely flipped on its head. That table was there, but nothing caused it to be there. Imagine if that sort of thing were to happen to you so often that you start expecting it. Now imagine that it happens to everyone, and it's not just tables, but rooms, houses, office buildings."

"That would cause a lot of confusion."

"And it might also affect natural features like lakes, hills, islands, continents."

She stared at him. "Are we talking about the end of the world?"

"Could be."

How could they be talking about this so calmly? The surreal feeling persisted, insulating Dani from the hugeness of it all. "How much time do we have to work with?" she asked.

"Probably months. Worst case, a little less than a month," he said.

She swallowed. "But no big deal, right?"

He stood up and put his hands on her shoulders. "Dani. We get do-overs, remember? We're going to fix this. We're going to figure our way through any difficulties. What would happen to this timestream in the next several months is just theoretical. It'll never happen."

He kept his hands on her shoulders, searching her expression, until she nodded. "I know. I just don't have any experience with saving the world."

He grinned. "You and me both. C'mon. Let's go get that device. And then, I think, dinner will be ready, if you care to join us."

"I hadn't even thought about eating." She realized she wasn't hungry. "Honestly, I think I'm too wound up to eat. I'll go in and give my apologies to Doc, but then would you mind if I just saw myself out?"

It was hard to explain, but she had to narrow her focus to just the job that lay before her. So much depended on her success the next day. Her emotions had been wrenching her back and forth, and she couldn't afford that kind of ambivalence any more.

His expression showed that wasn't at all what he was hoping. "Okay. If you're sure?"

She nodded.

"I've got the device in the library. What time are you going to be using it?"

"Just after lunch. We need to make sure all the scanners are back online." She followed him to retrieve the device. They walked around a big world globe. Had that been there before?

"Kat will be coordinating with the guy who is going to call in the bomb threat?"

"Yes. She wondered if you and Doc would like to come to their place, since none of you can actually be inside the institute with me. She invited her uncle too." She wrinkled her nose. "I don't see that it matters where people are when I run the program. Everything will change anyway."

"True, but it might be good to have us all together, in case something unexpected comes up. Here's the device. Take care of it. We don't get a second chance," His tone was somber as he handed it to her. He caught her eyes and held them. Was he talking just about saving the world? Or was he talking about the two of them? Second chance, funny. They wouldn't even get a first chance.

"You think I don't know that? What do you think is making me so nervous?" She realized she had snapped at him. She softened her tone. "Hey, I'm sorry. I just think I need to be alone for a while tonight."

He opened his mouth and then closed it without saying anything. Finally, he nodded, and she brushed past him to find Doc in the kitchen.

"Hey, Dani. Are you going to join us for dinner?" he asked cheerfully. He was chopping fresh cilantro.

"No, Doc. I just came to say goodbye, and thanks for everything."

He put down his knife and ran his hands through the rinse-and-dry near the sink. "You're leaving? Come here and give an old man a hug."

She set down her belongings and returned his hug. It was big and warm and comforting, but just for a few seconds. Then it was done. She sighed.

"Are you all right?" Doc searched her expression. "Do you want to talk about it?"

No. No, she didn't want to talk about it. She wanted to ignore it. She wanted to do her job, and do it well, and save the whole world somehow. And in the process, never see this delightful old man and his adopted son again.

Change the subject. Talk about something else. She glanced around. Lexil's notes lay near her hand. She patted them. "Lexil made copies of his notes for me. I want to read them, but I can't help thinking how useless it is to learn anything. If only we could take what we know and transfer it to the other reality!"

Doc raised his eyebrows. "You'd have to stay in the observation box while the insertion program was running. You're not—"

She shook her head. "No, no. I'm not stupid. But if there was some way—" Her gaze lit on her copy of Lexil's notes. That gave her an idea. Could it work?

"There isn't, Dani. It's too dangerous. Don't even think about it."

"Okay, but what if it wasn't a person?"

He looked up at her sharply. "What do you mean?"

She pointed to the notes. "What if it was, say, a stack of papers? If we left these in an observation box for the other Lexil to find, would he—and the other you—understand what they meant?"

Doc pursed his lips and squinted one eye while he thought. Then he nodded. "That could work. And our other selves would most certainly be able to understand it. We just wouldn't understand where they came from. Which parts did he copy?"

"The parts that show that matter is being removed from the past."

"That is a wonderful idea! It gives the other timestream, the right one, a fighting chance."

"What do you mean? Is it in danger too?"

"Yes, of course. If the procedures continue as before, it's only a matter of time before something important is removed, and the timestream is diverted again. But in another such occurrence, there might not be a Dani to notice the difference."

The lighting changed subtly. The wall color switched from gray to a soft yellow.

"We need to leave it here," she said, "in one of your sensor boxes. Whichever one you would notice first."

"We check them all every day. Anything inside their domes would be obvious immediately. This will work! It has to!" He frowned. "Of course, opening a sensor dome will affect the readings slightly. You'd have to do it quickly. Get Lexil to show you how."

She gathered up the notes and her worktablet and went to find Lexil. He had left the library. Probably in the lab. The globe had moved over by the window. Now that she knew what was going on, the changes weren't so alarming.

She glanced outside. A tiny bird banked its wings to land on a branch that, abruptly, wasn't there any more. It fell several inches before recovering enough to fly off and find another perch. The changes were definitely accelerating.

Would the notes be enough to warn the other Lexil of this danger? Why not spell it out? She found a pen on a table. Her handwriting was rough, unpracticed, but she could certainly leave a message. What should she say? "Hello from another reality"? No. "Your world has been changed, and changed back, based on the observations in these pages." Better. She wrote that.

What else? "RIACH must be warned." No. That was too broad. The message might go to people who wouldn't understand or who wouldn't act. Who in RIACH would care and have the power to do anything about it? Kat's Uncle Royce? Dr. Brant? No, neither of them had the kind of pull to stop anything, from what she could tell. It was the blackmailer who would need to be stopped, and it would take someone outside the institute to do it. Marak. Marak would follow the data through to the end. And he'd need the financial information too. "Contact Marak Wallace and Detective Tom Rayes to stop this," she wrote.

There. That should do it. She started to put the pen down, but then, smiling, she scrawled one more line, down near the bottom of

the page. It couldn't hurt.
    She went to find Lexil.

29
ESCALATION

WALLACE HOME, Lower Queen Anne, Seattle, WA. 1145, Wednesday, June 14, 2215.

"Things are crazy out there," said Lexil, as he and Doc arrived at the Wallace house. "We came in the helicar. When I stepped out, a parrot flew by my nose. Oh, and your irisscan has disappeared."

"What?" Kat asked. "A parrot?"

Doc nodded. "The changes to the environment caused by the disturbances are accelerating. Good thing we're doing this today. In another day or two, we might not recognize things, much less be able to count on them staying in place.

"How's Dani?" Lexil asked. "Have you heard from her?"

"She called on one of her mandatory breaks," said Kat. "Everything is on schedule at the institute. She'll be eating in the cafeteria. She's just waiting for the threat and the evacuation order."

Doc cleared his throat. "Dani said you invited Royce."

"Yes, I did." Kat nodded. "I wanted to include him, since he was the first one to take all this seriously. I've talked with him a few times in the last few days. He's been very interested in how our investigations of the timestream differences have been coming along. He was horrified to learn that the institute's equipment was responsible for the shift, and he was relieved to hear you were helping. He thinks very highly of you."

Lexil looked around. No Royce. Well, they had arrived fifteen minutes before lunchtime. Probably wasn't here yet. "When will he arrive?" he asked.

"He won't be coming," she answered. "He said he had a lunch commitment. He offered, at first, to try to get out of it. It seems odd that people still have plans and appointments, but of course he didn't know anything when he made the appointment. I just told him today."

"I said she should tell him it was the end of the world," said Marak. "What else could be more important?"

"So I told him what Dani was going to be doing," Kat continued. "He asked some questions about timing to be sure people there wouldn't interfere. Asked if we needed him to request a special assignment for her. I said no, and told him how we had arranged to empty the lab and free her up. And then he said his lunch meeting was with someone from the institute, and he'd better keep it so things would seem as normal as possible."

Doc nodded. "I was looking forward to seeing him again, but that makes sense. He has always been a big picture kind of person."

"He was worried that Dani would try to stay in the lab at lunch, but I reassured him that she was going to eat in the cafeteria. I should send her a message to remind her of that." She raised her hand to her temple. Then she put it down again. "Can't. The institute blocks all the signals from outside. She can't get incoming calls."

"Why would he care about her staying in the lab?" asked Lexil.

"He said the institute has been increasing the monitoring of employees lately, due to concern about the protests. They're feeling political pressure. It might flag something if she was seen in the lab, and they might escort her out."

"Nice to have someone on the inside, even if he can't make any changes," said Marak.

"Wait. I'm getting a call. Maybe Dani? Nope, Neferyn." Kat made a face. "Probably calling to confirm. I'll switch to the house connexion so you can hear."

She accepted the call. "Everything ready?" she asked.

"Yes," said the voice on the other end. "The timing was a little tricky, but everything is ready to go."

"What was the tricky part? Making an anonymous call?"

"No." He laughed. "That will be easy. This is an external connexion, untraceable, or I'd never be talking to you! The next call will be to the institute. No, the tricky part was last night. They had some additional monitoring devices set up when we went to place the bombs."

"You planted fake bombs?" Kat frowned. "I think the threat would have been enough to clear the place, without those."

"Fake? You think I'm going to waste an opportunity like this on fake bombs? Not a chance. These are real, and there's nothing small about them. They are going to tear the place apart!"

Kat inhaled sharply.

The voice on the other end continued. "If it were me, I wouldn't have called in the threat. I'd have let them all die."

"Neferyn!" she said desperately, "this whole arrangement was to clear it out so my friend—my best friend—could be there alone. She will be in the building. You can't set those off!"

"Too late." His voice was calm. "They're on timers. Can't get close enough to change that. If you want to call your friend and get her out of there, better do it now."

Lexil reached up to call Dani. Kat saw him, and shook her head. He remembered. Dani was off the nexus. He started for the door, then hesitated. "Find out where the bombs are," he whispered. She nodded.

"We can't reach her. We're going to have to go find her. Where are the bombs?"

"You're going to have to hurry, then." He laughed. Laughed! "One is right by the front entrance. It'll go off at 1:20. Just enough time to clear the building after my guy calls at 1:05. There are ten others timed at three-minute intervals. They are planted all the way around the perimeter. Yup. Blaze of glory! The whole thing will collapse. I'm going to watch from the hill!"

Kat ended the call with a look of disgust. "Go!" She told Lexil.

"Take the helicar!" said Doc.

"I'll go with you. I'll drop you off right at the door," said Marak.

Kat started to protest.

"They'll be telling me to go report on it soon anyway. Might as well be on the scene where I can help." He kissed her. "I'll see you—and Jored—this afternoon!"

30
DIVERSION

RIACH LABS, Alki Beach, Seattle, WA. 1250, Wednesday, June 14, 2215.

Dani barely noticed what she had for lunch. She ate only to give herself a reason for sitting in the cafeteria. Lunch would be over soon and then she could make her way to the lab.

Just a few more minutes now. She picked up her tray and headed toward the exit. If she could be first to arrive in the lab, it would make it easier to hide when the bomb threat came in.

She left the cafeteria three minutes early, hoping no one would stop her. So far, so good. The back hallway, lengthy as it was, would give her the best chance of getting to Lab D undetected because it bypassed the lengths of Labs A and B, taking her directly to the shorter hallway that contained the doors to all the labs.

She felt in her pocket for the memory rod. The whole plan, the entirety of the timestream repair, depended on an object that could hide completely in a closed hand. There it was, among the other four objects that she hadn't been able to bring herself to return to the store room. Soon she wouldn't need a metal disk to remember Jored. Her spirits lifted. So close!

The back hallway would take her past the VAO converter. She marveled that such a simple process—recording, rather than just letting someone experience—the past, would have become the source of so much havoc. She hoped that the notes in Lexil's notebook would be enough to point out its dangers to those in the other timestream.

It will have to be enough, she thought. It was all they could do from here.

"Dani!" A voice interrupted her thoughts. She looked up, startled.

It was Kat's Uncle Royce. "Kat updated me on all that you've discovered in the last few days. I have to say, I'm impressed."

"Thank you. I had a lot of help."

"So I hear. Seebak and that boy of his. Both of 'em geniuses, if I'm not mistaken."

She nodded. "They are amazing."

"You've been to their lab, I hear."

"Yes. It's impressive. Nothing like here, of course." She wondered how much Kat had told him. So much had happened in such a short time! Did he know what she was doing today? He was a sweet old man, and she wanted to be polite, but she was getting fidgety. She needed to let him know she had to hurry.

"So this is the day, is it? You're putting us back on track?"

Oh good. That made it easier. "Yes, I'm heading for the lab, right now. Did Kat tell you about, uh, getting people cleared out?" She wasn't sure how to phrase that. She didn't want to say anything about a bomb threat if he didn't already know about it. She could just imagine the confusion that would cause, and the explanations it would require, and she couldn't afford the delay.

Just then, the speakers in the hallway clicked on. "All personnel, please move to the nearest exit in an orderly manner. This is not a drill. Repeat, this is not a drill." The announcement continued with more specific instructions. She was behind schedule. She was supposed to be hidden in the lab by now.

"Oh yes. That's your cue, isn't it? Will you need any help?"

"No, I don't think so. But thank you for the offer."

"All right then. I'll let you get back to it."

She nodded, and watched him head back the way she had come. Now she would have to hurry. She passed the door to the VAO converter at a fast walk. She heard the machine doing its wind-down noises. It always took so long to shut off! Hurry, don't stop, she chided herself.

But the delay had cost her the minutes she needed to get ahead of the crowd. In desperation, she watched the stream of workers go past her on their way out. She needed to cross the hall. She could see the doors to Labs C and D right across from her. But if she stepped into that river, she'd be carried far down the hallway and might not be able to get back until the stream stopped.

"Excuse me, I need to get across the hall," she said, trying to push through.

"This is not a drill. Didn't you hear the message?" A tall, thin intern grabbed her by the arm. He was stronger than he looked.

She finally wriggled her arm out of his grasp. "You go ahead. I'll be right there."

"You're crazy." He shrugged and moved on down the hallway.

Others were looking at her, wondering why she wasn't following. She needed to hide somewhere until the hall cleared enough for her to cross without attracting so much attention. She decided to go back to the VAO converter room and wait. It would only be a few minutes. It wasn't as if the others would be allowed back into the building before the bomb crews had combed it, looking for the explosives. She would have plenty of time.

The machine had finished its shut-down routine by the time she got there. Had it been only yesterday that she had coaxed it into revealing its secrets? She wondered how Detective Rayes was doing with the names of the blackmail victims.

It occurred to her that the easiest way to discover who the blackmailer was would be to happen upon him in this room during lunch. Too bad she couldn't have been there 20 minutes earlier. She'd have known then.

Not that that would do any good. Whatever she learned here wouldn't survive the timestream fix anyway.

31
APPREHENSION

RIACH LABS, Alki Beach, Seattle, WA. 1255, Wednesday, June 14, 2215.

"Go, go, go!" Lexil muttered. It didn't help. A tree that suddenly popped up in the middle of a restaurant had attracted onlookers, and the flyways had been completely rerouted as a result. Traffic was snarled.

He and Marak finally arrived just before the first threat was to be called in.

"You get out; I'll go find a place to park," Marak said.

"Park anywhere," said Lexil. "Doesn't matter if you get a ticket. Doesn't even matter if the helicar is stolen while you're gone or damaged by the explosion. If Dani succeeds, we have do-overs. If she fails—"

"—the car may grow horns and a mermaid tail anyway," Marak finished. "I know. Now go! Help her finish before this whole thing goes down."

Lexil knew he'd have to get inside the building with the lunch crowds if he was to have any chance at all. He bypassed the irisscans by dropping his hat and bending down to pick it up. Then he stood up on the other side of the scanners. Nobody noticed. He was surprised by how easy it was. Royce had said there was heightened security, but he didn't see it.

Now, in through the door. He didn't see signs to the lab, but he saw people putting on powder blue lab coats. Dani had one of those. He guessed that they would be heading where she would be heading. He followed a big group of the blue coats down a display hall. Memories from childhood flooded back. It was his mother's display hall, he realized. But no time to stop and remember. He had to find where the lab was before the alarm sounded and they all turned around to go out the doors they had just come in.

He did his best to look like he belonged. Look straight ahead. Walk purposefully. Don't run, no matter how much you want to.

And then he saw the sign to the labs. He wished he knew which one she'd be in, but at least from here, he could find the labs, even if the alarm—

And there it was. Every person in the crowd stopped abruptly to hear the announcement. "All personnel, please move to the nearest exit in an orderly manner. This is not a drill. Repeat, this is not a drill. Pass through the irisscan at the exit to assist us in accounting for all employees. All personnel, please move...." The message repeated several times.

Lexil could hear the deliberate rhythm in its instructions. It was almost hypnotic. He marveled at how calmly people walked, almost marched, to its cadence. He could see signs to two exits. One was just before the first lab, Lab A. It pointed to the right, down a long hall. The other was beyond the last lab, Lab D. The distances looked about the same. Half of the group he was with diverted to the right. Among those who remained, he slumped and bent his knees so his head and his lack of a lab coat wouldn't be so obvious, preparing to enter Lab A as they went past.

The door to the lab was closed but unlocked. A part of his mind was counting off seconds since the alarm was announced. He knew the first bomb would be at the front entrance, and the others would go off in intervals. But he had no way of guessing how long he had before the one at the end of this hall went off.

He entered Lab A. The pieces of equipment were more elaborate than he was used to, but their functions were easy to recognize. First were the projectors, with big screens for groups of people to experience the same recording at the same time. Then were the scanners.

According to the plan, Dani should be at her scanner in one of the labs, setting it up for the procedure, or in the object library, getting the padlock. The scanners had tinted glass, so he could only see inside the nearest ones. He stepped up on the raised platform in front of the projectors. It didn't help, and she could as easily be in the aisles, hidden between them, as inside. He'd make a quick tour of the labs and then head for the library.

Halfway down the first aisle, he heard, then felt, the shock of the first explosion. Three-minute intervals, Neferyn had said. He started running. Noise wouldn't matter now. Two aisles later, he knew for certain: No Dani in Lab A. He would have to check the other labs, then the object library.

Where would the library be? Probably a room that was easily accessible from any of the four labs. In the back, he guessed. And he spotted a likely door.

But the door to Lab B was closer. He'd check that first. He dashed through the door and started checking the scanners.

It happened in a split second. The blast and the wall hit him simultaneously. Then the floor came at him and he blacked out.

32
EXPLOSION

RIACH LABS, Alki Beach, Seattle, WA. 1310, Wednesday, June 14, 2215.

As Dani waited in the room with the VAO converter, a boom from the direction of the front entrance startled her. The floor and walls shuddered, the hall windows rattled. She poked her head out the door and looked down the hallway. The remainder of the crowd was moving much more quickly now. Could Neferyn have set up some kind of sound effect to make the bomb threat more realistic? But that was so loud!

An uneasy thought occurred to her. What if that was not a sound effect, but an actual bomb? Would he have done that?

Either way, she would need to finish her job here. She stole another glance down the hallway. Only the stragglers were left inside the building now, and they were running toward the exit. No one would notice her. Time to get across the hall to the labs.

She had passed by the door to Lab C when she heard and felt the second explosion, much closer than the first, followed by the screeches and rumbles of metal girders and cement walls giving way, collapsing. So loud! The floor heaved, and instinct cried out for her to turn and run. But danger didn't matter now, she reminded herself. Speed did. She braced herself against the wall as the waves died down. Cement dust filled the air, and she coughed.

That was when she heard the moan, followed by a scream that started in agonized pain and ended, inexplicably, with her name. She knew that voice. Horror propelled her toward it. Whatever her mission, whatever her goal, she could not let Lexil be alone with that kind of anguish.

She found him in Lab B, just inside the door, buried in rubble, crisscrossed with girders. In the seconds it took her to reach him, she saw his right foot jutting from the rubble nearby, but it couldn't be his. Impossible for a leg to bend that way! Her eyes shifted back and forth between the foot and his face, too pale, too gray. She choked back a scream of her own as she understood.

"Dani..." he said again, between groans that tore at her soul. "The bombs... every three minutes... your connexion... blocked." He fought to keep his eyes open.

"More?" she shuddered. She didn't want to think about bombs. She wanted to pull the girders off, stop the blood from draining out of his beautiful body, wish him safely back home. Now there was no gentle good humor in his glance, no flash of brilliance. But his brown eyes still held tenderness and trust.

It was a horrible time to realize she loved him. She would do anything for this man! With a surge of desperate strength, she heaved at the top girder. It took only a second to discover that any momentary gain disappeared as soon as she stopped pulling. What could she use as a lever?

Lexil reached, grabbed her wrist. "No, Dani." He grimaced. His eyes closed against the pain. She had to lean close to hear him whisper, "Go. You have to go."

Everything in her protested. She would stay by his side! She could not let him die! A world without Lexil in it was unthinkable.

An explosion rocked the floor. More of the ceiling tore loose and fell on either side of them. One chunk broke loose from overhead, and she instinctively threw up her arms to shield her head. A piece of something metal tore at her left forearm.

Bloody, but superficial. She ignored the pain.

More walls were crumbling, this time back near the library, making it inaccessible from here. She had to reach the padlock. She hoped the door from Lab C or Lab D was still intact.

She looked back at Lexil. She knew he was dying. Why did he have to come? His warning came too late to have done her any good. If only she could go back before he left, tell him not to come.

"This wasn't supposed to happen," she whispered.

"So go. Make it... unhappen."

She knelt beside him, cupped his face in her hands, and gently kissed his blue lips. "I love you. I won't even know you there. But you'll be alive."

When she pulled away, his eyes were closed, and she couldn't hear him breathing. But she thought she saw him nod.

The hallway to Lab C was still passable. As long as there was a chance, she had to try.

RIACH LABS, Alki Beach, Seattle, WA. 1320, Wednesday, June 14, 2215.

Dani picked her way through the debris in the hallway. A new concern surfaced. Even if she could get to the library, would there be a scanning recorder in Lab C or D that had survived the blasts? Lab B, where Lexil lay dying, was a total loss. Lab A, just beyond it, was sure to be worse, since it was closer to the exit where the bomb had gone off.

When she got there, she found Lab C was easier to step through, but almost all the scanners in the front were crushed under a slab of concrete that had dropped from the ceiling above. Fragments were still falling onto the few remaining scanners.

The whole upper floor could come down at any moment, but the back section appeared to be largely intact. Perhaps she could find a scanner there! But when she got nearer, the usually glowing panels were dark, telling her the power was out in the back. None of the scanners were on line.

Another explosion, more distant, rocked the building. She steadied herself on the nearest support pillar. Those, at least, were holding up. Now, she needed to make her way to the library for Object 097113, the padlock. One more time.

Just past the area with the VAO converter was the library. It was in shambles. Case after case was toppled, objects spilled everywhere. She would be horrified at the loss to researchers if she hadn't finally and completely convinced herself that this chaos and destruction would all go away soon, and everything would be restored. If only she could find the padlock. This mess would definitely make it harder.

The soft lights emanating from the panels in the walls were flickering. Case 90 lay in front of her. She climbed over it, and then over Case 91. Case 92 was still standing, and she started hoping that Case 97 would be too. Just a little farther.

There. Case 97 had toppled over partway and was leaning on the one next to it. Dani would have to go underneath, between the two, to see if Object 097113 was still in place. Just as she got herself wedged between the shelves, the floor shook. The wall lights flickered again and went out.

"No, not now! Not this close!" she yelled, to no one in particular. She felt in her pocket for her worktablet and switched on the white background. In its light, she could see, just barely, the numbers on the shelves. Spot 109, 110, 111 had objects in them, but spots 112 and 113 were empty. Dani swallowed, willing away the panic that was rising in her. This had to work. Where was that padlock?

She got down on her knees on the floor, picking up containers and labels and fragments of ceiling tile. She mourned the quiet efficiency of the library she'd always known, remembering how easy it was to reach up and gather ten or fifteen objects at a time just a few days before.

She took a deep breath to steady herself, then started searching the floor methodically from the wall backwards toward the passageway, picking up debris, checking it, moving it aside. About halfway to the passageway, she found the label: "097113." It must have been stripped from the padlock during the upheavals. She wished it had been the padlock. She calmed herself, taking the label as evidence that it was here somewhere.

But she worked her way all the way back to the passageway without finding it.

For the first time since the explosions had begun, she began to consider that this might be the world she had to stay in. They knew her role in it. They probably knew the names of everyone involved, even the West Seattle kids. She had almost completely brought down an entire institute. She gripped her hair, trying to steady herself, trying to stop the tremble in her hands.

A rumble signaled another detonation, more distant. Lexil had said they were set to go off every three minutes. She wondered how he knew that. She took a deep breath. This had to work. She had to find that padlock.

And then she saw it. Two shelves up from the floor on Case 98. It must have been flung over there when its own case tottered. She recognized it immediately. Same keyhole at the bottom. Same band across the top, and fine lines down the sides.

It looked a little newer. In a fleeting thought, she attributed that to the effects of the timestream breaking apart. Everything was changing. She was lucky it hadn't turned to a sausage or something.

Would the power still be on in Lab D? Like Lab A, it was near an exit door, but if there was a bomb planted there, it hadn't yet gone off. Please be working, she begged it silently, and breathed a sigh of relief when she entered to find the back corner, where her usual station 3 scanner was located, apparently undisturbed. The lighting and air systems were still functioning.

She dared to hope that she could pull this whole thing off, because the idea of not hoping, not believing this would all go away, was unthinkable.

RIACH LABS, Alki Beach, Seattle, WA. 1330, Wednesday, June 14, 2215.

Dani braced herself at the entry to Lab D, riding out another explosion. How many of these were there going to be?

The lights in the lab continued, uninterrupted. Her observation box should be intact, but who knew how long it would last?

She was so focused on getting to her destination that she almost didn't see him, standing behind the box, leaning against it. She jumped at his voice.

"That one won't work."

"What one? What do you mean? What are you doing here?"

He ignored her last question. "The padlock. It's not the right one."

"What? How do you know that?"

"You'll need this one." He held out a nearly identical padlock. She recognized the faint patterns of scrapes and gouges immediately. He was right.

"But how—?"

"There's no time to explain. Go fix this." He waved his hand in a circle. Fix this. The lab. The city. The whole rippling world. Yes. She needed to fix it.

But something in the back of her mind nagged her to stay, to find out why he, of all people, would have the item she had spent so much time searching for, and why there had been a different padlock in the library for her to find.

Her hesitation lasted only seconds, and then she remembered. The VAO converter, winding down as she passed it, right after lunch. The only other person who would have any reason to be down here during that time would be the blackmailer. Everyone else would have left when the evacuation sounded—especially when the explosions began.

She was looking at the man behind it all.

And for some reason, their goals had meshed. He wanted her to succeed here as much as she did.

"You're the blackmailer." It wasn't an accusation. It was matter-of-fact, forced past her natural filters by urgency: a surreal interval of perfect clarity in the midst of confusion and uncertainties, meant to be acknowledged and forgotten. Whatever she knew now would be useless soon.

He was surprised. She could tell by the way he drew back, just for a moment. And then he laughed. "Congratulations! I didn't even know you were looking for me. Does it matter?"

She shook her head, slowly. "Is this yours, then?" She held out the newer padlock.

He nodded. "If it weren't for the bombs, I'd have let you go ahead and try to repair time with that one. It wouldn't have worked, of course. It was made just a few months ago. It wouldn't exist yet if you sent it back."

"You knew about the damage to the timestream, and you wanted to keep me from fixing it? Why? Why would you do that?"

"Things were going so well here, you see. No one suspected me, and my accounts were growing nicely."

She couldn't decide whether to be furious that he had so little regard for others or relieved that he had changed his mind and brought her the padlock.

A bomb at the exit just outside the lab door detonated. She braced herself as walls folded in and pieces of ceiling fell in widening circles inside the door. Plaster dust mixed with the smoke in the air. Her last exit was blocked. No matter. She wasn't planning to leave here anyway.

The reverberations made it hard to stay standing, and harder to see. Through the greenish dust that filled the air, she saw his legs buckle, watched him slide down the side of the box, observed the red smear left behind where he had been leaning.

"You're hurt." Again, matter-of-fact, despite the dangers around her. This was a thing she knew. She was strangely calm.

"Fatal, I'm afraid." He was almost apologetic as he lifted his arm to reveal a blood-soaked shirt from what looked like multiple wounds.

A shard of broken glass jutted from his abdomen.

He followed her gaze. "Spleen. I scanned it. And internal bleeding. No hope, even if we could get out of here. You'll have to come get the lock." He held it out, and she could tell his strength was fading.

How was he even talking? She picked her way around fallen chunks of ceiling and retrieved the padlock. A bony hand, stronger than it should have been, grabbed her by the wrist.

"I had all the evidence, you know." His voice had dropped to a whisper. "All the recordings, from the VAO, from hundreds of cams and mics recording live, under my personal account."

"So we could have found it, if we'd looked there?"

He laughed again, but now it was a sort of gurgle. "Would you have ever looked?"

She shook her head and stepped back. No. She would never have suspected him.

"Go save my life."

She felt no pity for him. He had made life miserable for hundreds, maybe thousands, of people. He had polluted the science that she loved. He wore the face of someone she had cared for, someone who had seemed to care for her. But that was all a lie.

As far as she knew, though, he had never killed anyone. Save his life? That might come, along with saving Lexil and Jored and the whole timestream, but she made no promise about saving his lifestyle.

Dani left him there and entered the observation box. She placed the padlock in the chamber, making sure she got the right one, and inserted the memory rod in its place. With quick motions of her hands, she set the date and time. Only one more thing before she stepped out and let herself and everything around her fade into "never existed." She reached into her pocket for what she needed. That done, she set the timer for five seconds, just enough time to step out of the box and close it up tight.

She hoped it would work.

33
CONFIRMATION

RIACH LABS, Alki Beach, Seattle, WA. 1336, Wednesday, June 14, 2215.

Dani whistled on the way back from the library to her observation box. Today was a good day. Lunch with Kat had been great, especially when she had found out that Jored's team had actually won their last game. So funny to hear about his squeals of delight, and how he and his holographic teammates had run around the play area in their respective houses, sometimes slapping hands, sometimes using ghost mode to go through each other's 'grafs, all the while yelling and whooping.

Tonight, she'd be meeting with Anders again. Every time they met, they grew closer. So far, they were just friends, but Dani knew she would be quite willing to consider more, and she thought he would too. He was smart and funny, and they worked really well together.

She frowned a bit, thinking of their last meeting when they'd gone over the high school kids' discoveries and her own follow-up investigation. It was frustrating to be so close to finding the blackmailer and still not know who it was. They had lists of his/her victims. They had amounts of payments. They even knew which of the RIACH accounts was holding the money. But all their efforts to discover who was in charge had failed. So far.

Nobody was ready to give up. They all felt that the solution was just around the corner. She smiled again. Slow progress couldn't drain her good mood this afternoon.

With her thoughts in the background, she had been mechanically sorting through the objects to scan. She selected a brass belt buckle from the 1880s and set it on the ledge to scan first. But something was already there.

Strange. Had someone come by while she was in the library? She poked her head out to look around. Three other interns were working in observation boxes, but none of them acknowledged her. Not likely that they had made the trip over to her machine.

She looked back at the four objects: a plastic leaf, a scrap of leather, a small stone, and a metal disk. They looked exactly like the objects she had recently returned with the school demo kits. Was there something wrong with them? Maybe someone had left her a note on her worktablet. She checked, but there were no new notes.

She picked up the stone and rolled it over in her hand. She couldn't see anything wrong, although it seemed lighter than it should be. She shrugged that off, looking for any kind of reason that someone would take these objects from the kit and place them here.

No matter how many presentations she had made, how many objects she had examined, she still found it fascinating that piece of geology could have its entire chronetic history imprinted within it. This stone, which existed in some form in the earliest stages of earth's history, could tell her everything from that point to the point when she just picked it up. Or—a sudden thought—to the point just before she found it, when someone was deciding she should have it back, and upon not finding her in her observation box, had placed it on the ledge.

Why not? she thought. She could find out who left the objects here by reading the chronetic imprints from the last ten minutes. She put down the stone and selected the metal disk for maximum sensory input.

Immediately, she was overwhelmed with the smell of dust-laden air and burnt electronics. It felt hard to breathe, although she knew objectively that she was breathing just fine. She couldn't see anything, except for filtered light. Fabric. Inside a pocket, if she had to guess. This wasn't going to tell her anything. She reached to turn the time back further when she heard the voices.

"That one won't work." She recognized the voice. Odd. Why would he be here in the lab? Then her own voice! How could that be? She checked the time settings, but they were correct.

She heard some words about a padlock, and fixing something, none of which meant anything to her. But she understood the next sentence perfectly.

"You're the blackmailer," she heard herself say. She shook her head. She must have heard wrong. There was no way…

"Congratulations."

He was admitting to it? As she listened to more of the words, her mind raced. She knew she had not said those sentences. She had been whistling while the words were supposedly spoken. What else could it be? Could someone else have imitated their voices to produce these? She knew chronetic recordings couldn't be falsified, so the sounds were genuine. But what made the sounds could be fake.

Now the voices were talking about bombs, damage to the timestream, and something that needed to be fixed. And then an explosion, which was so vivid she braced against things that might fall on her. But everything was calm outside the box.

She paused the playback. Damage to the timestream. Seemed far-fetched, but at one point chronography was science fiction too. So what if this whole sequence was from a different timestream, and found its way, somehow, into her observation box. How much of it would be true in this timestream?

She swiped, and the playback resumed. As she listened, her eyes widened, and she smiled. If there was anything useful here, it wouldn't require much work at all to confirm it. She activated "Notes" on her worktablet and spoke a few words.

She and Anders would have a lot to talk about tonight.

INTERRUPTION

RIACH LABS, Alki Beach, Seattle, WA. 0943, Thursday, June 15, 2215.

Only a few hours into the work day, and Hunter had already made two large deposits into the Research and Development fund, and he had a dozen objects to check into the library that showed high potential. Secrets to be uncovered.

He had never had a job he enjoyed as much as this one, and everything he did secured his future a little bit more.

His face darkened as he thought about his previous career. Decades of doctoring, caring for other people's whiny kids who came in complaining of sniffles, coughs, sore throats, itches, or crying about broken bones which could easily have been avoided. He had only entered medical school for its promise of wealth, and he'd planned on a lucrative cosmetic surgery practice, but circumstances had forced him to settle on pediatrics.

He'd practiced smiles until he could keep a fake one on his face, even while he was resenting his patients' stupidity, even while he was looking for expensive procedures that he could order to justify bigger bills. Nobody would refuse a "necessary" medical procedure, and he was a master at convincing them they had no choice.

He had discovered a lot of family secrets, too, and made some forays into blackmail (in the form of family counseling charges) by threatening abusive parents with exposure. They knew the court systems would take their children, so they gladly paid his fees. As a side benefit, he saw those children frequently to set broken bones and prescribe salves for burns. Their parents dared not take them anywhere else.

As a ten-year-old boy, he had watched his father leave for a short trip to the store. His cocaine-addicted mother said he had been shot in a robbery. The neighbors told him his father had boarded a bus for California with another woman and a baby. He hadn't known what to believe, but it was then that he had decided to devote his life first to learning everything he could, and then making enough money to always be able to afford the best. Once that was achieved, he had set his sights higher, and stepped into the position on the board of the institute.

It only took him a few months to refine his blackmail methods and start making more money. At this point, he knew he would never again have to deny himself anything.

He leaned forward in his chair to inspect the list of items and make the afternoon's assignments. He was so absorbed that he didn't notice the red flag on his viewwall that signaled the admission of an unexpected visitor to the institute. He first became aware of the intrusion when he heard his secretary say, "You can't go in there!" and then splutter to a stop. Hunter looked out to see his secretary with his back to the door, blocking an older man and two uniformed police officers.

A detective, he realized. The man held out a badge. Probably looking for some chronographic investigations. Those requests usually went through one of the other directors, but perhaps they were not available this morning. He cleared his throat.

"That's fine, Richards. Clear my appointments for this morning." He knew, and Richards knew, that he had no appointments, but Hunter was never one to pass up an opportunity to make another man appear obligated to him.

"What can I do for you, Detective...?" He trailed off, letting the other man supply his name.

"...Rayes, Tom Rayes. Actually, what I need you to do is come downtown with us."

Decidedly out of the ordinary. Now he was regretting having Richards "clear" his schedule. "I'm afraid I can't do that today. I have obligations here at the institute."

"I'm afraid you will have to." Detective Rayes tilted his head toward the two officers, and and they stepped forward to flank him. "We can do this the hard way, if you prefer."

"All my equipment is here. How can I help you without the resources of the institute?"

The detective looked up at the ceiling and gave a barely-audible sigh. "Royce Hunter, you are under arrest for the crime of blackmailing, multiple counts."

35
RESTORATION

WEST SEATTLE HIGH SCHOOL, Seattle, WA. 1000, Saturday, June 17, 2215.

The members of the Political Action Club were buzzing with excitement when Ms. Harris led Dani and Anders to their meeting room. She counted faces: full tally of students, and Detective Rayes was here too.

She nodded to him.

"Hey, everybody, this is my friends Anders, who dug up all the financial details for us."

The kids applauded and whooped.

"Anders, these are the kids who helped me take the possibility of blackmailing seriously."

"So you're the ones who started it all," said Anders. He looked around. "Which of you are Joph and Lora?"

Dani pointed them out. Anders strode over to them and shook their hands. "You two did a great job. That was a lot of work!"

Joph shrugged, but he couldn't hide the broad grin on his face. "We had fun."

"Yeah, it was fun," said Lora. "Many, *many* hours of fun. What I want to know is: Did it help?"

Detective Rayes stepped forward. "I'll answer that one. The work you all put in helped us determine how the perp was getting his information. We were able to identify several of the victims, and find where the funds were being stored. But we didn't have anything to tie any particular person to the crime. The victims we interviewed claimed they knew nothing. After we showed them evidence of their fund transfers, they admitted to making the payments, but all three of them said they were afraid to tell us more."

"None of them had any proof to convict a blackmailer anyway, did they, Grandpa?" Ronny asked.

"No, they didn't. We were stuck, waiting for a break in the case, when Dani got a mysterious tip."

"Crazy mysterious!" Dani agreed. "Recordings of things that had never happened, the voice of the blackmailer confessing, and my voice responding — although I had never spoken those words. As it happened, the voice of the blackmailer was one I knew well, someone I had trusted to be one of the good guys. It seemed impossible. But it pointed in a certain direction, and when I gave Anders a name, it was easy for him to confirm what we had heard. The man had numerous files of blackmail material stored in his personal account."

"He left a record every time he accessed the material, and those access dates and times corresponded with dates and times of deposits," Anders said.

"Anders was able to report it to me under the whistleblower law, and that gave us a reason for a search warrant and enough justification to make an arrest."

"You actually made a real arrest?" Jazz sat up straight from where she had been lounging in a chair. "Not as a joke?"

Detective Rayes laughed, a big hearty laugh. "Yes, a real arrest, Jazz. One of the institute's board members, in fact. And we have most of the rest of them in custody as persons of interest. It's very likely they were aware of the whole scheme. They have been suspended from their duties and restricted from access until this whole thing is sorted out."

"Who will direct the institute in their absence?" asked Ms. Harris.

"Well, they're not *all* gone. The directors who were not implicated will remain. As I understand it, they're meeting this morning with a few prospects to fill at least some of the empty spots."

"Yes, they arrived just before I left," said Anders. "I overheard several of them talking. Apparently, there's a risk involved with chronography that we weren't even aware of, but someone working independently has discovered." He turned to Dani. "Dr. Seebak. I'm sure you've heard of him, from your studies."

She nodded. "Of course."

"What will happen to the blackmail victims?" Anders asked the detective. "Obviously, they'll be relieved of having to pay him, or whatever he was demanding, but will they be prosecuted for crimes he'd discovered?"

"For the most part, no. We can't use evidence that we obtained without a specific warrant for that crime. It might open up other cases, though. We'll have to see. We're facing weeks, if not months, of work to go through it all."

"This is really a big deal, isn't it?" Shard asked. "I mean, we've been meeting regularly for a long time, but this time we really did something, didn't we?"

"We did indeed," said Ms. Harris. "And I think that's worth a celebration. I've ordered pizza, and I just got notified it's here. Figured you all wouldn't mind an early lunch."

Their enthusiastic response immediately confirmed it.

RIACH LABS, Alki Beach, Seattle, WA. 0930, Monday, June 19, 2215.

It felt strange to walk the halls of the institute, to be welcomed again after hiding for so many years. Lexil remembered visiting his mother here, before the accident, when she was bright and witty and drew people to her with charismatic warmth. Before she lay in her hospital bed, dying.

He shook his head to bring himself back to the present. Here they were, at the large conference room. On Saturday, they had met with the few remaining directors in the small meeting room next door. But today, they would meet with all the full-time employees to let them know about what he and Doc had discovered on Wednesday.

Those employees were streaming in now, taking seats. The research scientists took places up front. Most of the questions would come from there. In the back was a section reserved for interns. They needed to hear the presentation, but if they had any questions, they would meet with the research scientists later. It was easy to spot the interns; they all had light blue lab coats on.

The plan was to open up communications between the researchers and the interns as an attempt to restore the free exploration of ideas that the institute had been known for in its early days, when his mother was the inspirational head.

With the audience seated, Doc stepped up to the presentation platform.

"Good morning. I'm Dr. Mitchum Seebak, and I've been appointed to direct the transition after recent events. I'm assuming most of you have been notified, or have heard from a friend or co-worker, about what happened, but I wanted you all to get the full story, and have a chance to ask questions."

A wave of murmurs swept the audience. Doc waited for it to die down.

"One of your directors, Dr. Hunter, has been arrested on suspicion of blackmail. I can't give you details about the investigation, so hold those questions and wait for the official police announcement. Some of the other directors have been suspended until we know more about who was involved." He stepped back and gestured to the three women and two men sitting behind him. "These five, who we know were not complicit in any way, remain to continue the work of the institute. They asked me to come help."

More murmurs. Someone among the research scientists in the audience stood up. "Excuse me for interrupting, Dr. Seebak, but many of us recognize your name, and we know you were dismissed from this instituton some years ago, and you're..." The man hesitated.

"Discredited?" Doc offered.

"Well, yes. I wasn't going to use that word. But since you said it, I'll ask the question that is going through all our minds: Why should we listen to you?"

"I can answer that." All eyes turned toward another scientist. Good, thought Lexil. Marielle would tell them.

"You all know me, and most of you know I was here both before and after Dr. Seebak left. I can tell you with certainty that the grounds for his discreditation were completely fabricated—by the same people who are currently in police custody."

The murmurs swelled to loud voices. She raised her voice to speak over the noise.

"In addition, his ongoing work with chronography has revealed a significant danger to the timestream. The question is not why you should listen to him, but how you could possibly refuse!"

"What do you mean, danger?" the man demanded.

"That's what we're here to find out," said Marielle. "Dr. Seebak? Please continue."

"The danger is with the use of the VAO machine." Doc held up the papers they had discovered in the sensor box. "We have a packet of research here that describes in detail the mathematics behind a timestream disruption that could make the stream collapse."

"Hypothetically." The man was certainly persistent; Lexil would give him that!

"No. There has already been a timestream disruption, and it was barely—barely—repaired. Because of the repair, we have no memory of it, but these papers document an actual occurrence."

More murmurs. A woman rose from her seat. She glared at the other questioner until he sat down. "How could the VAO machine cause damage?" she asked.

"We need to study it more, but we believe that when the VAO conversion is recorded in permanent form, it removes objects from the timestream for that brief instant. At my private lab, we have ways of measuring disruptions. A small one might have no lasting effect. But remove the wrong object at the wrong time and you'll have major consequences. We will be making no more VAO conversions until we understand when it is safe to do so."

Another woman stood and spoke over the buzz of voices. "Excuse me, Dr. Seebak, but what kind of work are we supposed to do, if we can't record anything? Are we all going to be laid off?"

The room fell silent.

Doc shook his head. "Ten years ago, before they named it RIACH, the founders of this institution were engaged in scientific research. I remember that, because I was one of them. It's different now. You focus on gathering evidence in criminal investigations and sampling thousands of objects with the hope of finding something historically significant. That's appropriate. You have 'Anthropology and Chronographic History' in your name, after all. And that kind of research will go on, but we will stop at the VAO conversion step, for now. There will be no recordings, not until we figure this out.

"But who better to figure it out than chronographic scientists? I propose that some of you, who want to return to scientific research, form a division to dig deeper, learn more, and open all our eyes to what can still be an exciting new field of scientific inquiry. Are any of you interested in that? Could I see a quick show of hands?"

Hands went up, a few at a time, and Lexil counted, because he knew he would be working with some of these people. Twenty-five, twenty-six, twenty-seven. A good number, he thought, but he was disappointed that almost all of them were from the intern section. From the way Doc had described their jobs, the interns must be tired of the tedium. I would be too, he thought. But he had hoped for inspired minds, and he was going to have to settle for glorified flunkies.

Doc was speaking again. "Good! Please come see me after this meeting so I can get your names. We'll set up some interviews later. If there are no further questions, I'd like to introduce my associate, Lexil Myles. He has been working alongside me since he was a teenager. His research in temporal distortion, while unpublished, is leaps and bounds ahead of anything else in the field. This packet of papers that details the specifics of the disturbance from the altered timestream came to us in his handwriting, presumably from the Lexil that existed there."

He paused, then grinned. "Good thing I had one of my own, because almost nobody else can read his handwriting!"

"Hey!" Lexil said. "It's not *that* bad."

Chuckles from the audience. He'd have a warmer reception when he got up there than Doc had faced.

His mentor was still speaking. "He'll be heading up the new division, and reporting to the new board of directors."

That was his cue. Lexil stepped over two steps straight up onto the platform. Long legs had their advantages. He took the packet from Doc and glanced at it. Two scrawled lines at the bottom of the first page, in an unfamiliar handwriting, reminded him he had one more project of his own.

The first line instructed them to take their findings to Marak Wallace and Detective Tom Rayes, and they had done that. The detective had already been working an angle on a related case, which ended up with Dr. Hunter's arrest. Marak Wallace had cut through all the scientific data to the heart of the matter and used his considerable reporter's influence to get the ear of lawmakers, the mayor, and the governor himself. As much as he disliked government oversight, Lexil had to admit that in this case, it had shut down the VAO conversions much more effectively than they would have been able to do on their own.

The second line was more puzzling: "D. Adams will be helpful with further study." After the meeting was over, he meant to go to the administrative offices and check the employee lists for someone with that name.

People were waiting for him to speak. He held up the packet. "The research we've been doing at our lab ties in neatly with these records. We have a series of sensors that have been sealed for the last fifteen years, much like your observation boxes. We've paired them with sensors that are left open to whatever changes the timestream undergoes. The differences appear as blips—for want of a better term—on a viewwall and serve as a warning that something has changed."

"Will you move those sensor pairs to this lab?" The voice came from the back of the room. As he was scanning the room, trying to spot the speaker, a young woman in a blue lab coat stood up. She continued, "Or will we be going off site?"

He glanced at Doc. Should he answer questions from the interns? There were so many of them, the meeting could get confusing quickly. But Doc nodded.

So he answered. "We'll be bringing them here, and also installing new ones, with improvements we will be developing as part of the project. Those who work with us in the new division will get familiar with the sensors and their output very quickly. I have to warn you, though: We won't be taking many interns."

"I'll look forward to the interview, then," she answered, looking at him steadily. Cheeky, but kind of appealing, he had to admit.

She sat down and another man stood up. Not one of the interns this time. Good.

"I wasn't able to post assignments this morning. Is this part of the changes?"

A better question for Doc, but he knew the answer. "As I understand it, we're encouraging research groups to meet together at the beginning of each day, for now. We want you all to be fully informed as we make changes, and have an avenue for asking questions and getting answers. You'll be able to assign responsibilities at those meetings."

He answered a few more questions. Then they dismissed the group, inviting those who were interested to stay behind and leave their names. They were down to the last intern. It was the bold one who had spoken up during the questions. She reached out her hand to introduce herself.

"Danarin Adams. I'm very interested in working with your team."

Lexil froze and took her hand automatically. He liked her handshake. It was firm, confident, totally competent.

This could work out well.

WALLACE HOME, Lower Queen Anne, Seattle, WA. 1730, Friday, June 23, 2215.

Marak welcomed her at the door, as usual. "Hey, Dani. How bad were the upheavals at RIACH this week?"

"You want to know the results of your handiwork?" she asked, wrinkling her nose at him and trying to hide a grin.

Kat came out of the kitchen, carrying a glass of iced tea. "Thirsty? He's been pestering me all week to find out if I've talked to you."

Dani took the iced tea with a nod of thanks.

"And she keeps saying, 'Yeah, I've talked to her,' and then clamming up. Sure glad I don't have to interview *her* for a living."

Dani laughed. She couldn't ask for better friends. "Lots of changes. Seems like everything's for the better, though. Except..." She looked at Kat. "...except finding out that your uncle was involved."

"That's hard to get my head around," said Kat. "That person who did all those things—that's not the uncle I know."

"It's hard for me to understand too," said Marak.

"I'm so angry about what he's done. On the other hand, he's the reason we met! I wish I could sit down with him and ask, 'What were you thinking?' But he won't even talk to me."

"Give him time." Marak gave her a little side hug. "He'll see you when he's had some time to think."

"I hope so."

"What about you?" Dani asked Marak. "After all your work, you didn't even get to submit the whole story of the timestream repair to the paper, did you?"

He grimaced. "No. They said it didn't happen, so it wasn't news. The news was that it *didn't* happen." Then he smiled and winked. "But that's all right. I'm already working on the book."

"How will the changes affect you, personally?" Kat asked Dani. "You didn't know much when we had lunch on Monday."

"Well, for starters, we meet in groups every morning and interact directly with a researcher. We hear about the projects we're working on, and the assignments feel more like part of a group effort than isolated tasks. Sometimes it's even the same type of task, but because we're working together, there's more opportunity for discussion and sharing what we've found."

"Wow, that's a big change, isn't it?" Marak asked.

"It is! And there's a bigger change coming." Dani paused to draw out the suspense, but the dramatic moment was spoiled utterly when Jored tore through the force-field screen over the back door.

"Dani! I heard your voice! Can we play chess? Did you bring me anything? Are you staying for dinner? Wanna come see what I built outside?"

She returned his enthusiastic hug. "Hey, bud! Slow down. I'm here for the evening. There'll be lots of time for all that."

"Okay! I'll get it ready for you!" And before she could respond, he dashed back outside.

"It's like you're his playmate, instead of his grown-up friend." Kat was shaking her head.

"And you love it," Marak told his wife.

"Yeah, I love it." She smiled at him and turned back to Dani. "Let's go sit down and you can tell us about the big change at work."

"They've started a new division, dedicated to researching temporal disturbances. How to monitor them, what causes them, how to stop them, even how to fix them, if necessary. It's real research with lots of promise."

"How will that affect you?" asked Kat. "Will you have a part?"

"Yes, I got the notification today. At first, they were saying they didn't want interns involved, but I guess I made an impression."

"At your interview?" Kat wanted all the details, of course.

"No. They didn't even call me for an interview."

"That's unusual," said Marak.

"Yeah, it was. I think they may have decided at the first meeting." Dani paused to remember. "And that was weird, because it sure seemed as if he didn't want me to put my name on the list at all. They were already packing up to go."

"He? Who?" asked Kat.

"Lexil Myles. He's heading up the division."

"He's a little young for that, isn't he?"

"Yes, that's what I..." She glanced at her friend, sharply. "How did you know that?"

Kat shrugged. "I've just heard of him, that's all. Through my...uncle." Her face darkened again.

"You're right. He's not much older than I am. He didn't look interested at all, until I said my name. And then—the strangest thing—he acted like he'd heard it before, and then he smiled." Dani trailed off.

Kat leaned forward. "Yeah?"

"Yeah," she looked up at her friend and blushed. "I mean, it was probably nothing. Anyway, four days later, I got my notice. Oh, and it comes with a promotion. No more blue lab coat."

"That calls for a celebration," said Marak. "I've got a secret stash of chocolate hidden away for just such an occasion."

"You have chocolate that you're hiding from me?" Kat frowned at him.

"If I hadn't, I wouldn't have it now to celebrate with, would I?"

"No, probably not."

"Okay then. Dani, would you like some chocolate?"

Jored stepped through the force-field screen. "Chocolate? I would! I would!"

Dani laughed. "Let's save it for dessert, okay?"

"Aw." His face fell. He looked so much like his dad sometimes.

"Hey, you want to play a game of chess while we wait for dinner?"

He beamed. "Yeah! Right now?"

"Yes, right now. Which do you want, white or black?"

ABOUT THE AUTHOR

Kim K. O'Hara is a high school math and publications teacher who lives in Lacey, WA, and relishes frequent visits from two irresistible granddaughters. She loves reading, writing, and recreational math, but seldom gets in the mood for housework. You can reach her by email at kimkohara.author@gmail.com. Sign up for new book notifications at www.pagesandnumbers.com.

AUTHOR'S NOTE

Hey! You made it to the end. What do you think, will Dani and Lexil stand a chance in the restored timestream? I am excited about writing the next book in the series, and your comments can contribute to the story that's told. What and who would you like to see more of?

On the next page, Kindle will give you the opportunity to rate this novel and tell your friends on Facebook and Twitter that you've just finished it. Please take a few seconds to help make my book more visible by rating it or leaving a sentence or two as a review. I'm eager to hear from you, and I'll be reading every comment!

With gratitude, Kim

Made in the USA
San Bernardino, CA
28 October 2015